Chalet Craggy

THE SNAKE

"There are 'disaster' novels and 'disaster' novels. Some work. Some don't. This is great. Enjoy Central Park, but stay away from those rocks, especially after you read the last 15 lines of *THE SNAKE*."
— *Publishers Weekly*

"GODEY KEEPS THE SUSPENSE GOING RIGHT UP TO THE LAST PAGES..." — *Library Journal*

"GODEY IS SUPERB." — *Chicago Tribune*

"A DOUBLE-TWIST SHOCKER!" — *Cosmopolitan*

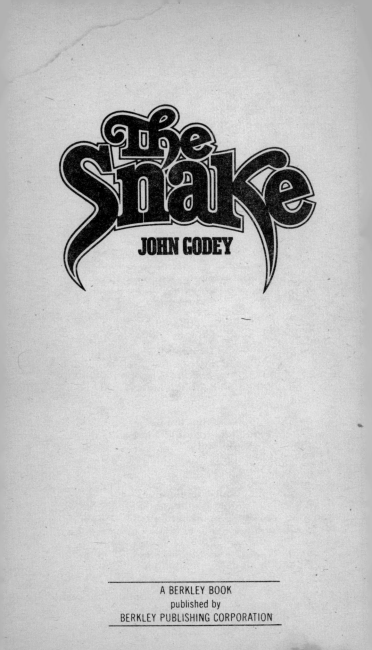

The Snake

JOHN GODEY

A BERKLEY BOOK
published by
BERKLEY PUBLISHING CORPORATION

This Berkley book contains the complete
text of the original hardcover edition.
It has been completely reset in a type face
designed for easy reading, and was printed
from new film.

THE SNAKE

A Berkley Book / published by arrangement with
G. P. Putnam's Sons

PRINTING HISTORY
G. P. Putnam's Sons edition published August 1978
Berkley edition / August 1979

A BERKLEY BOOK® TM 757,375
Berkley Books are published by Berkley Publishing Corporation,
200 Madison Avenue, New York, New York 10016.
PRINTED IN THE UNITED STATES OF AMERICA

Author's Note

I am deeply indebted to a number of people —police officers, firefighters, herpetologists, a distinguished physician—for expert and generously given advice. I thank them collectively rather than by name to spare them embarrassment in the event that I have committed any unpremeditated errors of fact.

Various existing New York City departments and institutions are represented in this book. But the characters who portray members of these departments and institutions are purely fictional, and not intended to represent any actual officials. All other characters in the book are fictional, as well.

CENTRAL
PARK

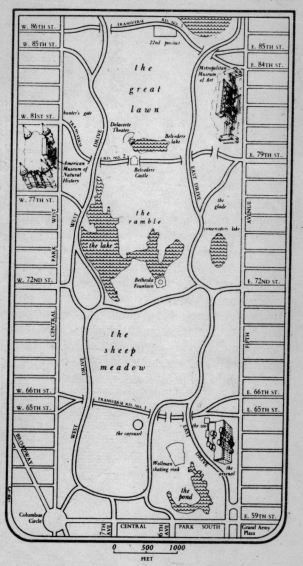

CENTRAL PARK
BELOW 86TH STREET

W. 86TH ST.
W. 85TH ST.
W. 81ST ST.
W. 77TH ST.
W. 72ND ST.
W. 66TH ST.
W. 65TH ST.

TRANSVERSE RD. NO.
22nd precinct

E. 85TH ST.
E. 84TH ST.
E. 79TH ST.
E. 72ND ST.
E. 66TH ST.
E. 65TH ST.
E. 59TH ST.

the great lawn

Metropolitan
Museum
of Art

hunter's gate

Delacorte
Theater

Belvedere
lake

American
Museum of
Natural
History

R D. NO. 2

Belvedere
Castle

the ramble

the glade

conservatory lake

the lake

EAST DRIVE

Bethesda
Fountain

the sheep meadow

CENTRAL PARK WEST

WEST DRIVE

FIFTH AVENUE

TRANSVERSE RD. NO. 1

the carousel

the zoo

EAST DRIVE

Wollman
skating rink

the arsenal

the pond

BROADWAY

Columbus
Circle

7TH AVE

CENTRAL

6TH AVE

PARK SOUTH

Grand Army
Plaza

0   500   1000
FEET

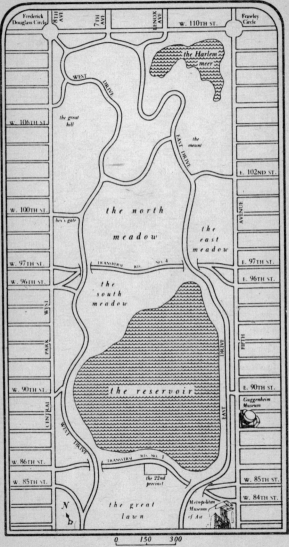

Frederick Douglass Circle

8TH AVE.

7TH AVE.

LENOX AVE.

W. 110TH ST.

Frawley Circle

the Harlem meer

WEST DRIVE

the great hill

EAST DRIVE

the mount

W. 106TH ST.

E. 102ND ST.

W. 100TH ST.

AVENUE

the north meadow

boy's gate

the east meadow

TRANSVERSE RD. NO. 4

W. 97TH ST.

E. 97TH ST.

W. 96TH ST.

E. 96TH ST.

the south meadow

WEST

PARK

the reservoir

CENTRAL

WEST DRIVE

FIFTH

EAST DRIVE

W. 90TH ST.

E. 90TH ST.

Guggenheim Museum

TRANSVERSE RD. NO. 3

W. 86TH ST.

the 22nd precinct

W. 85TH ST.

W. 85TH ST.

N

the great lawn

W. 84TH ST.

Metropolitan Museum of Art

0   150   300

METERS

ONE

THE BOX WAS two feet long, a foot and a half wide, and a foot and a half deep. Its outside was plywood, its inside a lining of burlap stitched into cardboard. There were airholes drilled into the top and sides. Together with its contents, the box weighed sixteen pounds. For anyone less than Matt Olssen's size it would have been an unwieldy burden, but Matt carried it comfortably under his long arm.

Even so, a few times along the way it became a drag, and he was tempted to walk away from it. Once, without meaning to, he had actually forgotten it. By the time he got back to where he had left it, two characters had hefted it up onto the bar and were struggling with the knot in the blond sisal twine looped around its width. He had been half inclined to let them get a look at what was inside the box, but he had been warned that, although it would probably be lethargic, he wasn't to count on it; it might come out of the box like a shot. So he kicked ass, picked up the box, and moved along.

He had taken it—box and animal together—from some Greek or other in a poker game in Lourenço Marques (Maputo, they called it now, a no-class name) in exchange for a handful of markers in Malawi dollars, which was the funny-money they were playing for. The Greek claimed it was a rare specimen that he had bought at a bargain price from some nigger cop in Elisabethville who was said to have confiscated it in the bush country from another nigger, who had staked it out as a booby trap on a dark path in front of his brother-in-law's house, with intent to kill. It hadn't worked out. The brother-in-law had a flashlight and spotted it in time, and then hollered for the cops. Matt had accepted it, as an alternative to beating up on the Greek, with the notion of turning it loose in the downtown area of the city for laughs. But later, sobering up, he decided instead to bring it back to the States and try to sell it to a zoo. He stowed the box away under the bunk in his cabin, and aside from sprinkling some water through the airholes a few times, paid no attention to it on the ten-day voyage back from Africa.

His ship had docked in Brooklyn in early morning. By the time he had finished supervising the off-loading it was noon, and 92 degrees, and he was nearly dehydrated. He cleaned up, put the box under his arm, and staggered to a waterfront joint a block away from the ship's berth. It wasn't until three o'clock that he remembered to phone his wife.

"Betty? It's me."

"Oh, Christ."

"What does that mean?"

"Well, you come and go, don't you?"

So it was going to be an uphill fight. Tuning his voice up to a little boy's sweet upper register, he said, "Baby, your little Mattsie is dying to see your beautiful face. You know?"

"Look, you bastard, don't come on with that cutie-pie act. You ask me if I know? I *know*."

"Hey, baby, be nice to me. I been six months at sea—"

"Six? I haven't heard from you in over a year."

"—and every single night when I turned in I dreamed about my beautiful Betty."

She snorted. "Well, dream on. I'm hanging up."

"Wait, no, I have to tell you something."

In the steaming phone booth he was pouring sweat and booze vapors. He glanced through the glass of the door at the box, standing on end near his bar stool. Nobody was paying any attention to it; he had promised to break the nose of any man who went near it.

"What you said about not hearing from me?" He wiped a rill of sweat off the side of his face with the phone. "I swear to Jesus Christ God I wrote you once a month like clockwork. Don't tell me you didn't get my letters."

"You lying bastard, I'm hanging up on you."

"You can't hang up on me. I'm your husband."

"In name only. I'm hanging up."

"I have to see you, Betty. God, how I missed you."

"I'm busy. I have to go now."

"No. Listen. . . ." I know the way to your heart, you bitch, and to everything else, too. "I got something for you. A present."

She paused for a moment. "Well, if it's another dumb statue like last time, you know what you can do with it."

"Every port we made I worked my butt off, so I didn't even have time to buy you something." He smiled slyly into the transmitter. "So I'm just gonna have to give you cash instead. You mind, baby?"

Her voice came alive. "You're gonna give me money?" How much?"

"Ah, don't let's spoil the surprise. But I'll give you a little hint. It's in the four figures."

"I could certainly use some money. You got no idea what it's like, just keeping up the apartment, and buy a few clothes once in a while."

"I would have mailed you money, like I promised, but these crummy ports, they would steal it right out of the envelope in the post office. I'll be over in an hour or two, soon as we're finished unloading the ship. Okay, sweetheart?"

"Well, okay. But don't get rolled or anything. I really have to have the money."

"See you in an hour, baby. Wear a see-through, willya?"

Ten hours later he had drunk better than a quart and a half of whiskey, spent almost three hundred dollars, and had two or three causeless fights. He had moved from joint to joint on a course that led in slow stages generally northward through Brooklyn, across the East River into Manhattan, and on up the West Side to Columbus Avenue in the Seventies. Now he was the last remaining customer in the dump, and the bartender had just shut off the air conditioner to chase him.

"You want me to go, tell me man-to-man to go,

and I'll go," Matt said. "But don't lie the air conditioner broke down, you crumb."

"I don't want no more trouble with you," the bartender said. His right hand was under the bar, and he gave Matt a glimpse of a fat sawed-off bat. "Whyn't you just call it a night, sailor?"

"You crumb, if I felt like staying here I would *make* you turn it on again." He was pouring sweat again even though the air conditioner hadn't been off more than a couple of minutes. "But my dear little wife is waiting for me, and man, I got a terrific load saved up for her."

He heaved the box up on the bar, paid his bill, and threw the bartender a ten-dollar tip. The bartender mumbled his thanks and then, as if to underline his gratitude, pretended to be curious about the box. "What you *really* got in there, sailor?"

It was a question that had been put to him often during the long hours since he had left the docks. Depending on the variable temperature of his mood, his answer had been either "a little pussycat" or "none of your fucking business." In all cases he had made it evident, by virtue of his size and attitude and general air of recklessness, that the subject was closed. In the only instance when a questioner had persisted, Matt had grabbed him by the collar and run him out the door.

Now he simply winked at the bartender, hiked the box up under his arm, and went out into Columbus Avenue. The September heat had hardly relented since sundown, trapped by pavement and steel and concrete. Considering that it was nearly 2 A.M., there were a surprising number of people on the streets. In front of him, a couple slouched along with their arms clasped limply around each other's waist. Across the street, a man and two women were standing at the curb singing. Before him, a young man, barechested, wearing floppy shorts, bore down toward him on a collision course but sheered off at the last moment. A few cars were heading south, their headlights bouncing on the ragged road. Here and there, above the street, people leaned out of darkened windows, their arms and elbows cradled on pillows on the sills, trying to distill some refreshment out of the hot moist air.

He turned east toward Central Park, his gait rolling, part swagger, part stagger. The street was dark, with almost every other one of its lamppost lights shattered. The curbs were lined with garbage, some in plastic bags, some simply strewn. A few windows were dimly lit, and there were sounds of voices or music drifting into the street. Near the end of the block, a cluster of Hispanics sitting on a stoop, wearing shorts and nightgowns, laughed at him and called out insults. He stopped, and challenged them to come down off the stoop and fight, the whole lot of them, men, women, children, and knives. They laughed, and saluted him with their beer cans.

He told them that they were a bunch of dirty *cabrones, putas,* and *bastardos*, and when they applauded his command of their language, he bowed to them and moved on. He wasn't ignorant of the streets of New York—and of Rio and Genoa and Marseilles and a hundred other ports—but they held no terrors for him. He knew that his size was intimidating; and if it failed to intimidate, he was ready to fight, confidently and with enjoyment.

At Central Park West he checked the street sign and looked at the building on the corner in bafflement. From the lobby, a uniformed doorman looked out at him cautiously. He checked the street sign and the building number again. Dumb ass. She lived east, the other side of the park. He set the box down near the curb and waved his arms wildly at an approaching cab. The cab slowed and stopped, then suddenly shot off. Matt took a wild swing at the trunk of the car as it went by. In the next five minutes two more cabs passed him up.

He glared into the street, cursing loudly. But he knew what the problem was—the yellow bastards were scared of him. He was wearing what he called his "shore uniform." He had begun to put it on, item by item, at that dockside joint in Brooklyn and now, fifteen hours later, he was fully dressed. There was a footprint on the crown of his white nautical cap, and the yellow braid on the black bill was hanging by a couple of threads. A sleeve of the white linen jacket was separated at the shoulder. The T-shirt beneath it was grimy and soaked with sweat and spilled drinks. The duck pants were filthy and ripped at one knee. He had a smear of dried blood at the corner of his mouth from a cut lip, another smear on the lapel of the linen jacket, and spatters on his white shoes.

Like his size, his shore uniform proclaimed a violent man, and it was forbidding.

A cab stopped for a red light on the north corner of the street. Matt picked up the box and ran toward it. The driver watched him for a moment through the windshield, then put his car in gear and shot the light.

"Fuck it. Fuck you all, *cabrones*," Matt yelled.

He tipped the leading edge of the box forward and shook it for balance, and the animal slid drily inside.

"Don't get restless, pussycat," Matt said. "Relax and you'll live longer."

He tucked the box securely under his arm and crossed the street toward the park.

Torres, sitting on a bench backed against the stone retaining wall that bordered the park, watched with sour lack of interest as the big sailor tried to get a cab. But he came alive as the sailor started crossing over to the park side of the street. When the sailor hitched up the box he was carrying, and started walking north, Torres had to talk to himself to keep from running after the guy and jumping him right then and there.

"Wai', stupid, see what he gonna do."

When the sailor was fifty or sixty feet up the street, Torres eased off the bench and began tailing him, walking close to the retaining wall, so he could crouch against it if the guy looked back. But the sailor didn't turn around. He stopped once, and looked across the street at the Museum of Natural History, but only for a second. He kept walking north, and a couple of times he paused and looked toward the park, as if he was thinking of going in.

"I'll wait if you promise to go inna park," Torres said softly. "You wanna know how to go in? Transverse coming up on Eighty-first."

The sailor was a giant and looked tough—he carried that box under his arm like it was a feather—and Torres realized that it would be risky to tackle him one-on-one, but he was desperate for a score. The way the weather was, people were wearing hardly any clothes, and they didn't have noplace to carry their money so they left it home. That was what had happened the last two times, and he got mad the second time and pistol-whipped the score real good.

But pistol-whipping didn't put no money in the bank.

So he knew he wasn't going to let the sailor's size or anything else stop him. Besides, the way the sailor was walking he looked pretty drunk. Torres made up his mind. Even if the sailor went past the transverse without going in, he was gonna hit him anyway. There wasn't nobody walking on Central Park West, and only a few cars, mostly cabs, and no goddamn cab driver was gonna stop if he saw somebody being worked over, unless it was one of those moonlighting cops that drove a hack, and even then he might look the other way. Still, it was dangerous.

The sailor stopped at 81st Street, at the entrance to the transverse.

"Go in," Torres said. "Go inna park, you stupid fuck. It's bullshit what you hear about danger. Ain't no danger, it's real safe, anybody can walk through and be safe. Don't be afrai', go on, walk inna park." But the big guy crossed the street past the transverse opening. "Aw ri'," Torres said, "aw ri', I'm gonna do it to you anyway."

The sailor stopped again. Torres held his breath. The sailor was turned toward the pedestrian entrance, a broad entry between two squat pillars. Better than the transverse, Torres thought, no cars, no nothing. Go on, go in, man, he pleaded silently, and in an agony of wishing used body english, like with a pinball machine, to get the sailor to turn into the park.

It worked. The sailor turned into the entrance, and as he hurried after him, Torres said, "Beautiful. Thank you, God."

He touched the short-barreled .38 he carried in his belt under his loose shirt.

• • •

A short while after he began walking through the park, Matt Olssen realized he should have gone through the transverse, which would have taken him on a direct line to the east side. Here, the walkways branched and wound, and he would have to use a little navigation to keep from wandering in circles. Well, he was a sailor, wasn't he? Steer by the stars. He looked up. The sky was overcast, with a reddish tint, and there wasn't a star in sight. He thought for a second of going back, of trying to retrace his steps to the entrance and then taking the transverse, but it seemed like too much trouble. Screw it. At least the park smelled a little better than outside.

As for little Betty, she'd wait no matter how long it took him. Expecting money, she'd wait all night, and then some. Little Betty. He smiled, envisioning her in the apartment, probably fallen asleep, lying on her back in the air-conditioned bedroom in her see-through. He would have to lean on the bell to wake her up, and she'd be pissed off, but not fatally, because she would be thinking about the money he had promised her. He would take a nice slow shower—maybe get her to take it with him—and then into the kip. When she wanted to, Betty could fuck up a storm, and with the prospect of money she had the incentive.

Except for the sound of his own footsteps on the pavement, the park was silent. If there was anybody else around, they were keeping real quiet about it. He knew you weren't supposed to walk in the park after dark, but it didn't bother him. Any mugger got a good look at him he'd probably run away and hide. And if he didn't, well, another fight was just another fight, and he'd bust the sonofabitch up good.

There was motion in the box. He reached around with his free hand and tapped the cover sharply.

"Lie still, pussycat."

He tilted the box back and forth a few times. The movement inside became briefly agitated and then subsided.

It was clear to Torres that the sailor didn't know what the hell he was doing. First he went to the left, toward the kids' playground, then wound around back to the main path, heading east. He never once looked behind him, or even to the right or left. Nice sailor, Torres thought, you gonna win the medal for easiest score of the year. He let the guy get out of sight a few times, laying back, knowing that when the curving walkway straightened out, he would be there. No hurry. Let him get nice and deep inside the park.

No way of losing him. Even if he got invisible in the shadows once in a while, it was easy to pick him up again when he passed into the light of the streetlamps every few hundred feet.

When the sailor lurched across the West Drive, Torres whispered to himself, "Watch yourself, stupid, don't get hit by no car." The sailor crossed the roadway safely, and after a while Torres followed. When he saw him again, the sailor was stopped, facing to his right, toward the path that climbed up to the Belvedere Castle. "Hey, that's a good one, nice and lonesome up there," Torres whispered.

But the sailor turned away and went straight on. Ahead, on the right, was the Delacorte Theatre, and on the left the Great Lawn, with the baseball backstops sticking up and the patterned dirt infields, stretching north for about four city blocks. The sailor moved on past the big round theater without even looking at it.

Because the path was straight here, Torres hung well back. Above him, nailed to a tree, was one of those green signs: THIS PARK CLOSES AT MIDNIGHT. What's a matter, sailor, Torres said to himself, you can't read? You breaking the law, *amigo*, you committing a crime, so I don't feel sorry for you, what's gonna happen, you fucking criminal. He smiled to himself in the darkness, and closed up the gap a bit as the sailor lurched past the little Belvedere Lake, they called it, with the castle on the other side, sitting on a rocky bed, looming up against the sky like something from olden times.

After a while, as the sailor wandered deeper into the park, something occurred to Torres that made him worried. What if there was another mugger someplace, and he picked off the sailor while Torres was laying back? And suppose, from the way he was heading, suppose he stumbled into the Ramble, where all the fags hung out? Some of those *maricons* were rough people, and could rob the dumb bastard, besides cornhole him, too. *Cristo*, Torres thought, I better pull the job before he gets hijacked.

He started to quicken his pace, and just then the sailor turned around. Torres dove for the pavement. Sonofabitch had seen him! No, he was looking up, maybe checking out the buildings on Central Park West to see which way he was going. Just ahead was one of those arches, like a little tunnel. Go ahead in the tunnel, Torres said to himself. But instead, the sailor veered off to his left.

Good enough, Torres thought. He got up, drew his piece out of his belt, cocked it, and took off after the sailor at a light run. He had closed in to within a dozen feet when the sailor heard him and turned around. Torres edged toward him a little.

"Aw ri', man" he said. "This wha' they call a mugging, okay?"

The sailor's eyes were blinking in surprise. He didn't look scared. Torres raised the piece so the guy could see it.

"You be a smart guy and you don't get hurt. Ri'?" He waved the pistol. "Else you get blowed away. Okay? I wan' you lay down on your face. Okay? Lay down, man."

The sailor laughed.

"You hear me, man? Lay down." When the sailor kept laughing, Torres began to feel uncertain. Sonofabitch was like an apartment house. But then the sailor laughing at him made him mad. He pushed the gun out at arm's length toward the sailor and yelled, "You lay down, motherfucker!"

"Okay, greaseball, I lay down."

The sailor shifted the box from under his arm and threw it at Torres, shoving it out from his chest with both hands, like a basketball pass. Torres saw the box coming at him, tumbling in the air, and, behind it, the sailor moving toward him fast. An edge of the box caught him on the shoulder, and then it went sailing past him and he heard something crack as it hit the pavement. The sailor was right on top of him when he pulled the trigger. He shot three times, the last two with the muzzle of the gun right against the sailor's chest, and then the sailor's weight was bearing him backward.

They hit the ground hard, with the sailor on top, and Torres heard his own breath whoosh out of him. He struggled wildly, threshing with his legs, chopping at the back of the sailor's neck with the barrel of the gun. He braced his feet against the pavement, arched his back, and heaved upward, and the sailor rolled off him. He scrambled to his feet and trained the gun downward at the sailor's head. But the sailor wasn't moving. His eyes were open and staring up at the sky. His shirt was bloody, and Torres realized that all three bullets had gone into his chest and that the sailor was already dead when he fell on top of him.

"Sonofabitch," Torres said. He felt awed. It was the first time he had ever wasted anybody. Then he felt a surge of pride. Big like an apartment house and he had wasted him! Okay, beautiful, but think about it later on. Three shots, and if there was cops cruising through the park they maybe heard it. Hurry up and make the score and split.

The sailor was lying a couple of feet in front of the box. The wood had split when the box hit and the cover was broken. Torres started toward the sailor, and his eye was caught by something moving in the box. He saw two points of gleaming light and a dark shape moving slowly from side to side. The dark shape moved upward on a long column, and Torres, staring, realized that it was the head and neck of a snake. As he watched, frozen, the snake started to slide out of the box. It slithered over the rim, pouring out in a continuous motion. It kept coming, slow and smooth, no end to it, and Torres thought he must have been dreaming.

"Madre de Dios!"

He looked on in fascination as the snake poured out of the box, drawing itself into a loose coil until finally a thin tail flipped out. Then the snake raised its head up high on its stiffened neck and stared at Torres. Its head was small and flattened and its eyes were bright and shining in the darkness. Some of the coils were practically touching the sailor's body. The snake was flicking its long tongue in and out, and its head swayed over the sailor's body, like, Torres thought wildly, it was guarding it.

Torres couldn't believe his eyes. He had seen some big snakes before in Puerto Rico, in the interior, but never one like this sonofabitch. It scared him. He wanted to turn and run away, but he wasn't gonna split without getting the money. He thought of trying to shoot the snake, but he knew it would have to be a very lucky hit, and if he missed it might get the snake mad.

The snake kept looking at him with its gleaming eyes, and the tongue kept sliding in and out. It was like they were both hypnotized, Torres thought, staring at each other across the sailor's body. But Jesus, man, Torres said to himself, you can't stay here all night. The cops might be trying to locate where the shots had come from. He had to make a move. The snake had started to hiss at him, and it had its mouth wide open. Suddenly, remembering a movie about India, Torres had an idea. He held the gun out in front of him and moved it to the right, and the snake's head swayed to follow it. He moved the gun back to his left, and again the snake's head moved with it.

"Stupid snake," Torres said, and, to himself, Hey, man, you got it made. He edged forward to within three feet of the sailor's body. Cautiously, he moved the revolver left and right a few times, and always the snake's head followed it.

"Okay, man," Torres said, "now we make the score."

He extended the revolver as far out to his right as his arm would reach, and when the snake's head turned to stare at it, hissing, he quickly crouched, and with his free hand reached inside the breast pocket of the sailor's bloody coat. His fingertips had just touched the wallet when the snake's head shot forward, so fast that it was a blur, and he felt a sharp stinging pain in his thigh. Before Torres could move, the snake struck again, launching itself over the sailor's body, and he felt it hit in almost the same place.

Torres shouted hoarsely and jumped back. The snake was erect again, hissing, its mouth gaped open. Torres retreated half a dozen paces and looked at his thigh. His beige pants were slightly reddened by a few tiny spots of blood. It didn't hurt there, just a feeling like pins and needles. When he looked up again the snake's body was in motion, curling forward over the sailor's body, moving toward him.

"*Cristo*, save me," Torres screamed. "*Cristo*, please save me from this fucking snake!"

He turned away and began to run at top speed.

The snake crawled off the walkway into the grass. It held its head high, and its black forked tongue darted in and out. It disappeared into the darkness.

Two

FIVE MINUTES AFTER the start of his panicky flight, Torres stopped running long enough to rub the surface of his revolver with his shirt, and drop it into a trash basket. Then he began to run again.

He had been running headlong, as fast and hard as he could, from the moment the snake had crawled across the sailor's body toward him. For a while, he kept turning his head to see if it was chasing him, though he knew that no snake could possibly travel at that speed. From time to time he reached down to touch the place on his thigh where he had been bitten. It wasn't swollen and it didn't hurt—just the little pins-and-needles feeling—and he took comfort from that. Maybe the goddamn mile-long whore of a snake wasn't even poisonous.

But he began to feel lightheaded, like he had been drinking too much wine, and he was having some trouble breathing. Also, it was taking him too long to get out of the park. He had stayed on the winding footpaths except for once, when he tried to take a shortcut through an uphill bushy area, and he had lost his bearings and almost gotten hysterical until he found his way back to the paths. He always thought he knew the park as well as he knew his own asshole, but now he couldn't seem to find the way out.

After he found the paths again he felt played out and had to take a rest. So he just sat down on the pavement, facing in the direction he thought he had come from, so he could see the snake coming if it was still following him. *Estupido!* He had lost it a long time ago. But the fucking animal had scared him shitless, and he couldn't free his mind of the way it kept sliding out of that box, and the way it bit him so fast that he couldn't hardly see it move.

Sitting down and resting didn't seem to do much good. If anything, his breathing was getting worse, and his mouth was filling up with some sticky kind of crap. He couldn't spit the stuff out and had to try getting rid of it with his fingers. He got scared all over again, and he knew he better get to a hospital fast, but he had a hard time standing up. His legs felt weak, and he was starting to feel sleepy. But he finally pulled himself up and took off again, though he was staggering more than running, and he couldn't breathe good, and the gummy stuff in his mouth was dribbling down his chin now.

He began to sob, and tried to beg some saints to help him, but he couldn't think of any of their names. He was sucking for air, and his arms and hands felt so heavy that he could hardly move them. At last he remembered his name saint, but when he tried calling out to him he couldn't talk, only make sounds like a frog.

He couldn't feel his legs at all now, just saw them going up and down like in slow motion. The pins and needles were spreading upward in his body, and his head kept falling down until his chin bobbed against his chest. After a while it got too hard to try lifting his head, so he just let it hang down. He didn't feel like running no more, either. All he wanted was to lay down and go to sleep. But he kept going, and a little bit later he saw an exit out of the park onto Fifth Avenue. It puzzled him that he was way down near 64th Street, when he should have come out in the high Seventies.

He stumbled through the exit, but couldn't stop himself at the curb. His momentum carried him into the middle of the street, where he collapsed.

Through his closed eyelids he saw the brightness of headlights coming toward him, but he didn't try to move. He knew his legs wouldn't work, no part of his body would work. He heard the bad noises he was making when he tried to breathe, and he knew he was gonna die, right there, laying down in the middle of Fifth Avenue.

Patrolman John Nebbia, driving sector car Boy-3, saw the figure stagger out of the park and into the street, where it collapsed.

"See that?" he said to his partner, Patrolman Frank Finnerty.

Finnerty nodded. "Look at the cars. They go right around him, like dodging a pothole. Nobody stops."

"Who stops and gets out of his car at three-thirty in the morning? I'm not crazy about it myself."

Nebbia sped up a bit until he reached the figure sprawled in the street. There he made a short U-turn that brought the car around in front of the figure, setting up a barrier to protect it from the oncoming southbound traffic. Finnerty was out the door before the emergency brakes were set. Nebbia turned on his revolving roof light before he got out.

Finnerty was down on one knee, leaning over the man. "What's the matter, feller?"

Nebbia watched the man's brown eyes open and stare upward. He was having trouble breathing, and a heavy gluey mucous discharge glistened on his lips and chin.

"OD'd" Nebbia said. "One more Hispanic OD. I'll call for an ambulance."

"He can hardly breathe," Finnerty said. "See how blue his face is? Probably a heart attack."

"Me, I diagnose it overdose," Nebbia said. "He's too young for a heart attack. I'll call an ambulance." He straightened up, but instead of going back to the car, yelled at a driver who had stopped alongside them, with his window turned down, to watch the scene. "Move along, move along, chrisesake. You got no home to go to?"

"He looks like he might go out any second, John," Finnerty said. "Let's put him in the car and take him ourself."

"I don't know," Nebbia said.

"What don't you know? He could go any second."

"That's what I don't know," Nebbia said. "You know as well as me that if he dies on us we have to hang around and wait for the M.E., and Christ alone knows how long it takes the wagon to get here, and then we have to inventory his possessions. . . ." He paused, and assessed the tightening of Finnerty's spare Irish face, and shrugged. "Okay, okay, we'll take him ourself."

They carried him to the car. Finnerty got into the back seat with him.

Nebbia spoke into his microphone. "Nineteenth Precinct sector car Eighteen-twenty to Central. K."

In the back seat, looking down at the slumped figure beside him, Finnerty heard Nebbia inform Central that they were transporting a serious OD to East Side Hospital. After Central acknowledged, Nebbia turned his siren on.

Not OD, Finnerty said to himself, not OD but a heart attack. He tried to remember the emergency procedure he was trained to follow. The only thing he could think of right now was mouth-to-mouth resuscitation, and he wasn't sure he could bring himself to do it with all that crap that was clogging the victim's mouth and oozing down over his chin.

"Move it," he said to Nebbia. "Will you move it?"

As the snake headed into heavy brush, a squirrel fled before its approach. The snake was hungry, and it might have taken the squirrel, but its primal impulse was to seek a place of safety. It crawled deeper into the brush, constantly probing with its deeply forked black tongue. It paused at the base of a tree, erected its head on the taut anterior portion of its body, and looked upward. Then it began to crawl up the trunk of the tree, winding around it swiftly and smoothly, using its prehensile tail for leverage.

It stopped two-thirds of the way up the tree in an area of heavy foliage, and draped itself over the branches in a seemingly patternless arrangement of loose random loops that were designed to distribute its weight evenly.

The snake was eleven feet, two inches long, and

slender. Its head was coffin-sided and comparatively small for the length of its body. Its eyes, dark brown and round, were wide open. It was unable to shut its eyes because it had neither eyelids nor nictitating membrane.

The snake was asleep.

With the exception of weekend nights, when the traffic was heavy and continuous until dawn, the emergency ward of East Side Hospital was normally at its busiest between 4 P.M. and midnight. Those were the hours when most of the patients flocked to emergency for nonemergency treatment they would normally have sought in the clinic, which closed at four o'clock.

Now, at 3:45 A.M., the reception room was empty except for a sleeping wino with a stiffly bandaged forefinger. He had been treated more than an hour ago, but showed no disposition to leave. Probably, Nurse Rosamund Johnson thought, glancing at him from behind the reception desk, because of the air conditioning. Well, he was peaceful enough, poor old bum, so let him hang around.

She was working on a sheaf of Blue Cross claim sheets when two cops came in with a patient. His feet were dragging, his head lolling, and he seemed to be semi-comatose.

"Found this on Fifth Avenue," one of the cops said. "He's got the blue face."

Nurse Johnson punched a key on her intercom and said, "Billy, bring out a stretcher, stat," then punched another key and, after a moment, said, "Dr. Papaleo, we have a patient in a cyanosed condition who's having trouble breathing. Come immediately, please." She listened for a moment and then said sharply, "Look, doctor, you better come immediately. Stat."

"Overdose," one of the cops said. "I seen hundreds of them."

The nurse, grimacing at the intercom, said, "How's he ever gonna be a doctor if he don't learn how to wake up?"

"He can't breathe," the other cop said. "My opinion, it's heart attack."

An attendant came through an inner door rolling a stretcher.

"Put the patient in Room D, Billy," Nurse Johnson said. "Dr. Papaleo is on his way."

The two cops strained, helping the attendant lift their burden onto the stretcher. "Dead weight," one of them said, arching an eyebrow. "If you know what I mean."

Nurse Johnson said, "Can you fellows hang around a few minutes in case the doctor wants to ask some questions? There's a coffee machine around the corner."

One of the cops nodded, and the other one said, "I'll çall it in."

Dr. Charles Papaleo disliked the emergency ward almost as much as he disliked the surgery, which, in turn, he disliked more than obstetrics and less than medicine. He recognized that in terms of gross experience emergency ward service was invaluable for a first-year intern, but that didn't change his view of it. His problem was that he was abnormally shy, and had trouble in his dealings with people. Left to himself, he would have chosen another profession, something reclusive, no doubt, but his father and brother, both of whom were physicians, wouldn't hear of it, and they were overwhelming. Nevertheless, he had prevailed in making his own choice of a specialty—radiology. As a radiologist he would rarely have to face a patient from one year to the next, just his shadow imprinted on a sheet of film negative.

The patient on the table in Room D, Papaleo thought wryly, posed no problems in the personal sense. He was obtunded, semicomatose. On the other hand, his inability to respond to questions that might provide helpful signposts into the diagnostic process did pose medical problems. Looking down at the man, Papaleo thought, Overdose, I'll bet it's good old overdose. But he put the notion out of mind. Physicians were expected to follow form, especially first-year interns, who were discouraged from making snap judgments. "Even if you turn out to be correct," one of his professors was fond of saying, "the lightning-flash diagnosis in fledgling doctors—the Kildare syndrome—is either brilliance or dumb luck. Our science is based on neither brilliance nor dumb luck but knowledge."

So—attend to the symptoms. Cyanotic. Marked hypoventilation—the patient was breathing poorly, although he didn't seem to be fighting desperately for air, as people usually did who couldn't breathe. Meaningful? Maybe, but file it away for the moment. Meanwhile, *the airway receives first attention.* Oxygen. He found a nasal catheter and inserted it. Nostrils filled with heavy mucus—have to check to see that it didn't clog the catheter.

A nurse came into the room. Kelly, an old hand. It figured. They liked to have someone around to keep an eye on the first-year interns, and if no doctor was available, an experienced nurse was next best.

Without looking at her, Papaleo said, "Blood pressure cuff, please."

He opened the patient's mouth—slimy, thick mucous discharge, like the nose—and checked the tongue. No falling back of tongue—takes care of that. Didn't seem to be any obstruction, either. He sniffed the patient's breath. No alcohol smell, just a strong bouquet of . . . what? Chili peppers.

Nurse Kelly was winding the blood pressure cuff around the patient's arm, her movements deft, practiced. Papaleo said, "Never mind that for a moment. The airway is more important. Will you get the suction apparatus, please?"

Kelly nodded and moved off briskly. Papaleo, suddenly remembering the old yarn about the green intern who had diagnosed a day's growth of blue-black beard as cyanosis, examined the patient's fingernails, lips, and tongue. All blue. Cyanosis, not need of a shave.

Nurse Kelly came back with the suction apparatus: a vacuum to suck up the mucus via a tube running into a clear bottle so the matter could be examined. Kelly maneuvered the tube in the patient's mouth with her right hand, and with her left wiped up the mess on his chin and lips.

Papaleo, his forehead ridged, fitted his stethoscope into his ears, opened a few buttons of the patient's shirt, and listened to the heartbeat. Fast but fairly regular. The speed was nothing like tachycardia, exertion could even account for it. He picked up the man's wrist and counted his pulse. Fifteen seconds on the sweep hand of his watch: twenty-four or twenty-five. Call it an even hundred. He finished winding the blood pressure cuff around the patient's arm and pumped up the auto-valve bulb. He released the bulb, and took the systole and diastole reading. A hundred over forty. Combined with the pulse rate, it was slightly under normal, and it failed to suggest anything of substance to him.

"The oxygen doesn't seem to be helping his breathing any, doctor," Nurse Kelly said.

"Yes, well . . ." She was right. No answer for her. He frowned and said, "Let's give it a chance to take."

Nurse Kelly was silent for a moment before saying primly, "Shall I check the catheter to see if it's clogged?"

"Yes. Will you please do that, nurse?"

He waited until Kelly had removed the catheter. She stepped back from the table and began to clean it. Silently disapproving. Mustn't let her bother me, Papaleo thought. What now? Neurological check.

"Neurological check," he said aloud, and stepped back to allow Kelly to reinsert the nasal catheter.

Okay. Test for sensation—pinch and poke and press. Knee reflexes, okay. Bang the tendons—okay. Response to pain, okay. Check head for trauma: lots of black hair, wavy, but can't feel anything amiss. Okay. Shine flashlight into eyes—pupils normal size and contract under stimulus of light. Heroin out.

The patient's hand rose feebly, reaching for the mouth. Trying to clear it of mucus. But Kelly had vacuumed most of the mouth clean. She was looking at him sidelong now, and fidgeting. She opened her mouth to say something, but Papaleo intercepted her. "Lungs. Help me to get him into a sitting position."

He started unbuttoning the rest of the man's shirt. Unbutton? He remembered what another professor had said: "Don't waste time with buttons, cut the garment off or rip it off—the moral being that saving a shirt is no substitute for saving a life.'' Balls. All he had to do was push the shirt up over the patient's back. Two birds with one stone—save the life *and* the shirt. Maybe.

The patient was dead weight as they tried to sit him up. His head lolled forward against Papaleo's chest. Kelly held him steady and Papaleo leaned over him, placed his ear against the smooth brown skin and tapped. Sounded all right, but what could he really tell with the patient unable to breathe deeply?

"Let's get him back down, nurse, shall we?"

"Doctor, I think we—"

He cut her off with a frown. Got to keep them in their place, especially the old-timers, mustn't let them get ahead of you.

He picked up the patient's arms and studied them. No needle tracks. Well, the normal pupils had told him that. Overdose of some kind of pill? a possibility. Do a gastric lavage? He realized that he was sweating profusely. He wiped the sweat from his face with his forearm. Kelly watched, her lips pursed.

He said, "Who brought him in?"

"The police. I think they're still around."

"I'll step outside for a second and talk to them." Should have thought of that earlier, dammit. He started away from the table, then returned. "Maybe some kind of overdose, though the signs are absent. Still . . . get some Narcan, will you, please? Yes, and set up an I.V. with five percent dextrose and saline."

Nurse Kelly nodded her head and her lips softened. Good, Papaleo thought, I'm on the beam, Kelly approves.

"Oh yes, let's protect against an insulin overdose. Add fifty percent glucose."

• • •

He found the cops in the anteroom, drinking coffee and chatting with the security guard. They told him what they knew. No help.

"What about his movements. Was he jerking? You know—you've seen epileptics."

The cops agreed that although he had been staggering he hadn't appeared to be convulsed.

"It looks like overdose to me," one of the cops said. "A lot of Hispanics overdose these days."

Kelly maybe, but a dumb cop no. Papaleo returned through the reception room to Room D. Kelly had already hooked up the I.V. and she was back working with the suction apparatus, picking away at the mucus in the patient's mouth.

"Not alcohol," she said. "No odor."

"I'm well aware of that. I have a nose, too."

Kelly's lips tightened up again. Papaleo looked down at the patient blankly. What else was there, chrisesakes? Take a blood sample, check for sugar? But it would take at least a half hour. Some kind of GI hemorrhage?

"Could be inapparent bleeding," he said aloud.

"Doctor," Kelly said, "I think we're in trouble."

He thought so himself, but the declaration would have to come from him, not from a nurse. What the devil could it be? He ticked off items in his mind. Alcohol, no. Overdose, none of the signs. Trauma, no. Stroke—who knows? He decided to listen to the heart again. There was some change, and it was for the worse—beat more rapid now, and weaker. The patient's chest barely seemed to be moving. Paralysis, some kind of paralysis?

Kelly said, "Doctor, I think we want a Code Blue."

Code Blue was the emergency call that mobilized a surgeon, an anesthetist, the Chief Resident, extra nurses. It was clearly indicated, Papaleo thought, but suppose they all piled in and made a sure, quick, easy diagnosis? Christ! Better hold the Code Blue for another minute or two.

"Presently," he said to Nurse Kelly, and studied the patient hopelessly. Why should he resist just because they might think he was a dunce? That's what everybody thought of first-year interns anyway. They would come in, fire questions at him with the same sort of hauteur he had used with the two cops outside. . . .

"Well, doctor?" Kelly looked grim. "I think we're about to lose him."

Sweat was pouring down the sides of Papaleo's face. "Very well. Let's do a Code Blue."

Dr. Shapiro, the Chief Resident, was down in less than a minute. He ran his hands over the patient's chest, almost abstractedly, while Papaleo, earnest, sweating, filled him in. Shapiro's face was a mask. Before Papaleo was quite finished, Shapiro interrupted.

"Let's tube him," Shapiro said. "He needs air. Nurse, get hold of a respirator." Nurse Kelly, looking righteous, moved away from the table. "He can't breathe because his muscles aren't functioning properly. We want a mechanical aid to help the chest muscles do their work."

Should have thought of it, Papaleo told himself, when I noticed that he didn't seem to be fighting for breath. Mechanical respirator: endotracheal tube pushed into the windpipe, attached to a cock on wall that pumped oxygen directly into lungs.

Shapiro removed the nasal catheter when Kelly

arrived with the respirator. He had some initial
trouble intubating the patient, and Papaleo thought,
Christ, if *he* has trouble, what would have happened
to me? Other members of the Code Blue team had
arrived, but there was nothing for them to do, as yet.

With the tube emplaced in the patient's trachea,
Shapiro stepped back a pace and shook his head. "I
don't know." He looked worried. Then, frowning,
he stepped forward to the table again. "What's this,
on his thigh?"

The light summer trousers were stained with a
scuffing of grime, sweat, and a little blood. Papaleo
hadn't noticed it before.

"He must have scraped it when he fell. The
policemen who brought him in said he collapsed in
the street."

"Hand me a scissors. We'll cut them off."

But, abruptly, Shapiro bent over the patient with
his stethoscope.

"I swear," Papaleo said, "I can't figure out
what's wrong with him," and then shut up because
Shapiro was still auscultating.

Shapiro straightened up. "I can't raise a heartbeat.
Let's get going."

The entire Code Blue team pitched in. Everyone
worked with great intensity, injecting, kneading,
pounding—Papaleo, with a shudder, felt a rib break
under his fist—but to no avail. The patient's heart
refused to start up again.

"You can all go," Shapiro said. "We've lost this
one."

Before he left, Shapiro reminded Nurse Kelly to
phone the Medical Examiner's office and ask them to
send the death wagon around to pick up the body for
autopsy. In death from an undiagnosed cause,

Papaleo recalled, no permission from next of kin was required.

"Death from cardio-respiratory failure due to unknown causes," Shapiro said to Papaleo. "Don't forget, the M.E. gets a duplicate of your report."

"I should have thought of the mechanical respirator earlier," Papaleo said. "I'm sorry."

"Well, you'll think of it next time." Shapiro took a last look at the corpse on the table, said "Good night," and left the room.

The surgical resident, wearing white ducks and a dirty sweatshirt, shuffled into Room D. His yawn turned to a scowl when he was told that the patient had died and that the Code Blue had been canceled. He charged Papaleo and Nurse Kelly with wantonly disturbing his sleep.

"I'm doing a very difficult abdomino-peritoneal resection at seven o'clock and if I'm not at my best during the operation . . . Christ!"

Nurse Kelly flushed and said defensively, "Well, I'm sorry doctor. The patient's condition indicated a Code Blue, and we didn't know he was going to die."

"Well, *somebody* should know those things," the surgical resident said, giving Papaleo a dirty look. He turned abruptly and shuffled out. He was barefooted.

"Five minutes late for a Code Blue, and *he's* mad," Kelly said. "Surgeons, they're *born* that way."

Papaleo had once heard someone say that surgery residents begin getting difficult in their third year so that they could open their own practice with their arrogance at full bloom. But he had seen plenty of arrogant first-year interns who were preparing for surgery, so Kelly was probably right, they were born that way.

"It's a fact of life," Kelly said, "the way heart specialists are dangerously overweight and plastic surgeons are handsome, and orthopods are built like football players."

And radiologists are shy of people, Papaleo thought. While Nurse Kelly picked up the pieces—phoned the M.E.'s office for the death wagon, and got an orderly to wheel the body to the hospital morgue near the truck exit—Papaleo went to another room, where he put a butterfly suture under the eye of a man who had been kicked decisively in a brawl. After that, his tour of duty was finished. But instead of going to bed, he went down to the morgue.

The patient's eyes were open, and they seemed to Papaleo to be bewildered, as if he too was trying to fathom the cause of his death. Papaleo closed the eyes, not from sentimentality but because—he told himself with a nervous smile—he preferred working without anyone watching him.

He ran his hands over the torso absently, as Shapiro had done earlier. The skin had begun to cool, and to gray down from the smooth brown of a young man who had been, Papaleo guessed, in quite good health. The mouth was open in a crooked gape, and the lips and chin were smeared with hardening mucus. He ran his eyes down the body from top to bottom, as if taking inventory. Then his eyes traveled upward again to the thigh, to the patch of bloodied grime on the trousers.

After a moment's hesitation he opened the belt buckle and started to roll the trousers down, but changed his mind. He took a scissors from the pocket of his jacket, and firmly slit the trouser leg up from

the cuff to the hip. He spread the material carefully
to the side and bent over the thigh. The skin was
abraded and slightly stained by blood. Bending still
closer, he noticed four small perforations in the skin,
partially obliterated by the abrasions. So it was overdose after all, despite the contraindicative symptoms!

But his certainty was short-lived. Why would an
addict use his thigh when his arm was clear? And
how could he be thought of as an addict if there were
only the four marks, and no signs of needle tracks?
And why four marks, of equal freshness? The four
perforations seemed to be in two sets: one pair about
six inches above the knee, the other two or three
inches higher. The perforations in each set appeared
to be about twelve millimeters apart.

With his nose almost touching the thigh he studied
the marks. They certainly could be an injection of
some sort, though with a rather large needle. But
who would inject in pairs? Bites of some kind? Fang
marks? But fangs would make much bigger and more
ragged holes. Insect bites? Too large, and not with
that spacing. No insect he had ever heard of bit that
way, in pairs. Besides, who would stand still for *four*
such bites or stings?

Fangs, then. What had fangs? Dogs, cats, lions,
tigers . . . come on, Papaleo. Snakes? A poisonous
snakebite in Manhattan? Anyway, snakes didn't
strike that high. They might bite a hand or finger if
they were held, but they usually struck the foot or
lower leg. Besides, so far as he knew, snakes secreted
a hemotoxic poison, which destroyed the red blood
corpuscles and resulted in discoloration and swelling
of the affected area due to local hemorrhages.
Nothing like that here. Snakebite? Forget it,
Papaleo. Still, shouldn't he tell Shapiro about the

perforations? Yeah, sure, wake him up, wake up the boss and face that curled lip and those glittering eyeglasses. . . . Forget it, Papaleo.

Nevertheless, he decided to read up on snakebite in *Beeson and McDermott* before he hit the sack. But by the time he got back to his room he was feeling too damn exhausted to start rummaging for a book. Instead, he fell on his bed fully clothed and went to sleep.

A half hour later the M.E.'s death wagon backed into the receiving bay. The attendant signed a receipt for Torres's corpse, and took it away for storage in the city morgue until the M.E.'s office could schedule it for postmortem examination.

THREE

THE SNAKE WOKE shortly before dawn. At once, its long tongue began to flick in and out through a rostral opening in the margin of its upper jaw that allowed it to emerge even when its mouth was shut.

The two tips of the forked tongue fitted into ducts communicating with the snake's Jacobson's organ, which lay in a depression in the roof of the mouth. The sensory epithelium of the Jacobson's organ responded to odor substances conveyed to it by the tongue, and interpreted them as a chemical computer might do, in terms of the quality of the atmosphere, of the presence of another animal, of prey.

The findings of the Jacobson's organ disquieted the snake. And so, when it slipped through the branches of the tree and down the trunk, it chose not to wander off in search of water. Instead, moving in slow ripples, it drank the dew from the grass. Then, despite its hunger, it did not go in search of food, but wound back up the tree until it found the place where it had been before.

It slept again.

At much the same moment, Arthur Bennett stumbled on a body. His first thought, when he saw it lying on the walk, was that it was some other wino sleeping it off. But when he saw its size, he decided that it was that big bastard who had beaten him up a month ago and damn near punched his eye out.

His immediate impulse was to cut out, but when he touched his eye, still scabbed in the process of healing, he got mad. Stepping forward a pace, he launched a thudding kick to the ribs. He was bringing his foot back for a second kick—although by now he had remembered that the bastard who had punched his eye was a black guy—when he saw the dark blood staining the front of the T-shirt and the linen jacket.

Bennett recoiled, then stepped forward again and looked at the body. The eyes were open and glassy. One arm was bent back underneath. The white captain's hat had fallen away and lay nearby, incongruously balanced on its rim. There was a good-looking box a little distance away. He looked dead, but to make sure, Bennett let him have a couple more kicks in the ribs.

He found the wallet, first try, sticking up from the breast pocket of the linen jacket. He cackled with pleasure. He leafed through the wallet quickly and gasped with delight: bills a half-inch thick—twenties and fifties and even a few hundreds. He slipped the money into his pants pocket, and looked around him. Nothing in sight. He began to work feverishly, eager for what other wonders he might discover. In the jacket pockets he found a pack with half a dozen cigarettes in it, some keys, a crumpled dollar bill, two packages of matches, a disposable lighter, a packet of salted peanuts, a bloody crumpled handkerchief, some foreign coins. In the body's left-hand pants pocket he found a package of condoms, in the right a handful of U.S. coins. Everything went into his own pockets. When he had picked the body clean he put the sailor cap on his matted white hair, and giggled when it slid down over his ears. He picked up the box—the cover was busted, but it was still a fine box—and put it under his arm.

He decided to get out of the park real fast. He had entered on Fifth Avenue near the Metropolitan Museum, not too worried about walking through, because no self-respecting mugger would waste his time on an old wino bum (though some of the mean ones would hurt winos just for laughs), but now, with his loot, he felt different.

He pushed the hat to the back of his head so it wouldn't swamp him, tucked the box under his arm, and hurried along the path toward Central Park West.

The snake basked on the surface of a large black rock a short distance from the tree it had sheltered in, its eleven-foot length spread out to the sun in an extended sigmoidal flex. At 7:30 A.M. on the third day of the heat wave, the sun already burned relentlessly through the city haze.

The snake was poikilothermal—a cold-blooded animal. Its temperature was not constant, like that of most animals, but modulated with the temperature of its environment. Because cold exerts a narcotic, potentially killing effect, snakes predominate in the tropics and subtropics and thin out in number and

species in the temperate regions moving toward the
poles. Yet, a common viper is known to inhabit an
area above the Arctic Circle and parts of Siberia.

Scarcely stirring, the snake warmed up its blood
until some instinctive thermostatic reflex warned it
that it had reached the optimum temperature. Then it
slid away from its exposed position on the rock and
into the shaded underbrush near its tree.

Matt Olssen's body was discovered a little after
8:30 in the morning by a Parks Department truck
carrying grass-cutting equipment. The police were
notified, and an RMP car was dispatched to the scene
from the Central Park Precinct, located in the 85th
Street transverse. The Medical Examiner's office sent
out its death wagon to collect the remains, which
were brought to the morgue on First Avenue, near
Bellevue Hospital, and assigned a refrigerated drawer
not too far removed from the remains of Ramon
Torres.

Examination of Matt Olssen's effects, which had
been stripped from him at the scene and placed in a
transparent plastic bag, offered no clues to his identification. A label in the linen jacket indicated that it
had been purchased in Hong Kong. The shoes were
of French make. There were no labels on the T-shirt,
the underpants, or the socks. The pockets were
empty except for a few crumbs of food; there was not
so much as a handkerchief in them. The only hint as
to the victim's identity, if it could be called that, was
a red and purple tattoo across one buttock, reading:
BETTY.

But, later in the day, the corpse was identified by
its fingerprints, which were on record as the result of
a number of arrests over the past five years, all for

aggravated assault. An address on the East Side was given for one Betty Parker Olssen, listed as the victim's wife.

Arthur Bennett locked himself in a booth in a washroom of the main branch of the N.Y. Public Library, and counted the money in the wallet he had taken from the dead sailor, whimpering with disbelief as he tolled off the numbers in a hoarse whisper. He stuffed the money (nine hundred and eighty-four dollars) into the pocket that held the coins, the disposable lighter, the keys, the salted peanuts, the matchbooks and the bloodstained handkerchief.

He left the library, bought and drank a pint of muscatel, and then wandered down to the Bowery, picking up eighty cents in handouts along the way.

He sold the peaked sailor hat for seventy-five cents, but couldn't dispose of the box, for which he was asking a dollar. When he became too persistent in pushing the sale of the box, someone became annoyed, grabbed it away from him, smashed it by jumping on it, and then threw the remnants into the street where, in time, passing cars splintered it further.

Near noon, two men cornered him in a doorway, beat him unconscious, and took his money.

The olive-slate color of the snake's top blended with the shadowed leaves of the tree, and the starling, lighting on a bough, did not see it.

The snake's vision was highly developed, with particular acuity to perception of movement, and, because of the placement of the eyes at the side of the head, commanding a large field of view. It had picked up the starling in flight and watched it flutter to its perch.

The bird was four feet from the snake's head and facing outward from the tree. The snake's darting tongue picked up the odor of prey. Unmoving, alert, tensed, the snake stared at the bird. Then, anchoring itself by its prehensile tail, mouth wide open, it shot forward in a blur of speed, and sank its fangs into the bird's body. The bird squawked and flew off. But before it had gone twenty feet its wings began to flutter erratically and it dropped to the ground.

The snake did not pursue. It stretched out on the tree, its head hanging downward, its eyes focused on the movements of the bird. Even when the bird struggled feebly into a patch of undergrowth and out of sight of the snake's vision, the snake did not follow. It waited patiently for perhaps five more minutes before it circled down the tree. On the ground it trailed the bird unerringly by means of the special scent left by an injected prey.

The snake's poison organ was a digestive juice in the form of a highly specialized proteinacious saliva. Thus, the snake's venom, in addition to killing the prey, had at the same time begun the process of digesting it.

The starling was dead when the snake found it in the brush. The snake maneuvered its length until the bird's head lay directly in front of its mouth. The bones supporting the snake's lower jaws moved in the skull, the elastic ligaments between the halves of the jaw stretched, and the mouth opened to an astounding width which would accommodate the swallowing of a prey far bigger than the starling, and even larger than the diameter of the snake itself.

The snake hooked the teeth of one side of its

mouth into the bird's head. Using this purchase as a fulcrum, it pushed the other side of the mouth forward a short distance, engaged the teeth (which were useless for chewing and hence required the snake to swallow its prey whole), then repeated the ratcheting process, opposite side after opposite side. The recurved shape of the teeth, acting as hooks, would have prevented a struggling prey from escaping once it had been engaged by the teeth.

The snake gradually ingested the starling, not so much swallowing it as drawing itself over it.

Around 4:30 in the afternoon, two policemen arrived at Betty Olssen's small apartment house to perform the uncomfortable duty of informing her that her husband had been killed. As always, in such instances, they sought the cooperation of a neighbor, on the theory that the involvement of a familiar face would somewhat cushion the shock. But of the first three people they found at home, one claimed not to know Betty Olssen, and two declined, on the basis that they didn't get along with her. One of these, the superintendent of the house, was quite emphatic in his refusal to help. The bitch was nothing but trouble, and, what's more, in the seven years she had lived in the house, had never tipped him as much as a thin dime, even at Christmas.

The policemen decided to proceed without assistance. They rang the widow's bell and, after an awkwardly oblique approach that she fathomed in the first seconds, broke the news of the discovery of her husband's body. They asked her to be so good as to accompany them to the morgue to complete the identification.

The widow, who was pretty, and wearing a

revealing nightdress, took the news calmly, even with a certain grim satisfaction. "I knew the crazy sonofabitch would get himself killed sooner or later."

One of the cops was red in the face. Betty Olssen thought at first it was because of what she had said, but then realized from the way his eyes kept wandering away from her, that he was embarrassed by her near-nakedness.

"Wear a see-through, he told me," she said. "So I put on a see-through and I fell asleep in it. So it shouldn't entirely go to waste, officer, I wish you would take at least one good look at me."

Her face was stolid as she stood in the echoing room in the morgue and waited for the chilled drawer to be pulled out. Mátt Olssen came out feet first, with a tag tied to his big toe. His hair was neatly combed. She looked down at his face with no emotion showing on her own, and simply said, "That's him," and then turned away.

When she asked about the contents of his pockets and was told that there were none, that he had obviously been shot in the course of a robbery, she nodded her head, as if in confirmation of some previously formed judgment. She seemed surprised when the attendant told her that the Medical Examiner's office would perform an autopsy before releasing the remains.

"What for? He was shot, wasn't he?"

"It's required by law. Besides, we sometimes turn up clues that help the police with their investigation. For instance, what position he was in when he was shot, whether the perpetrator was left-handed, maybe what height the perpetrator was. . . ." But the attendant saw that the widow wasn't the least bit interested. He rolled the body back into the refrigerated case. "Okay, miss, tell me where you want the remains sent."

"Feed it to the cats."

Not because he was shocked—after twenty years on the job he had heard everything—but because he had a duty to perform, the attendant said, "You want to give him a decent Christian burial, don't you?"

"He wasn't a decent Christian, so why should he have a decent Christian burial?"

"Well, it's the usual thing. . . ."

"I'll tell you something." Her round face hardened to show some of its underlying bone structure. "The sonofabitch never gave me anything but misery, he starved me out, he spent his money on whores, and I never saw a penny of it except once in a while when he was bombed and, you know what I mean, wanted my favors. So if you think I'm going to spend any of my hard-earned money to bury him, forget it. You got potter's field, right? That's where to bury him."

"Well, we don't call it that," the attendant said. "I can't force you to take the body, but if the city has to bury it, you'll get billed for the expense."

She shrugged.

Meaning, the attendant thought, that billing her is one thing, and collecting another. He said, "Look, he was a seaman, so there's probably a pretty good insurance policy, and union benefits too—right?"

She smiled. "It's the one good thing he ever did for me, and he couldn't help himself—the company took out the policy *for* him. I got that money coming to me, I deserve it, and I'm not gonna piss any of it away burying him."

"Aw, miss," the attendant said, "in the name of common decency—"

"Potter's field," Betty said. "He'll never know the difference."

FOUR

THIS EVENING'S PERFORMANCE at the Delacorte Theatre was to be Richard Brinsley Sheridan's *School for Scandal.* All 2,200-odd free tickets had been distributed by seven o'clock.

At least half the ticket-holders picnicked in the park, mainly in the areas adjacent to the Delacorte: up by the Belvedere Castle, on the banks of the small oblong Belvedere Lake, by the Shakespeare Gardens, and, in the hundreds, on the burnt-out grass of the Great Lawn. The grass was barely visible for the blankets that covered it, on which people sat or reclined or spread their picnic food and drink.

A certain segment of the crowd, notably the older people among them, were festive and uneasy in equal parts. As New Yorkers, trained in the ways of survival in the perilous city, they held it as an article of faith that one didn't enter the park after, or even approaching, dark. And so there was a heady, nervous pleasure in being here now, a sense of willful violation of common sense, like teasing a bull in an open field. They were aware that there was no real danger, of course, since they were part of a vast throng, and since there was a reassuringly sizable police detail on hand. Nevertheless, it was an adventure of sorts.

When the performance began at eight o'clock, it was not quite dark. The buildings to the east lay in dusk, and their windows were already sparkling with lights; to the west, the sky was hazily luminous with the setting sun. In a few moments that light would die away, and darkness would fall. Sitting on their wooden fold-down seats in the circular theater, the crowd was dressed for the stifling heat in light summer shirts and blouses, trousers and skirts and halters, and even, here and there, bikini bathing suits and bare chests. The house lights dimmed, and the audience prepared for its pleasure, knowing that, whatever standard terrors would surely transpire in the more remote regions of the park, here it was cozy and secure.

The snake crept swiftly through the darkness, its slender length always in direct contact with the ground, curved into a continuous flowing S-movement, each part of its body following precisely in the path of the part preceding it.

The snake's movement was by horizontal undulation, a series of gentle curves, with the body forced against the substrate at each curve. This method of locomotion was made possible by the hundreds of vertebrae that constituted its backbone. The scales of its lower surface were enlarged, forming transverse overlapping plates whose free edge was directed backwards, and to each of which was attached a pair of movable ribs. When the ribs moved forward they carried the plate, or scute, with them. Since the scute was smooth, and its leading edge was protected by the one over it, it slipped comfortably over any irregularity in the surface. There was one disadvantage: when the scute was moved backward, its free rear edge snagged. Thus, to all practical purposes, the snake could move in only one direction: forward.

Although it had no awareness of it, the snake was, in part, retracing its movements of the night before, after it had escaped from the box. It passed within a few feet of the place on the pavement where Matt Olssen had died, where it had bitten Torres. Its path took it across a segment of the Great Lawn. If the grass, burnt dry and tanned by the sun, was a familiar environment to the snake, nevertheless many of the odors its tongue carried to the Jacobson's organ were alien to it.

It glided over the edge of the grass, crossed a walkway, and slid toward the Belvedere Lake. It veered to the left, away from the great upward fling of light from the Delacorte Theatre, and then crawled down to the water's edge.

As it drank, a great shout of laughter rose from the theater. The snake didn't hear it. It lacked an external ear, an ear drum, a tympanic cavity, and eustachian tubes. It was deaf.

Roddy Bamberger leaned toward the girl and whispered, "Let's duck out of here and go to my place and turn on the air conditioner and bring out the fine sherry wine and . . ." He brushed her cheek with his lips. ". . . and anything else your heart desires."

Somebody in the row above shushed him. The girl herself didn't answer, didn't even seem to have heard him. She was sitting forward eagerly in her chair, seemingly transported by what was occurring on the lighted stage. Roddy groaned inwardly. Transported, for Godssake, by a bunch of inept emoters without the foggiest notion of how to speak the witty cadences of the great Irish—what else?—master of the English comedy of manners. Some of the speech was as flat as street talk, some of it so badly imitative of flutey mid-Atlantic English that it verged on parody. He had seen college dramatic society versions that were better. And, Christ, in London he had been privileged to be present at a National Theatre performance of *School for Scandal.* After that, this thing was sacrilege!

Looking at the girl, still gazing at the stage with idiot rapture, he couldn't imagine how he had ever thought that profile interesting. What had at first seemed to be an enchanting kind of delicacy was really more aptly describable as simpering. He was an ass to have been beguiled by a profile and a set of agreeable small breasts he had permitted himself to fantasize about in various pleasingly diverting ways.

It was all a bloody mess. He should have had more sense than to have allowed himself to be conned into coming here in the first instance. Free theater—like free anything else—was bound to be lousy theater. What you got for nothing was nothing. Nor should he have deceived himself into thinking that the profile and the quivery little tits might lead to a relationship of lasting (or *protractedly* temporary) value. The girl was worth exactly one dinner, a little arty talk, the air-conditioned bedroom. A one-night stand, and then goodbye forever.

It was all a bloody mess: the play, the girl herself, the ridiculous heat, the chicken and oversweet domestic wine she had put up, and which they had eaten on the buggy Great Lawn surrounded by hundreds of others eating the same cold chicken and hot wine. He despised the crowd around him—the way it dressed, the way it talked, its manners, its uproarious laughter when Sheridan's wit called for a quiet, appreciative smile. Not to mention its collective smell—a blending of sweat, greasy chicken, and pot.

"Arline. . . ." He breathed softly on her cheek, glancing downward at the tender curve of her breast, bra-less under green linen. She turned to him reluctantly, unhappy at being deflected from the play. "Arline." He tuned his voice to a persuasive whisper. "Let's go back to my place." Her eyes kept alternating between him and the stage. "I want to talk to you—seriously."

She made an abrupt gesture, stilling him so that she could catch the next line of the play. Above, somebody was shushing him again. He twisted around to glare back at an angry face covered by black beard. He faced front, but refused to look at the stage. He fixed his gaze on his knees, sharply outlined by the silk of his trousers. He placed his hands on his knees and molded them, feeling the bone of the patella, the indentation beneath, the hard bone running down his leg.

Okay. If he was reduced to feeling his own leg for excitement he had bought it. Chalk up the evening as a disaster and cut his losses forthwith. And, of course, take a solemn oath never again to be intrigued by a profile that was less than it seemed, a breast that might well be humid and clammy to the touch.

"I'm sorry, Arline, I'm feeling dreadfully sick."

He was already halfway to his feet. She looked at him in distress. For him, or for fear of having to leave the play? She glanced quickly at the stage before facing him again. The play's the thing! She started to say something to him, but he was already moving through the aisle, bumping knees, murmuring insincere apologies. At the end of the aisle he looked back. She was looking at him, discomposed, uncertain, but it was too late. Even if she were to chase after him, and offer to thrust those little tits into his mouth, he would have none of it.

It occurred to him, as he left the theater, that he would be walking through the park alone, but he wasn't overly nervous about it. There were lots of cops around, and, undoubtedly, the Muggers Benevolent Association had put out an advisory to its membership. The conceit amused him, and he smiled. A couple of cops, lounging on the brick walkway around the perimeter of the theater, smiled back at him.

He headed eastward between the Belvedere Lake and the Great Lawn, on a course that would take him in a direct line to Fifth Avenue. He walked alertly, his eyes moving actively from left to right and behind him—only a fool took anything for granted—but he still saw it an instant before he stepped on it. He saw it but didn't quite believe it, which was perhaps why, with his right foot on the way down to meet the pavement, his reflexes didn't react to compel the foot to step clear over it instead of coming down flatly on its tail.

The tail rolled under his foot (he felt its steely firmness through the thin leather of his sandal) and he no longer questioned the snake's reality. Revulsion ran through his body from his foot to his brain, and in his effort to step free—though perhaps the writhing of the snake had something to do with it—he lost his balance and fell on it.

The snake whipped back on itself, coiling and twisting to free itself of the man's weight. Its head curved back, mouth wide, and it struck. Its fangs sank into flesh. It bit again. It launched a third strike, but the man was rolling away from it, so that, although one of its fangs penetrated, the other only grazed the target.

The snake lost its balance and fell toward the man. Writhing, its light underside visible, it forced its coils back against the man, and pushed itself away. Quickly, with powerful surging curves, it slithered off the walkway and into the grass.

The sense of unreality persisted.

Roddy Bamberger lay still on the pavement after the snake had gone, as one did in the aftermath of a nightmare, waiting for logic to return, to dislodge fantasy, to reestablish a sense of time and place. Naturally, the details were vivid: the irrecoverable instant when he might have withheld his step, the horrible feel of the snake rolling under his foot, the contortions of those writhing coils, the savagery of the gaping mouth and the head poised to strike. . . .

It was real, it had happened. There would be no waking to thankful relief. The snake had bitten him. It was a real snake and it had actually bitten him. He recalled the incredibly long, swift strike, the impact of the fangs, not really all that painful, however. He had been bitten on the back of the thigh, not far below the first swell of the buttocks.

He eased his hand fearfully down to his thigh. Some blood, not much. Suddenly, he felt awful. He was having some trouble breathing—God, was he going to have a heart attack? He rolled over and with a good deal of effort got to his feet. He felt lightheaded, dizzy, and his legs were wobbly. He was weak, drowsy, and wanted to lie down. But he resisted the impulse because it filled him with revulsion to think of lying down where the snake had been, where it had left a trail of slime. But that wasn't true. Snakes were not slimy but dry. . . .

He began to run back toward the halo of light that marked the Delacorte Theatre. He ran poorly, stumblingly: his legs were trembling, he couldn't seem to draw a decent breath, his mouth was choked with saliva. But he kept on, driven by terror and the incomprehensible but dread certainty that he was dying.

He collapsed a hundred feet from the theater, and might have lain there until the performance ended if a cop, strolling down the walk for a smoke, had not seen him. He tried to tell the cop about the snake, but he was unable to talk. He was only barely conscious.

There was not even time to call a Code Blue; the patient died thirty seconds after being wheeled in. Dr. Pranay Mukerjee saw the breathing stop, although, in his stethoscope, the heart continued to beat for a measurable time afterwards, perhaps thirty or forty beats. It could not be started up again.

Dr. Mukerjee was an experienced physician. He had served his residency in the Philippines, and was now pursuing his specialty, rheumatoid diseases, at a hospital in Brooklyn. Nevertheless, several times a week he did Emergency Ward duty for the fees, which he dutifully passed on to his family in Calcutta.

He was folding his stethoscope away in the pocket of his white jacket when a nurse came hurrying in. "He's dead," Dr. Mukerjee said. "Will you inform the Medical Examiner's office, please?"

Almost for the first time, Dr. Mukerjee looked at the man on the table as a person. In his mid-thirties, well-nourished, extremely well-dressed. A rictus of fright on the face. As noted before, an unsightly dribble of thick mucus in the mouth, on the lips and chin. Dr. Mukerjee lifted the corpse's hand, looked at the fingernails and dropped it. Cyanotic. What was the cause of death? Respiratory failure. According to the police who had brought him in he had collapsed in the park. Drug overdose? Not likely. The heartbeat had been fast and thready, but not abnormally so. The pupils were not dilated.

Dr. Mukerjee's eye was caught by a small smear of blood on the table. But no wound was visible. Beneath him, perhaps? He turned the corpse over and saw it at once: a slight bloodiness on the trousers, high up on the inside of the left thigh. Doesn't look much, Dr. Mukerjee thought, yet—shall we see?

He cut the left leg of the man's trousers away from the cuff to the belt, spread the material apart and bent low over the thigh. After a moment, he straightened up. Shaking his head, smiling, he said aloud, first in Bengali, and then in precise English translation, "Ah, no, it is not possible, is it?"

The nurse, who had just finished her call, said, "Did you say something, doctor?"

"Yes, nurse. Some alcohol, please."

He swabbed the thigh clean of blood, and studied

the affected area intently. There were two pairs of perforations, and a third perforation by itself. No, not quite by itself—in company with a light surface scratch. Below each perforation he could make out a series of tiny indentations, dropping down in a straight vertical from the perforations.

"Quite possible, indeed," he said aloud. He was still smiling when he addressed the nurse, but his voice had an edge of urgency. "Please find Dr. Shapiro for me."

"You want to talk to Dr. Shapiro on the phone?"

"Ask him to come to Emergency, please. Stat, please."

The encounter with the man had left the snake irritable, so that, when a small garter snake crossed its path, it took a striking position and hissed. In a different mood it would have recognized that the garter snake was no threat, and ignored it. But now it bit. It remained in striking position, head high, mouth open, and watched the garter snake writhe and twist in agony.

It was not tempted to eat the garter snake. Unlike many other species, which would eat other snakes, it preferred a diet of warm-blooded animals.

The snake went around the dying garter snake and into its adopted territory. It climbed the tree, spread itself loosely on a net of high branches, and went to sleep.

Dr. Mukerjee apologized to Dr. Shapiro for disturbing him, and then described the symptoms of the dead man lying on the table.

Dr. Shapiro looked startled. "We had one like that

last night. Early this morning, rather." He walked to the table and frowned down at the body.

"It is thoroughly outlandish, of course," Dr. Mukerjee said, smiling, "but the clinical symptoms are remarkably consistent."

"Consistent with what?"

"I direct your attention to these perforations," Mukerjee said. "This pair here, and this second pair. . . ." His long brown finger touched the white skin. "And this single one here, a seeming anomaly which I will presently explain. You will also notice, please, the series of tiny indentations below each puncture, some of which have begun to fade—"

"Yes, yes," Shapiro said. "Do you know what those punctures are, Dr. Mukerjee?"

"I believe they are fang marks."

"Of what sort of animal?" Shapiro spoke sharply. He was very quick and direct himself, and he suspected Mukerjee of milking the suspense.

"Of a poisonous snake, doctor," Mukerjee said.

Shapiro made an ambiguous gesture, then said, "I've never seen snakebite. I presume you have?"

"Yes."

"What about the single perforation?" It was not an immediately pertinent question, and Shapiro was aware of it. He was temporizing, to allow his mind to catch up with the exotic diagnosis.

"I believe the snake struck twice successfully, and a third time inaccurately, so that only one of its fangs penetrated. The tiny small indentations are the impression of the animal's back teeth, which have no attack function."

"Okay," Shapiro said with a strained smile. "Somewhere in Manhattan there is a rattlesnake at large."

"Oh, no," Mukerjee said. "Rattlesnakes secrete a hemotoxic venom. In that case the flesh in the area around the punctures would be heavily swollen, discolored, and quite painful. From the condition of these—the cleanliness, if you will—and, of course, the patient's symptoms and probable cause of death, this would be a neurotoxic venom. If I am to venture a guess as to the identity of the animal, I would say Naja Naja, doctor."

You're something of a pedant, Dr. Mukerjee, Shapiro thought irritably. He said, "What is Naja Naja?"

"I have seen a number of the victims of its bits at home in India. It is the cobra." Dr. Mukerjee smiled. "Our national snake, as it were."

"A cobra? We're a long way from India, aren't we, doctor?"

"Outlandish, as I stated at the outset." Mukerjee's finger tapped the corpse's thigh. "The inner thigh is of course a rich vascular area. It is even possible that one of the fangs might have injected directly into a vein. Awfully bad luck. He could have died twenty minutes after being bitten."

"Outlandish is right," Shapiro said. "You're certain of your diagnosis, Doctor Mukerjee?"

"If I were in India, I would say yes, flat out. Here, I will simply say that the indications strongly suggest the bite of a snake distilling a powerful neurotoxic poison."

"Yes, well. . . ." Shapiro looked at Mukerjee sharply. "Caution is certainly indicated in such an unusual diagnosis, and it does you credit. This is not, as you say, India."

"Most assuredly it is not," Mukerjee said. He

paused. "Did you not mention seeing a somewhat similar case last night?"

"Paralysis of the chest muscles. Semicomatose, so he couldn't tell us anything. He died on us."

"Ah," Mukerjee said. "Fang marks, too?"

"No, there weren't any. . . ." Shapiro's voice faltered as he remembered the bloodstains on the patient's trousers. Damn that Papaleo! Mukerjee was looking at him politely, waiting for an answer. Well, he wasn't about to bad-mouth one of his interns to another physician. What he would say to Papaleo was something else again. "Not to my knowledge. We're waiting on the M.E.'s report. If that one and this—" He tilted his head toward the corpse. "Meanwhile, professional caution to one side, you're really convinced, aren't you?"

"I wouldn't stake my entire reputation on it, don't you know, but. . . ." Mukerjee shrugged.

"Yes, yes," Shapiro said impatiently. "The question is this—shall I tell the police about it?"

"I should do so," Mukerjee said.

Dr. Shapiro returned to his room and phoned the police, who said they would send someone around to see him. He phoned the Medical Examiner's office and requested a rush report on Torres, Ramon, and a second cadaver, Bamberger, Roderick, soon to arrive at the morgue; suspected injection of neurotoxic venom by snakebite. He tried to get hold of Dr. Papaleo but was told that he was not in the house, it was his night off.

It *would* be, Shapiro thought. He picked his copy of *Beeson and McDermott* out of his bookshelves and began to read up on snakebites and their treatment. Before he had gotten very far he was summoned to the main reception room of the hospital, where a stocky, hard-faced man wearing a flowered shirt and peg-bottom chino pants introduced himself as Detective Robert Dark.

Shapiro said, "Good evening."

"About this alleged snake?"

"Yes. We haven't established as an absolute fact that it *is* a snake, but from indications—"

"That was the squeal, doc, that somebody got bitten by a snake. You aren't sure?"

"That was *my* squeal, well, phone call, but I said we *suspected* snakebite."

"You're a doctor," Dark said. "You oughta *know*."

Shapiro felt himself growing annoyed. Dark's tone was peevish, even challenging. Tough guy. Or maybe, to be charitable, his precinct house wasn't air-conditioned. He said, "Detective Dark, two men have died of respiratory arrest that suggests paralysis due to injection of a neurotoxic substance. One occurred early this morning, the second less than an hour ago. On the body of the second one we found perforations that might have been inflicted by a snake's fangs."

"What about the first one? Did he have the perforations?"

Everybody asks the right questions, Shapiro thought drily. He said, "Because of certain factors, we haven't determined that yet." Certain factors: a first-year intern's failure to take off a pair of pants.

Dark shrugged. "These perforations. That means like holes. You think of overdose?"

"Overdose is contraindicated. The diagnosis of

snakebite was made by an Indian doctor who is familiar with cobra bite.''

"A cobra snake?" Dark almost smiled. "I can see why you're not standing on that diagnosis, doc.''

"We're standing on it, officer, unless we're contradicted by the autopsy report: I phoned the M.E. and asked them to expedite a report. The soonest they can get around to it is early tomorrow morning.'' He smiled sourly. "They say they're very busy.''

"Everybody's very busy,'' Dark said. "So what do you want me to do, doc?''

"Hell," Shapiro said, "that's your business. How do I know? Check out the various zoos, pet shops. . . .''

"This time of the night? When we don't even know for sure that there's a snake, which I personally doubt it's a snake? Tell you what *I* would do, doc—wait for the autopsy report. How long does it take them to do an autopsy?''

"Who knows? Some of those fellows can dawdle over their work for hours. It's like looking up a word in the dictionary and being waylaid by a dozen other words on the page that you get curious about. You know?''

"Well, doc. . . .'' Dark put away his notebook, in which he had hardly made an entry. "I honestly think we ought to wait for the morning. There ain't a thing we can *do* right now, anyway.''

"Two men have been bitten in the park—*allegedly* bitten, as you say, I'll accept that—and who is to say that by morning there won't be a third?''

"I tell you, doc, anybody who goes into that park at night is likely to get killed one way or another. If he doesn't get bit by a cobra snake, he's gonna get himself killed some other way. Fact, we had a guy shot dead in the park just last night around three in the morning.''

Shapiro sighed. "Well, I'm just trying to do what I think is best.''

"Me too," Dark said.

The snake lay on the black rock under the sun, its length spread out in gentle curves.

During the night, lying in its tree, the snake had lost its fangs, but new fangs had already moved up into position.

The snake's upper jaw contained only two teeth, the poison fangs, ankylosed to the inside of the jawbone. The fangs were connected to the poison gland, and conducted venom from it through a canal. The fangs of a poisonous snake were subjected to much wear, and had to be replaced from time to time. Sometimes, they broke off prematurely. But substitute fangs, always growing just behind the functioning ones, would move up to take the place of the lost fangs. This cycle of loss and replacement continued throughout the snake's life.

Because of the continuing heat wave—now in its fourth day—the snake had lost little of its body heat during the night. Now, in the fierceness of the morning sun, it basked for only a brief time.

It glided fluidly down the rock and into its territory. It climbed into its tree and spread out amid dense foliage, which provided concealment and shelter from the rays of the sun.

FIVE

WHEN DR. SHAPIRO finished his morning rounds he went down to the hospital cafeteria for a second breakfast. Papaleo appeared beside his table.

"Did you hear it?"

Papaleo seemed pale and nervous. Shapiro sopped up runny egg with a piece of toast and washed it down with coffee. Then he looked up and said, "Hear what, Dr. Papaleo?"

"On the radio? It came in less than five minutes ago."

"I don't make rounds with a radio, doctor."

Papaleo grimaced, as if in admission of his own clumsiness, then said, "The radio, a flash, they said two people had been bitten by a snake in the park and died at East Side Hospital."

Shapiro put his fork down with a clatter. "The *radio?* What else did they say?"

"That's all. That two people had died of

snakebite. It was one of those flashes. You know, 'This just in,' and 'more on the story as it develops.' "

"Did they say where the information came from?"

"I don't think so."

Shapiro nodded and turned back to his eggs, but Papaleo lingered, fidgeting.

"On the one I treated, tried to treat," Papaleo said. "I have to tell you. There were perforations on the thigh. I guess they were fang marks."

Shapiro stared at him.

Papaleo was sweating. "After you left, I cut the patient's pants off and saw the marks. I actually thought of snakebite, but it didn't make any sense."

"It was your duty to wake me and tell me."

"I know. But you had gone back to sleep, and. . . ." Papaleo made a helpless, self-incriminating gesture, then said with some dignity, "I'm sorry, doctor."

My fault, Shapiro thought. He didn't tell me because he was afraid I'd either ream him out or laugh at him. That tells me more about myself than it does about Papaleo. He said, "It's my fault for not insisting on removing the patient's pants."

"Oh." Papaleo tried to smile, then said, "Well, anyway," and hurried away.

Shapiro finished his breakfast and then phoned the M.E.'s office. He asked for the pathologist who had performed the autopsy on Torres and, after some phone switching, was connected with Dr. Borkowski.

"How do you like that?" Borkowski seemed tickled. "Fatal snakebite in the middle of Manhattan—isn't that terrific?"

"I've been waiting for your phone call, Dr. Borkowski."

"I was on the verge of it. In fact, I had my hand on

the phone when the phone rang and it was you. The phone rang just as I was picking up the phone."

"Yeah, sure, it's a thrilling coincidence," Shapiro said. "I don't mind your making hay with the media, but you might have done me the courtesy—"

"I resent the implication, doctor."

"It wasn't an implication, it was an accusation. And I don't give a fuck whether you resent it or not."

Borkowski was silent a moment, then said stiffly, "The report will be on its way over. Meanwhile, to sum up my findings, the spectral analysis showed—"

"Never mind. I'll get it from the radio like the rest of the public." He overrode Borkowski's protest. "What about the second one?"

"I'm working on it right now. Jesus, it hit him five times, and at least one of them must have caught a vein. What a hell of a shot!" Borkowski had recaptured his gusto. "I swear, a bull's-eye. He was probably dead in fifteen or twenty minutes after he got stuck. Some shot!"

"Your enthusiasm is infectious," Shapiro said. "Look, doctor, I'd appreciate hearing from you as soon as you've finished with him. Me first, and then the media. I promise not to take too much of your time."

Borkowski said, "I resent the implication, doctor. Or the accusation, which is even worse. If you're making an out-and-out accusation, I demand an apology."

Shapiro had been hearing a page for the last half-minute. He jiggled the phone, cutting Borkowski off, and asked the operator what she wanted.

"There are some gentlemen here to see you," the operator said. "From the press. And also . . ." her voice became breathy," . . . from the television, too."

"Oh, shit," Shapiro said.

In the normal course of events, the Police Commissioner would have read about the snake in the morning report of overnight events prepared for him by his staff; and Hizzonner the Mayor would have been informed of it promptly by one of his young aides. But, instead of driving him to his office at No. 1 Police Plaza, the P.C.'s limousine had taken him directly to City Hall, where he was to help the mayor formulate an optimistic statement on recent crime statistics for presentation at a noontime news conference.

Hizzonner had issued a stern fiat against being disturbed for any reason whatsoever. His aides, mindful of his unpredictability in an election year, were prudently obedient, even though it was their consensus that the story of the snake just barely came under the umbrella of "whatsoever."

The purpose of the news conference was to announce a radical decrease in the homicide rate for the first six months of the year (down a whopping 1 percent), thus more than offsetting a negligible rise in crimes of violence (19 percent) and felonies (14 percent). Hizzonner would also point with quiet pride to the absence of a major riot (and only one mini-riot) in the city's major ghettos—Harlem, Bedford-Stuyvesant, the South Bronx, and the East Harlem barrio—due to a forceful but understanding police presence, and it is high time that we fully appreciated the sterling professionalism of the city's cops, under the firm but sympathetic guidance of our sterling Police Commissioner. "Don't smile when I say that,

Francis, and don't look modest, either. Just stare straight ahead into the camera.''

At 11:30, terrified that the mayor might walk into his press conference unbriefed on the snake, one of Hizzonner's aides entered without apology, walked across the room with the early edition of the *New York Post,* and placed it on the desk beneath Hizzonner's eyes.

KILLER SNAKE SLAYS
TWO IN PARK

The mayor goggled. The news story on page three, to which the aide obligingly turned, was brief, and tricked out with photographs and quotations from Dr. Shapiro, Dr. Mukerjee, Dr. Papaleo, and Dr. Borkowski. There was a single-column cut of each, arranged in a circle around a picture of a semi-naked girl, the Maharani Santha Agnes Chowdhury, playing the flute to a swaying cobra in a Cincinnati nightclub.

A small inset box contained a few facts about Central Park. Acclaimed masterpiece of its justly celebrated architects, Frederick Law Olmsted and Calvert Vaux. One of the great parks of the world, unsurpassed for beauty of conception and design. Its 843 acres larger than London's Hyde Park, Paris's Tuileries Gardens, Berlin's Tiergarten, Copenhagen's Tivoli Gardens. Not as large as Rome's Villa Borghese or Vienna's Prater. Purchased for $5.5 million in 1856, real estate market value today: untold billions.

The lead editorial, obviously a last-minute insertion, consisted of three sentences.

● ● ●

THERE IS A SNAKE IN CENTRAL PARK.
IT IS KILLING PEOPLE.
WHAT IS THE MAYOR DOING ABOUT IT?

"Dirty pool," the aide said indignantly. "It's one thing for them to endorse your opponent, but—"

"The bastards," Hizzonner said. "I'll show 'em what I'm doing about it. I'm leaving no stone unturned, that's what I'm doing about it!"

He used the phrase, later, at his news conference, where it was greeted with a mixutre of awe and muffled hilarity. He amplified on this declaration by telling his audience that the Central Park Precinct, which knew the park the way you gentlemen know your wife's, ah, face (laughter), were out in full saturation force, combing every nook and cranny for the interloper, with the able assistance of park personnel.

"Give 'em the details, Francis," the mayor said to the P.C.

The P.C., who had only fifteen minutes earlier learned of the details himself by telephone, declared that the men of the Central Park Precinct were fine-combing the park in cars, on horseback, on scooters, and on foot, ably assisted by Parks Department gardeners and groundsmen, as well as one of the justly famous Emergency Service Unit trucks.

"How many men is that, all told?" a reporter asked.

It was a good question, and the P.C., frowning in annoyance at being interrupted, ignored it. He knew that the total muster strength of the Central Park Precinct was in the neighborhood of 120 men, which broke down to 40 per shift. Subtract from that number clerical personnel, special duty officers, anticrime detective units on stakeout detail, shop personnel, officers on vacation and sick call, and the Central Park Precinct probably had not more than 15 men available for fine-tooth-combing the 840-odd acres of the park.

"Many of the cars are equipped with loudspeakers," the P.C. said, "instructing people to stay on the walkways and out of heavily brushed areas, to keep to the more frequented parts of the park, to be alert at all times, to make no attempt to deal with the snake if they spot it but to inform a police officer immediately. . . ."

"Mr. Mayor," a reporter said, "are you considering closing the park for the citizens' safety until the snake is found?"

The mayor was too practiced a public performer to blink, but he did pause perceptibly before saying, "You may rest assured, gentlemen, the matter has been under intense study since early this morning."

After the news conference broke up, the mayor, alone with the P.C., permitted his emotions to show. "How'd you like that bastard asking me if I was going to close the park down? He knows the answer as well as I do. Close the park in the middle of a heat wave when the worthy poor—as if his lousy rag gives a damn about them—are gasping for a breath of air?"

"You'd need a thousand cops to keep people out," the P.C. said, "and even then you couldn't do it. You know people in this city? Try to keep them out and they'd find a hundred ways to get in. Believe me, they'd try to get in."

"Believe me," the mayor said, "I believe you."

• • •

After a brief opening citation of the weather—"near record-breaking heat for September with no relief in sight"—the early evening news program on the mayor's favorite television network ("they're somewhat less bad than the others") devoted a whopping eight full minutes of airtime to the story of the snake, exclusive of commercial interruption.

The sequence opened with a panoramic sweep of the park from a circling helicopter ("the most valuable parcel of real estate in the civilized world"). The helicopter swooped low over the Sheep Meadow, headed northward toward the Lake, then rose again for another long shot of the park to its northern terminus at Cathedral Parkway. The whirr of its motor was damped down to accommodate the voice of the anchorman: "Somewhere in the more than eight hundred acres of famed Central Park there lurks an unwelcome visitor to the city—a venomous snake whose deadly bite has already claimed the lives of two victims."

The mayor watched the screen from an armchair in his bedroom on the second floor of Gracie Mansion. From time to time he groaned rhetorically.

The helicopter, now flying very low to the ground, swept swiftly back from north to south. Its camera focused fleetingly on a policeman on horseback or one riding a scooter. "From noontime on, cops from the Central Park Precinct have been scouring the park, thus far without result. Here's Bill Arthur, direct from the park." The scene shifted to ground level, picking up a cop emerging from heavy undergrowth, moving gingerly, beating out in front of him with his nightstick. The camera closed in when the cop reached the walkway.

"Any luck, officer?"

The cop was breathing hard, his face was tomato red, his light blue uniform shirt was darkened by sweat. He looked at the reporter with murder in his eyes. But then, remembering the presence of the camera, he reassembled his features into a mask.

"No sir."

"How long have you been searching?"

"Noon."

The camera shifted to the reporter, who was nodding his head sympathetically. "Must be pretty hot work."

"Real hot."

The reporter studied the cop dispassionately for a moment, then gave up. "Back to you, Jerry."

"The police search continues," the anchorman said. "It's hot work, and dangerous, too. . . . Earlier today, reporter Bill Stevens was at East Side Hospital."

Dr. Papaleo, described as "the earnest young intern who treated the first victim of the snake, Ramon Torres," told reporter Bill Stevens how he had watched helplessly as the snake's first victim had died.

"At that time, you didn't know the cause?"

"Not at that time."

Dr. Mukerjee, soft-eyed and soft-spoken, reminded the reporter that his "brilliant snap diagnosis" of cobra-bite was as yet not proven. "It was a bite *similar* to that of a cobra, shall we say."

Dr. Shapiro, Chief Resident of the hospital, his eyes ringed with fatigue, his lips curling impatiently, answered questions brusquely and minimally. When

the reporter asked him what he would do if another
snakebite victim was brought into the hospital, he
opened the door of a refrigerator and took out a
small cardboard box.

"This is a polyvalent, wide-spectrum antivenin.
We received it from the curator of herpetology at the
Bronx Zoo, as did all other hospitals in the area. If
another snakebite victim is brought in he'll be injected with this serum intravenously."

"May I ask which snake this serum is effective
against?"

Consulting the lid of the cardboard box, Dr.
Shapiro said, "Bitis, naja, dendroaspis. Bitis covers
various species of vipers and adders, naja is the
cobra, dendroaspis are arboreal snakes, such as the
mambas of Africa. If our snake is not one of these,
the antivenin will be useless. If it *is* one of these, it
may be effective. The most effective antivenins are
the specific ones: cobra serum for cobra bite, gaboon
viper serum for gaboon viper bite, and so forth.
Identifying the snake in the park is still of paramount
importance. If you'll excuse me, I must attend to a
patient."

"From East Side Hospital, Bill Stevens."

"Where did the snake come from, and how did it
get into the park?" The anchorman answered his
own question: "Nobody knows." Zoos, pet shops,
laboratories, exotic animal farms—all of these had
been queried, none had reported a missing snake.
Nor had any individuals who owned pet snakes come
forward. Perhaps such an individual existed, who for
obvious reasons didn't wish to make a self-
incriminating admission? A plea from a Deputy
Commissioner of the N.Y.P.D.: "If you are such an
individual, and your snake has escaped, call

anonymously. It is vital that we know exactly what *kind* of snake the death snake is, so that the proper antidote can be stocked.'' The Deputy Commissioner made an appeal to the public for information, and gave a special police number, which the camera flashed on the screen.

''Where did the snake come from, and how did it get into the park? Thus far, we do not know. And perhaps we shall never find out.''

The anchorman's face faded, and a tinkle of music introduced a laundry detergent commercial. The mayor found it mildly interesting.

After the commercial, the news report continued, setting the mood with a brief shot of a cobra in its glass cage at the Staten Island Zoo, erect, hood spread, eyes glittering. Next came a close-up shot of the mayor ''at this morning's news conference at City Hall.'' Hizzonner leaned forward in his chair and watched himself with a blend of professional detachment and affection. ''. . . leave no stone unturned. . . .'' Hizzonner sat back again when the camera focused on the Police Commissioner's speech.

Hizzonner, speaking aloud, passed judgment on his performance. ''The one thing you can say for me is that I know where the camera is every second. It must be instinctive.''

From City Hall, the scene shifted to the American Museum of Natural History, where a herpetologist, holding a jar containing a tiny snake no thicker than a pencil, which he seemed to be using as a hand prop, since he made no mention of it, declared that a drastic sudden turn in the weather, a rapidly falling thermometer, was highly desirable. This would cause the snake to become lethargic, disoriented, thus

sharply decreasing the danger of anyone else being
bitten. Meanwhile, some general advice: Stay out of
the underbrush. Watch where you set your feet down
if you're walking in tall grass. Although many snakes
could strike with incredible speed, they could not
locomote swiftly: the average human could easily
outrun just about any snake in the world. Don't
worry (smiling) about the snake chasing you. Except
in very rare instances, such as during the breeding
season, or in protection of their eggs, snakes would
not pursue a man.

The herpetologist offered advice on what to do in
case of snakebite: avoid strenuous activity, alcohol,
panic—all of these speed up the heartbeat and cir-
culate the venom more quickly through the body. Lie
down, apply a tourniquet above the wound in the
direction of the heart, inject antivenin as quickly as
possible. As to incising and sucking out the venom, it
goes in and out of fashion with the regularity of
(smiling) breast-feeding. If you do suck the venom,
make sure there are no lesions in your mouth or lips.

Hizzonner paid little attention to the herpetologist.
He was waiting for the inevitable man-on-the-street
interviews, which, idiotic as they might seem, must
be read seriously by the politician, for, however
cracked and inarticulate, they were truly the voice of
the people.

The first interview took place in the children's
playground at Central Park West and 81st Street,
near the Hunter's Gate. A young woman in a halter
and shorts, filmed against a background of antic
swings and seesaws, and the penetrating screams of
toddlers, speaks aggrievedly: "Where do I go if I
don't come to the park with my child—the French
Riveria?" She turns her back to the camera and

screams: "Mervyn! Don't just stand there when he hits you. Hit him back." She faces the reporter. "Self-reliance. Young as he is, I keep drumming it into him. Where was I"

"You were intimating that you would continue to come to the park in spite of the snake."

"Where are my alternatives? I won't turn my son into a hothouse flower. Besides, can a snake be any worse than the winos that hang around here and drink and spit and curse and ogle and generally carry on like an eyesore?"

A middle-aged couple, coming up out of an Independent subway station. The woman: "Maybe the snake will eat up some muggers. If that's the case, they should have one on every street." Her husband: "Sylvia, it's nothing to laugh at!" Woman: "Do you see me laughing?" Husband: "Sylvia!"

Another man coming out of the subway, hot, disheveled, in a hurry, forcing the reporter to trot to keep up with him. The man: "It's a pure cover-up." Reporter: "A cover-up? For what?" Man: "For everything."

So far, Hizzonner thought, mostly comedy. But his intuition told him there was more substantive matter to come, and presently he was proved right.

On Central Park West and 73rd Street, the spokeswoman for an angry group of mothers, surrounded by milling children: "They must close the park. That mayor, he's trifling with human lives."

In front of his storefront headquarters, an activist state legislator: "Tomorrow morning, I shall lead a delegation of justifiably indignant citizens to City Hall to confront the mayor and demand that he close the park forthwith, and keep it closed until such time as the snake is apprehended. And we will also demand an all-out effort to apprehend it, instead of this transparent half-hearted effort.'' Applause from the legislator's constituents.

On Cathedral Parkway, a clot of several dozen women, black and Hispanic, many dark resentful eyes. The spokeswoman, a large forceful black woman: ''He close that park over our dead body. We stifling in our apartments, even the rats gasping. Where else we got to go to beat the heat? He close that park and he hear from us come election time.'' Flashing eyes in the circle around her, clenched fists, shouts of ''Right on! *Arriba!*''.

A man getting out of a taxi in front of an imposing apartment building on Fifth Avenue: ''They've got a handful of cops in the park. It's pitiful. They don't stand a chance in hell. What's called for is the mounting of a supreme effort. They're just not trying. What I'd like to know is where our tax money goes.'' Reporter: ''Where do you think it's going?'' Man, over his shoulder, as he hurries toward the building entrance: ''It's lining certain pockets.'' Reporter: ''*Whose* pockets, sir?'' Man: ''Don't ask me. Ask our mayor.''

The final clip was light in tone, as if to leaven the antecedent bitterness. Three teen-aged girls, giggling. One of them says, ''It's kicky.'' Reporter: ''Kicky? What do you mean by kicky?'' The girl: ''Kicky? It means, well, like a groove.'' She and her companions burst into laughter and run off down the street. Reporter, shaking his head and smiling: ''I'm kicking it back to you, Jerry.''

Jerry, the anchorman, smiling, ''You're in the groove, fella.'' He pauses, adjusts his face to appropriate sobriety, and says, ''To recapitulate, a deadly venomous snake, origin unknown, suspected to be a cobra, is at large in Central Park. Two men have already succumbed to its fatal poison. The city has the jitters. . . ."

The mayor pressed his remote-control device and shut off the television set.

Hizzonner tracked the P.C. down at a Holy Name Society banquet, where he was guest of honor, and where, in his opening remarks, he made opportunistic reference to the absence of snakes in Ireland, thanks to good St. Paddy. Laughter and applause.

"When are you going to catch that snake?" the mayor said.

"I wish I knew," the P.C. said. "It'll be dark in a half hour, and we'll call off the search until tomorrow."

"And what are you going to do tomorrow?"

"More of the same. A diligent, quiet search."

"Forget quiet, Francis. Do it noisy. You get my meaning?"

Normally a quick study, and sensitive to innuendo, the P.C. was presently dulled by Irish whiskey. A further sign of his befuddlement was the surfacing of his brogue. "Whatever do ye mean, Sor?"

"It's war," the mayor said. "Two people have been slain. War has been declared. They're mobilizing. Everybody is blaming the snake on the mayor. They're going to be swarming around City Hall tomorrow by the thousands."

"So soon?"

"It's all the TV's fault. They *make* everything go faster. They make news by getting the public all worked up. They're provocateurs. Are you listening?"

"I am, Sor. They're going to want the park closed?"

"Half of them are. The other half are going to want it to be kept open. The opposition is behind it, too. They're pushing it along to embarrass me. Who do you think is behind those people in Harlem?"

The P.C. made an effort to clear up his confusion. "What did you mean by noisy? We'll have police cars in the park with loudspeakers all night."

"Goddamit, Francis. The main issue is not the snake, per se, I can live with the snake. The main issue is going to be the closing of the park, and it's a no-win issue. I can't afford to say yes, and I can't afford to say no. I have to stand pat. Do you follow me, Francis?"

"Explicitly, Sor."

"Well, I'm not so sure." The mayor paused. "Follow me explicitly, Francis. One, the snake has become Topic A. Two, they're all putting the blame on the mayor, saying we're not doing enough. Your handful of cops was invisible in that big park. We have to make them visible, so they can see the mayor is working for them. That means a very big police presence, Francis. I want five hundred cops in that park tomorrow morning."

"Five hundred? Where am I going to get them?"

"Get them. I don't care if you have to bring off-duty cops back on emergency duty. Just get them, just get that five hundred."

"I don't dare. The PBA would crucify us."

"Then take them out of Harlem and Bed-Stuy and the South Bronx. I want the people of this city to see with their own eyes that the mayor is leaving no stone unturned."

"Sor, pulling the police presence out of them areas is an invitation to riot."

"No more excuses, Francis. I order you to put five hundred cops in the park tomorrow morning, and that's the bottom line. Good night, Francis."

The mayor hung up.

The special police number provided by the Deputy Commissioner on the news broadcast began to ring within minutes of the announcement. The prevailing tenor of the calls was established early in the evening. A woman's voice, dark with suspicion, said, "How come when you announced the special number you didn't say all calls would be kept confidential?"

"Okay, lady, your call will be kept confidential."

"That's all I want to know," the lady said, and hung up.

There was a predictable number of jokers.

"My old lady just saw the snake." "Where?" "When I unzipped my pants."

"The snake just got on a 65th Street crosstown bus, and when it asked for a transfer the driver bit it.".

"A couple of kids outside my house are using the snake for a jump rope."

It was a familiar story to the police, who had learned to practice patience as an art in these circumstances. Except for the most outlandish of them, they methodically logged every call that came in. There were calls from people who had spotted the snake in their apartment house elevator. Others had seen it climbing up a traffic light stanchion, crawling through a subway tunnel, sunning itself on a neighbor's terrace; in a restaurant, a branch library, a street excavation, a beach at Coney Island. A cab driver swore he had run over it in the street, and breathlessly gave the location of the incident. The snake turned out to be a cable stretched across the street to record the incidence of passing vehicles. A number of callers had heard it hissing in a room of their apartment and had fled to the street.

Several calls, all too obviously, came from shopkeepers who had spotted the snake in other shops, which invariably turned out to be those of their competitors. Several people denounced by name the culprit who had turned the snake loose in the park; in all cases the person they named was a neighbor who, as subsequent questioning brought out, happened to have children who urinated in the hallways, broke windows and cursed, or owned a dog that barked all night. Several individuals who preferred to remain anonymous, and a number of activist organizations which did not, claimed "credit" for introducing the snake into the park.

About 70 percent of the sightings were within the confines of Central Park. The snake was observed drinking at the Pulitzer Fountain at Fifth Avenue and 59th Street; swimming in the Wading Pool, where it was capsizing the children's toy boats; twined around the 107th Regiment Monument; slithering through the grass of the Sheep Meadow; riding the Friedsam Memorial Carousel; sunning itself on Cherry Hill; communicating with the beards and the pot-smokers at the Bethesda Fountain; biting at oars on the Lake; climbing the steps of the Metropolitan Museum of Art; at the top of the Obelisk; in the children's playgrounds near the Hunter's Gate at Central Park West and 81st Street, and the All Saints Gate at West 96th Street; running around the Frederick Douglass Circle at Cathedral Parkway; at the entrance to the Conservatory Garden, where it was preventing people from entering or leaving; on top of the Great Hill; near the Block House, the Harlem Meer, the Huddlestone Bridge, Nutter's Battery, Fort Clinton, The Dene, Bow Bridge, Belvedere Castle, the Shakespeare Garden, and, just beyond the northernmost perimeter of the park, on Lenox Avenue, where it was chasing pimps and whores.

The police checked out as many of the plausible reports as they could, given the limitations of their manpower. They knew that, as in all branches of police work, from burglary to homicide, there were a thousand false leads to a single authentic one; but the thousand-and-first might crack the case.

SIX

SPECIAL OPERATIONS DIVISION (SOD), with headquarters in Flushing Meadows, Corona, consists of
the following units: Emergency Service, Tactical
Patrol, Street Crime, Auto Crime, Aviation, Harbor,
and Mounted (known as Horse Soldiers). The most
visible and widely publicized is the Emergency Service Unit, specialists in the oddball assignment. If
there's a cat at the top of a pole, a smoke-out in the
subway, a sniper to be dislodged, a bomb to be
defused, a riot to be quelled, a building to be scaled,
a finger stuck in a soda machine, someone trapped in
an elevator, the ESU comes to the rescue. They are
equipped for every conceivable emergency: oxygen
masks and tanks, keys to the subway escape hatches,
crampons, stun guns, floodlights, generators, jacks
capable of lifting subway cars, rifles equipped with
sniperscopes. . . .

The man who was placed in charge of the field

operation to find the snake in the park was Captain Thomas Eastman. As a younger man he had reveled in shinnying up poles, sliding down elevator cables, and carrying overcome victims out of subway tunnels, but now, with a bad knee, a general lack of fitness (weight, 240), and a recent melancholic awareness of his age (48), he directed the men in his command from the sidelines.

Captain Eastman was presented with his assignment by his boss, Deputy Inspector Vincent Scott, who had been the penultimate recipient of a buck that had begun with the mayor, passed to the Police Commissioner, and then descended in orderly steps to a Deputy Commissioner, the Chief of Operations, a Borough Commander, and the Deputy Chief in command of SOD. Eastman, who had left his office at 6 o'clock for his home in Hollis, was recalled by telephone. He arrived back at SOD Headquarters at 8:45.

"About the killer snake in the park," the DI said sourly. "You know which killer snake in which park I'm talking about?"

"Yessir."

"We just been given it."

"I thought we were already working on it."

"Just a couple of trucks and truck personnel helping out. Now we're running the show. You know anything about snakes?"

"Nothing special." Eastman pondered for a moment. "You're supposed to catch them behind the head with a long stick with a clamp at the end that closes up when you press a handle. Like the things grocers used to use years ago to bring packages down from a high shelf?"

"You don't have to catch it," the DI said. "Just

get rid of it. Just get in the park and find this sonofabitch and kill it.''

"That's what they were trying to do today, and didn't do it. The big problem is the size of the park. You know how big it is, Chief?''

"Certainly, I know how big it is. Fifth Avenue to Central Park West, 59th to 110th.''

"Eight hundred and forty-some acres. I don't have any idea how to cover all that area.''

"You don't need an idea, you need manpower. These days, everything is manpower.'' The DI shook his head. "You know how we killed snakes when I was a kid? We grabbed them by the tail and cracked the whip with 'em, just snapped their heads against a rock. Turn up a rock, grab them by the tail, and crack the whip. . . .''

The DI's eyes were inturned, wandering in a distant and undoubtedly more agreeable past. Eastman curbed his impatience and waited for nostalgia to run its course. The DI's mood changed abruptly with a hardening of his eyes.

"You're getting manpower, as much as you need, and if you don't turn that snake up, it's your ass.''

Somebody must be kicking his butt, Eastman thought, so he's kicking mine. Definition of chain of command. He said cautiously, "You say I'm getting manpower? How much?''

"Five hundred.'' The DI paused to savor Eastman's astonishment. "They want that snake real bad.''

Eastman's face was impassive again. "Yessir.''

"Pulling them out of the high-crime areas, would you believe it? It's political. It's a red-hot item. You get my meaning? You better damn well turn it up.''

"Yessir.''

"Planning and Operations is putting the package together. You'll have the five hundred, or so they say, tomorrow morning. They're working late on it. You and me have a date to go down there." The DI's eyes gleamed with bitter amusement. "Not much sleep for you tonight, Thomas."

Who sleeps at night, anyway, Eastman thought, and said, "I wouldn't mind some technical help. There's a young fellow at the Bronx Zoo—"

"Two dead in less than twenty-four hours, that's one thing." The DI shrugged. "People die all the time. But the other thing, the politics, that's serious. Your hear the news this evening?"

Eastman nodded. "John Q. Public is bitching."

"Right. *That's* why you got a whole army of cops to play with. They want a big police presence in the park. You get the meaning?"

"About seven or eight months ago," Eastman said, "there was this rattlesnake some nut kept for a pet in a small apartment house in Washington Heights, I think it was. It escaped, and I went down with a detachment. That was before my knee. We had a couple of those snake-catching sticks, I think. Anyway, we evacuated all the tenants, and we tossed that house. I mean really *tossed* it, cellar to roof, every nook and cranny. We must have been four or five hours at it, walking on eggshells all the time, and we couldn't find it. Then this young guy from the zoo heard about it and came down with a stick and a bag, and inside of five minutes he found the snake curled up near the boiler in the cellar. He lifted it up on the stick, popped it into the bag, and took it off to the zoo."

"An apartment house," the DI said. "That can't compare to Central Park."

"What impressed me, Chief, was not only that he knew right away where to look for it, but he *saw* it. For some reason, it didn't rattle. I forgot to ask why." Eastman shrugged. "We checked out the boiler area several times, and it was there all the time, only we didn't see it. But he saw it right away."

"We already got one of these characters, herpa-something, from the Natural History Museum, he's supposed to be helping us."

"I saw him on the tube," Eastman said. "Maybe he's okay, but this young guy . . . well, he didn't fool around."

"Yeah. I know what you mean. The Museum character acted like a professor, like he did a lot of *reading* about snakes. Get hold of this kid, if you want to." The DI looked at his watch. "I hope you had something to eat, because we got to go downtown right this minute."

Molting was one of the imperatives that governed the snake's existence. Unlike most animals, a snake never stopped growing from the moment of birth to the moment of death. Because it literally outgrew its horny outer skin, it was obliged to shed at regular intervals, three or four times a year.

For several days now the snake's skin had been darkening and dulling, and its eyes, sheltered behind transparent protective lenses, had begun to dim. It was time to molt.

Because it was defenseless during molting, the snake sought the shelter of the topmost branches of its tree. It stretched its sinuous length out almost to its full extent, and began to rub its face against a branch of the tree. When the skin around its lips broke away, the process of molting was under way.

Squirming vigorously over the next few hours, the snake advanced laboriously, like a finger being pulled out of a tight glove, until it had worked itself completely out of the old skin, which ended up at the tail, inside out.

The new skin was bright, the colors fresh and attractive. The snake was at its handsomest. Its eyesight was keen behind its new transparent lens. The old skin, feathery, translucent, dropped a few feet after it had been discarded, and then caught and held fast in a net of twigs, undetectable from ground level.

As always after molting, the snake was hungry. In the darkness, it coiled down the tree and sped away in search of food.

Hizzoner was not awake for the eleven o'clock television news. It was just as well; it contained little that might have comforted him. The program opened with a sequence showing the cops who had been sweeping the park leaving as darkness came on: hot, dispirited, out-of-sorts, a beaten army executing a strategic withdrawal.

"Some of these policemen were on the verge of collapse, and those who criticized the effort—or lack of it—were on the whole sympathetic to the frustrated policemen themselves. Mostly, their barbs were directed at the mayor."

The mayoral candidate of the opposition party, wearing a white shirt and tie, his sparse hair ruffled by the breeze from the air conditioner in his elegant living room: ". . . sorry for this pitiful handful of sincere, dedicated men. The niggardly number of police assigned to hunt down the snake is only too typical of the halfway measures that have characterized this administration for the past four years. The hard-pressed people of our city deserve better. Their God-given right to enjoy the beauty of their park in safety and with peace of mind has been flouted by a mayor who. . . ."

A former mayor, said to be grooming himself for a run for the governorship: "I don't want to come down too hard on the mayor, but if I was still in office I would mount the most comprehensive dragnet ever seen in this city."

From Washington, a member of the New York congressional delegation: "The good people of my district are being bitten to death by this deadly snake, and it has got to stop. If the mayor is unwilling or unable to do the job, then I say let's get someone on the job who can do the job. I have been trying to reach the governor in Albany, requesting him to send reinforcements, whether it be the National Guard or a contingent of state troopers, or both. My constituency must be protected."

A half-dozen new groups pledge their support for the march on City Hall in the morning. Shots of militant women, clamoring for the attention of camera and microphone. Following a commercial, the telecast continues with a shot of the same cobra that had been seen on the 6 o'clock news, then of a giant anaconda being held in the air by six men, then of a sidewinder rattlesnake slithering across desert sands in California. Finally, a closeup of a Russell's viper being milked at a snake farm in Brazil. "Not all snake poison is malign. The venom being taken from this Russell's viper will be used as a coagulant for persons suffering from hemophilia."

An interview with the curator of reptiles of a Midwest zoo, filmed in front of the glass cage of a puff adder that had bitten him six months ago. The curator assures his interrogator that he harbors no ill feelings toward the snake. "I made him irritable, you see." Touching a scar on his forearm. "Fortunately, with the prompt administration of antivenin, I recovered without any lasting ill effects."

In her modest but thoughtfully furnished apartment, responding to a hushed and commiserative reporter, Ms. Arline Simpkin, friend of Roddy Bamberger, second victim of the snake in the park: "Although it was only our first date, I realized that he was a rare type of person—warm, cultivated, and so in tune with life." Large eyes brimming with tears. "And to be struck down in the full flush of virile manhood." She pauses, ponders, seems to wonder if her remark is open to sexual interpretation, and flushes. "It isn't fair. It just isn't fair."

The anchorman: "Ms. Simpkin's statement provided the police with their first clue as to the possible whereabouts of the snake. It is, or was, in the environs of the Delacorte Theatre."

In a cluttered kitchen, with two small, solemn-eyed children wandering in and out of camera range, Mrs. Carmen Torres, mother of the deceased Ramon Torres, pretty, plump, wearing her hair in a towering beehive, rattles away in animated Spanish that is translated by a tall lean man with a scarred face and deep black eyes. The interpreter says, "She say her Ramon is a good boy." Mrs. Torres rattles on. "Once or twice he is arrested and the police try to frame him because he is Puerto Rican, but God is just, and he is sprung." Mrs. Torres waits impatiently for him to finish his translation, regarding him with a glittering, wary eye. She spouts Spanish again. "He was the sole support of herself and his three little brothers and one sister. And now that he is gone, who is to pay the rent and for the food? She wishes to know this.''

The reporter asks the interpreter what Ramon was doing in the park at 3 o'clock in the morning. The interpreter puts the question to Mrs. Torres, who answers indignantly. He translates: ''She say he is in the park to cool off, and because it remind him of the verdure of his beloved Puerto Rico. So he stroll in the park, never expecting to be stung by a snake.'' Wrapping up, the reporter asks the interpreter if he is a member of the Torres family. ''I am Roberto Ortiz, lawyer. I represent Mrs. Torres in this matter. We are filing a suit in the morning against the city for negligence. One million dollars for depriving this fine lady of her sole support and darling son.'' Mrs. Torres says in English, ''Wuh mee-yun dolls.''

The anchorman presses his earphone with a finger, listening. ''We're going to take you to Columbus Circle for an on-the-spot report, live, from Marcia Brooks.''

''This is Marcia Brooks, live, from Columbus Circle, where, as you can see, there is plenty going on.''

The camera pans over a crowd milling around near the Merchant's Gate entrance to the park and clustered around the marble Maine Monument. Standing out among dark complexions, bare chests, shorts, is a group of young, well-scrubbed, neatly dressed young men and women who seem to be haranguing the crowd, or any part of it that will listen. They are jeered at, laughed at, mocked, but they seem impervious to it.

Marcia Brooks whispers into her microphone. ''These self-contained young people are Puries, members of the Church of the Purification, followers of the well-known religious sect led by the Reverend Sanctus Milanese. Let's listen.''

She insinuates her microphone near a pale intense young man in a white, open-collared shirt, who is speaking to a young black man wearing a colorful bandanna around his head and an earring in his nose. ''The snake is Satan, or rather Satan's messenger, who has taken the form of a serpent. It has been sent here to earth by the devil to subvert and proselytize and recruit sinners for the legions of hell.''

The young black man: ''Man, you full of. . . .'' His bad word is alertly blipped. ''Onliest thing it recruit so far is two stiffs.''

The crowd cheers, laughs, slaps thighs. The young black man grins and takes a bow.

Nearby, a young woman wearing a light blue, crisp dirndl, her eyes flashing, says, ''You are deluded if you think it is funny. The snake is truly Satan's messenger. It is wily, it is evil incarnate and it will easily elude the police. It fears only the pure in heart and spirit, the army of Christ.''

Marcia Brooks has edged toward the young woman, but before she can question her there is a commotion. The black man in the bandanna has suddenly become threatening. He is shouting, raging. He takes a boxer's stance, dances, draws back his fist. But before he can throw his punch, he is seized around the neck by a tall young man dressed in a dark suit, and hurled to the ground. The crowd surges backward, then forward, there is a flash of fists, some shoving, but by now six cops are there, pushing the crowd apart, breaking it open.

Marcia Brooks backs away from the fray. Somewhat breathlessly, she says that the Puries ap-

pear to be out in force, not only here in Columbus
Circle but near the Pulitzer Fountain at Fifth Avenue
and 59th, as well as at other locations on the
perimeter of the park. It is her impression that the
tall man who threw the man in the bandanna to the
ground is a member of the Purie security squad, who
call themselves Christ's Cohorts, but whom some
people have bluntly characterized as a strong-arm
squad.

Behind her, the police seem to have quelled the
outburst. "The Puries took to the streets about ten
o'clock this evening, and these ardent young
followers of the Reverend Sanctus Milanese have
been spreading the word that the snake has been sent
to earth from, well, I guess from below, to. . . ." She
pauses, listens to the voice in her earphone. She nods,
then says quickly, "I asked one of the Puries if they
would be among those represented at City Hall
tomorrow morning. I was told that they would not,
definitely not, because, and I quote, 'we do not seek
intercession from mortal man, but only from God
Himself, Who speaks to us with the voice of the
Reverend Sanctus Milanese.' That from a Purie—"

She is cut off. In the studio, the anchorman says
hurriedly, "Thank you, Marcia. We take you now,
live, to Purity House, the Fifth Avenue mansion of
the Reverend Sanctus Milanese."

A tall blond man wearing a black suit, a white
shirt, a dark tie, stands in the opening of a high,
carved, gleaming doorway, facing a thicket of
microphones. He says expressionlessly, "The
Reverend Milanese is not available. He is at prayer."
Reporters shout out questions. He responds, "Yes, I
believe he will make a statement." "When?" "When
God instructs him to."

The door is shut firmly. The camera holds on its polished elegance for a moment, then fades back to the studio.

"A final note, just in," the anchorman says. "Police cars will continue into the night to patrol the park with loudspeakers, urging the public to stay away." He consults a slip of paper. "We are informed that the Central Park Precinct has received over twenty calls from residents of the buildings rimming the park, on Fifth Avenue, Central Park South and Central Park West, complaining that the blaring of the loudspeakers is interfering with their sleep and, in some cases, the audibility of their television."

Frozen in that extraordinary fossil-like quality of total immobility peculiar to reptiles, the snake watched the rat move along the base of the wall. The rat, which might have been intent on some prey of its own, failed to see the snake until the very last moment before it struck, and then it was too late.

The rat reacted immediately to the venom. Its brown hair stood up spikily, its body curled in on itself in an agonized spasm, and it bit frantically at the site of the bite. It turned away from the snake in terror, and with erratic movement retreated along the base of the stone wall. The snake, driven by its post-sloughing hunger, followed swiftly. It overtook the rat, its head low to the ground now, its mouth gaped, but it did not strike again. It curled in front of the stumbling rat and faced it. The rat made an effort to retreat, but its legs gave out and it collapsed. It lay quietly, its teeth bared in a rictus, its eyes half shut. Although the snake customarily waited until its prey was dead, it did not do so now. It opened its mouth wide and took the feebly struggling rat between its teeth. With one side of its mouth hooked firmly into the rat's head, the snake pushed the teeth of the other side forward a short distance and engaged them. It did not take notice of the shudder that preceded the rat's death, but continued to push forward by alternate investment of its teeth until the rat was completely swallowed.

SEVEN

WHEN MARK CONVERSE opened his eyes, the python was in the direct line of his vision and appeared to be staring at him.

The python was under four feet long, just a baby, but lately it had taken to having notions about the cat. A few days ago it had curled down the lamp standard and begun to constrict the cat. The cat had raked a claw across its ventral area before bounding away, leaving a bloody streak on the python's body, but it could just as well have taken out an eye with the same effort. Eventually, Converse knew, one of them would have to go. Probably the python, considering the expense involved in keeping it fed with mice and rats and small snakes. The cat could make do with a can of something off the supermarket shelf.

Wait a minute. He'd have to dispose of both of them, wouldn't he, when he went to Australia?

Dunce. Better start thinking about it. He could probably farm out the cat, but who would take a python? So it would doubtless go to the zoo. Meanwhile, it had made a nice pet, and even seemed to show some affection, or at least tolerance, for him.

It was sprawled on the bottom of its glass cage, still with the appearance of staring at him, though he was sure it was asleep. The air conditioning was on, and the cold made it lethargic. Normally, out of the cage, it would have found a sunny place on the floor to bask. That was another thing: it was a nuisance having to cage it every time he had a girl around. He hadn't found a woman yet who liked snakes, and that included his ex-wife and both of his serious ex-relationships. Maybe, if he ever found a girl who liked snakes, he might marry again. Jesus, no! He bounded up off the pillow and looked at the clock. Quarter of seven. In the morning, most likely, though you couldn't tell one way or another with the dark-green, light-tight windowshades drawn.

The telephone rang. Must be evening. Nobody would phone him at quarter of seven in the morning. The phone rang a second time, and he reached for it across the red-gold head on the other pillow. She was buried to the nose under the blanket, and she hadn't stirred. She has earned her rest, he thought tenderly, and picked up the phone as it rang for a third time.

"This is Captain Eastman of the New York Police Department. Excuse me for calling you at this hour of the morning. I hope I didn't wake you."

Morning. Okay, morning. His heart began to thump. "Who?"

He meant who has died, which of my distant parents has had a fatal heart attack. But his caller misinterpreted his question. "Captain Eastman,

NYPD. Emergency Service Unit. Remember me? That rattle-snake up in Washington Heights last year? I guess I was still a lieutenant then."

Converse breathed out in relief. "Oh, sure." He didn't remember any Eastman, captain *or* lieutenant, only a faceless lot of jittery, blundering cops. "Got another snake?"

There was a very long pause, during which Converse thought he heard Eastman muttering to himself. But when he spoke it was still in an apologetic tone. "I got your home number from the night man at the zoo. He said you're not with the zoo anymore?"

"Yeah, I quit a few weeks ago. I'm supposed to be going off to Australia with an expedition, to bring back specimens. . . ." Autobiography at seven in the morning? Forget it. The head on the other pillow was stirring. Converse said, "Where's this one?"

There was another protracted silence, and now Eastman spoke very slowly and with exaggerated clarity. "I guess I must have woken you from a pretty deep sleep. I'm sorry. I'm talking about the snake in Central Park, Mr. Converse."

"There's a snake in Central Park?" The girl was turning toward him. Her eyes were circled. She was smiling, showing her small white teeth. "On the loose? Another rattler?"

Eastman's voice became suddenly edgy. "Are you putting me on, Mr. Converse?"

Converse reacted to Eastman's tone. He said peevishly, "I don't know what the hell you're talking about."

Eastman said, "Chrisesake," and then, with wonder in his voice, "Where the hell have you been since twelve noon yesterday?"

"In the sack. Is there a law against it?"

"In the sack for twenty hours? You're some hell of a sleeper."

"Well, it hasn't been all sleep." The girl's hand was moving slowly toward him under the sheet. "I mean, we got up and . . . I got up and had something to eat every once in a while. You know, it wasn't *all* sleep."

"Be damned," Eastman said. "Still, didn't you turn on the TV or the radio or see a newspaper?"

"Well, you know, there wasn't time." Converse reached under the sheet and captured the girl's hand, stopping its movement. "You mean this snake has been on the radio and TV? Honestly, I didn't know."

"Look," Eastman said, "I haven't got time to fill you in on everything you've missed, except to tell you that this particular snake has bitten two citizens and they're both dead."

"You're kidding." It wasn't at all what Converse had meant to say, or what the occasion seemed to call for, but he felt stupefied. He released the girl's hand in order to gesture. "*Killed* two people? Are you sure it's a snake? In Central Park? Christ—what kind of a snake is it?"

"We don't know. It's a snake, all right, and it's still at large. The reason I'm calling—I remember how quickly you found that rattlesnake, and I'd like you to help us out again."

"Christ, yes." The girl had turned toward him. The sheet had slipped down, or she had helped it slip down, baring her breasts. He faced away from her, and felt the soft warmth of her breasts against his back. "In Central Park? That's all you know about its whereabouts?"

"We *think* it's in the area of the Delacorte Theatre. At least, that's where it was when it bit one of the victims. So far as I know, it could be anywhere."

"Anywhere." The girl's arm had fallen over his hip and her fingers were trailing lazily over his stomach. "Do you know how big the park is?"

"Eight hundred and forty acres," Eastman said wearily. "That's the reason we need all the help we can get."

"It's incredible," Converse said. The girl's fingernails were nipping at his thighs now, and he was having difficulty concentrating. "It's absolutely unbelievable."

"Only if you've been in the sack for the last twenty-four hours," Eastman said. "The rest of us don't have any trouble believing it."

There he goes again, Converse thought. Since when is it anybody's affair how much time a citizen spends in bed? He started to ask the captain if he thought he was in fucking Russia or something, but the girl's fingers had grasped him, and all that came out of his mouth was a groan.

"I'm sorry, that was out of line." Eastman sounded more tired than contrite. "The point is—can you help us?"

"Of course. The girl had kicked the sheet off, and, looking down, Converse could see her fingers moving upward in slow, mischievous circles. "Look, can I call you back? I'll call you back in a couple of minutes. Okay?"

Eastman let his breath out in controlled exasperation. "To be perfectly frank, there isn't that much time. We've got a big search operation set up at nine o'clock. I'd like a chance to talk to you before we begin. But if you can't. . . ."

"I can. I can. Ah." Converse bit his shoulder to muffle a groan. "Where are you, where can I meet you?"

"I'm phoning from police headquarters, but I'm leaving directly for the park. Do you know where all those statues of Latin American liberators are, at the Sixth Avenue entrance?"

"I know it, I know it. I'll be there in half an hour."

But it was a half hour before he even got out of bed. He kissed the girl chastely, and told her that she was wonderful and that he would call her sometime. He dressed quickly in jeans and a T-shirt imprinted with the legend *Duchy of Liechtenstein All Stars*, and ran down the steps into Charles Street. He went around to Seventh Avenue and bought a couple of papers. The *Daily News* front page, under a headline that read SNAKE, SLAYER OF TWO, STILL AT LARGE, showed an aerial view of Manhattan being constricted by a giant boid. The *Times* was predictably more circumspect. Its picture was also an aerial view of the park. The caption under the photo said, in effect, try to find the handful of searchers in this vast expanse. The three-column, three-line headline read, POLICE SEARCH OF PARK FAILS IN EFFORT TO FIND SNAKE; TWO ARE DEAD OF BITES.

Converse found a cab cruising southward on Seventh. It picked him up and took Charles Street to Hudson, where it turned north. The driver slid back his safety panel. "The snake in Central Park?"

Converse said, "Yeah." He was trying to read his papers.

"What'll they think of next?" The driver shook

his head. "Tell the truth, it actually don't surprise me."

"Well, it surprises *me*," Converse said.

The driver gave him a pitying look. "Come on, Chrisesake. This city?"

An agglomeration of fifteen or twenty police vehicles, massed along Central Park South, clogged the Artist's Gate where Sixth Avenue ran into the park. Close by, just inside the park, were three huge television trucks and a few private cars with PRESS placards on their windshields.

The area was swarming with cops. Converse had never seen them in such numbers, barring the St. Patrick's Day parade. They stood in stolid groups, looking as if they wanted to smoke. Their short-sleeved uniform shirts were already soaked by sweat, darkened to a deep blue. Their waistlines, laden with equipment—revolver, manacles, keys, nightstick, cartridges—gave them the appearance of some modified two-legged beast of burden. A number of them were wearing thigh-high wading boots. Some were armed with shotguns, others with cans of Mace. A few carried crowbars.

Barriers had been put up on the south side of Central Park South, and a dozen policemen wearing the distinctive blue and white helmet of the Tactical Patrol Unit were trying to keep a crowd of spectators from overflowing the curb. Sixth Avenue had been closed off at Fifty-seventh Street, and traffic diverted to the east and west. A dozen radios were droning from the open windows of squad cars. Inside and outside the park, loudspeakers were urging the crowd to go about their business, or, if they must stay, to remain behind the barriers.

"We request the cooperation of all citizens, for your own safety and so that the police can perform their duty without obstruction. . . ."

Converse started into the park, but his way was barred by a TPU cop. He told the cop that Captain Eastman was expecting him. The cop eyed him with ritual suspicion. "He's waiting for me," Converse said. The cop hesitated for another moment, then guided him through a small mob—cops, deeply tanned men wearing the green livery of the Parks Department, television and still cameramen, newspaper reporters carrying notebooks or folded copy paper—to what he said was the Command Post. Its center was a large folding campaign table with a map of Central Park pinned to it. A half-dozen policemen were bent over the table, their faces obscured by the bills of their caps.

The TPU cop spoke to a tall dark officer wearing silver oak leaves on his collar and yellow braid on the bill of his cap. "This fella says Captain Eastman wants to see him, sir."

"My name is Converse. I'm the herpetologist."

"You say?" The officer stared at Converse's T-shirt with distaste, then called out, "Eastman, the ologist-something is here."

A face turned up out of the heads bent over the map. It was broad, pink, sweating. Converse didn't recognize it. "Yeah, well," Eastman said, "tell him to wait a minute."

"Stay put right here," the dark officer said, and scowled at him before moving off a few paces, folding his arms across his chest, and gazing around him dourly. The cops in his immediate area fell silent.

Eastman's head was bent to the map again. Converse yawned. He wasn't sleepy, exactly, just played out. Behind him, someone tapped his shoulder. It was a young woman. She was holding a shorthand pad and a ballpoint pen.

She said, "Aren't you that herpetologist from the Bronx Zoo? I'm sorry, I forgot your name."

"Mark Converse."

"I did a piece for my paper when you caught that rattlesnake last year. Holly Markham. I don't suppose you remember?"

"Hell, yes, I recognized you right away. How you doing?"

She was pretty, but in that cool, self-contained way that usually turned him off. He preferred outwardness, even a suggestion of mischief in a woman's face. But when she put out her hand and smiled, her face opened up. If it didn't exactly suggest abandonment, it had become immediately charming. He smiled back at her and shook her hand. Her grip was firm and without coquetry, like her nonsmiling face.

"Are you helping the police again, Mr. Converse?"

He glanced toward the campaign table. "Captain Eastman phoned me. I'll certainly help if I can."

She wrote his name down, and slanted her notebook toward him so that he could check the spelling. Except for his name, her notes were written in shorthand. She asked him to remind her of his title at the zoo.

"Formerly assistant curator of herpetology. I've joined an expedition to Australia to bring back specimens. Australia has some terrific species of poisonous snakes."

She smiled and tilted her head and said, "How

does someone get into anything as funny as snakes?
You don't mind my asking?"

"Funny is in the eye of the beholder. I've been into
snakes ever since I was a kid. I'm twenty-nine now, in
case you're wondering. How old are you?"

"Twenty-five, but I guess I didn't have your ad-
vantages. Snakes make me crawl."

"Yeah." Converse sighed. "That's how people
feel about them. Not me. I like them."

"Because they're cute and cuddly?"

He looked at her sharply. Maybe there was some
mischief there, after all. "Because I understand
them. And maybe because I'm for the underdog."

"What makes them underdogs?"

"They're seriously disadvantaged animals. No
limbs. No hearing. No true voice. No teeth for
chewing, so that they're obliged to swallow their
food whole. No lids or nictitating membrane—can't
shut their eyes. Coldblooded, meaning they're at the
mercy of the environment for survival. No charm.
The number-one villain of myth and legend, from the
Bible onward. Underdogs, right?"

She looked up from her notebook. "That underdog in the park has killed two people."

"Accidents happen. Snakes don't bite people,
people get bitten."

"And there are no muggers, just people who get
mugged?"

He sighed again. "Look, I'll tell you something
about snakes. They have three defensive attitudes,
and they use them in this order when they're
threatened. One, they try to hide. Two, if they can't
hide, they try to run away. Three, if it's impossible to
hide or run away, they defend themselves by biting.

It's a last resort. Snakes are shy of people. They don't hunt them, don't hate them, don't eat them. It's the other way around."

"I read somewhere that those huge constrictors do eat people."

"That's crap. The very largest reticulate constrictors, which can manage to engorge a whole line of animals of quite surprising size, can't swallow a man, no matter what you've heard. The shoulders are too wide for them."

"It's a comforting thought. Unless . . ." Her face was solemn, but there was a twitch at the corners of her lips. "Unless every constrictor has to find that out for himself?"

Converse saw several of the cops at the Command Post straighten up, salute, and move off. Eastman was still bent over the map.

"I spoke to the Museum of Natural History herpetologist yesterday," Holly Markham said. "He doesn't think the snake is a cobra."

"It probably isn't. According to the news stories, the perforations are very clean and precisely defined. Injection-type bites, in and out quickly. Cobras have a tendency to hang on and chew, so the perforations usually aren't all that neat."

"Do you have any idea of what kind of snake it might be?"

He shook his head. "I just know what it *isn't*. American snakes like rattlers or copperheads or moccasins distill a hemotoxic venom. The eastern coral snake, the only other poisonous snake in the States, does secrete a neurotoxic venom, like the venom that killed those two people. But the coral is a chewer like the cobra, and not all that deadly."

"What makes it so important to know what kind of snake it is?" She looked up at him and said quickly, "I guess that's a dumb question."

He nodded, and listened to a loudspeaker: "All police personnel, attention. All police personnel, take up your positions. Follow your sergeants. Sergeants, all sergeants, move them out to their assigned positions."

The sudden movement, in response to shouted instructions from cops wearing sergeant's stripes, was like a mob scene. Everyone seemed in a hurry now, and there was a great deal of muttering. But Converse could see that out of the shifting and milling of bodies, the near collisions, a sort of purposive order was evolving.

"They're going to form a single line abreast," Holly Markham said, "all the way from Central Park West to Fifth Avenue, and sweep across the park from end to end."

Converse was shaking his head in wonderment. "They'll never find it that way."

She tilted her head inquisitively. "Why not?"

"How many cops have they got out here?"

"Five hundred."

"That's why. Too many. Four hundred and ninety-nine too many." Eastman was sitting on an edge of the campaign table, watching him. Their eyes met, and Eastman beckoned to him. "I have to go now." He pointed toward Eastman. "Nice talking to you, Markham."

"Too bad. It was just beginning to get interesting." She tapped her teeth with her pen and looked at him appraisingly. "Just in case this thing fizzles, how do I get in touch with you?"

He told her his phone number and she wrote it

down. He walked over to Eastman, who said, "Sorry to keep you waiting. But I hoped you might get here earlier so we could have had a talk."

"Yeah, well, I kind of got stuck."

The tall officer with the oak leaves moved over to join them. Eastman introduced him as Deputy Inspector Scott. Converse put out his hand. The DI, his arms folded across his chest, merely nodded. Eastman said, "Do you have any suggestions, Mr. Converse?"

Sure, Converse thought, call off your cops. He said, "I might, if I knew what kind of snake it was."

The DI, his lip curling, said, "We find it, we'll know what kind of snake it is."

Eastman said, "He's the snake expert I told you about, Chief. That found the rattlesnake in that apartment building in Washington Heights?"

The mass of policemen was fragmented now, attenuating, spreading toward the east and west ends of the park. Those close by were already in place, waiting for those on the distant flanks to get in position. Sergeants were busy dressing up their lines.

The DI said, "A park is a hell of a lot different from an apartment house. It's eight hundred and forty goddamn miles."

"Acres," Eastman said cautiously. The DI shrugged the correction off, and moved away.

Converse said, "I've never seen this many cops in one place."

"Neither have I," Eastman said. "It tells you something about how bad we want that snake."

"Well, I hate to tell you this, captain, but it's the wrong way to find it."

The loudspeakers blared, directing vehicles to "move into position." A dozen squad cars and two emergency service trucks wheeled in through the Artist's Gate past the statues of San Martín, Simon Bolívar, José Martí, all of them worked in bronze, all of them on horseback, as befitted Latin-American liberators. They spread out to the right and left down the walkways, behind the waiting line of cops.

Eastman said, "I asked for suggestions, not conclusions." His blue eyes were bleak. "I would appreciate any help you could give us in finding and killing this snake."

"What do you want to kill it for? It's no harder to capture it than it is to kill it."

"It's a murderer," Eastman said, "and I believe in capital punishment."

Converse shook his head. "It has to be caught before somebody else is hurt, but it's a fact that a snake doesn't attack out of malice. Whenever it bites something it can't eat it's because it felt threatened."

Eastman smiled, but his eyes were blue ice. "Whose side are you on—ours or the snake's?"

As it happens, Converse thought, I'm playing both sides at the same time. I want to prevent anybody else from being bitten and I want to save the snake if I can. But it would be best to leave Eastman's question unanswered. He waved toward the line of cops. "You can beat an area and drive a tiger out into the open, but not a snake. Snakes hide. They're among the most accomplished hiders in the animal kingdom."

The loudspeakers were blaring again, and their echoes rolled back. They were urging speed on the flanks. "Shake it, find your places, get on the stick, shake it. . . ."

"Poor bastards," Eastman said, "I'm shedding fat just sitting here in the shade. Imagine what it's like out there in the sun? They're going to be dropping like flies."

"Once, in my office at the zoo," Converse said, "and it was just a little cubbyhole, mind you, I misplaced a two-foot-long snake, and it was missing for three weeks. I turned the place upside down and couldn't find it. Eventually, it turned up in a desk drawer."

"We're going to toss the whole friggin park," Eastman said, "and not overlook any desk drawers. Every last inch of it, excluding nothing except water. . . ." He stopped abruptly. "Christ. Do snakes swim?"

"They sure can. In fact their motion, in which they push against the substrate, is essentially the same as the way a fish curves back against water. But this one obviously isn't a water snake, so you can skip the water."

"Thank God. There's a hundred and fifty acres of water, and we would have had to bring in divers."

"How many trees are there?"

Eastman groaned. "They hide in trees? Sure, now that you mention it, I've seen it in the movies."

"All snakes can climb trees. Some of them live in trees and never come down to the ground. Others are strictly terrestrial. Still others are *both* arboreal and terrestrial. And some of those also live underground in burrows."

"Trees and burrows." Eastman shook his head uneasily. "Anything else I ought to know?"

"Snakes live by stealth, and they have to be caught by stealth. As it happens, snakes are deaf, but they're sensitive to vibrations of the substrate. Five hundred heavy-footed cops are going to sound like an earthquake to that snake out there. It'll hide, and that's that. You don't need five hundred men, just one man who knows what he's doing."

Eastman barked a short unamused laugh. "One *modest* man, right?"

"Look, captain, I was walking along a downtown street with a cop I know one day. An ordinary street on an ordinary day, quiet and peaceful. But all of a sudden the cop tensed up and said, 'That character up the block, he's going to pull something.' The man he was talking about was casual, well-dressed, strolling, nothing suspicious about him. But in the next ten seconds, this guy turned into a jewelry store with a gun in his hand. Okay. Turn it around—you and I, we can both look at an innocent meadow, and if there's a snake in it I'll know it and you won't."

"Okay. I get your point. Come along and give us the benefit of your knowledge."

A series of loudspeakers burst into sound, all along the police line from the west to the east limits of the park. "Attention, all sergeants, attention. We're moving out. Remember your instructions. Walk as straight a line as you can, keep the line dressed up, eyes down to the ground, concentrate on the wild and heavily brushed areas. . . ."

"Eyes down," Converse said, "and they won't look up in the trees."

". . . everything is included—playgrounds, ball fields, walks, buildings, inside everything, behind everything. . . . Move on out. Move out."

Nearby, a sergeant shouted an order, and the line began to move forward. Converse said, "The guy on the street didn't know a cop had his eye on him. If there were five hundred cops, he'd have known about it and just kept walking."

The loudspeakers were addressing themselves to

people in the park, visible in the near distance: "Folks, please keep back. For your own safety and the success of the operation, please keep back and do not impede the officers. If you do not have business in the park at this time, we ask you to please leave the park. . . ."

Eastman stood up. "I'd better put that dope about the trees into the loudspeakers. Come along?"

Converse shook his head. "No sense to it. After this is over and the dust settles, I'll come back here."

"I apologize for waking you up. You can go back to bed now."

Eastman turned abruptly and walked away. Converse watched the police line at his right mass together and start to flow around the Pond. A group of winos and addicts sitting on the nearby benches gave them a cheer. Eastman had stopped to speak to the DI. Together, they hurried toward a communications truck.

Converse walked out of the park. There was a group of reporters at the exit, surrounding the Police Commissioner and four uniformed cops with yellow braid on their caps and stars on the shoulders of their uniforms. He wondered if Holly Markham was among them. She wasn't.

EIGHT

THE TURNOUT AT City Hall, doubtless because of the heat, was considerably smaller than expected, to the relief of the police guard, which was dangerously thin and might have been overwhelmed by a large aggressive mob. The operation at the park had strained police manpower to an unacceptable limit.

The demonstrators who did appear—the police estimate of their number was 150—were highly vociferous and reasonably energetic in waving their home-made banners and placards. There were a few clashes between bodies representing diametrically opposed viewpoints, a rough division between those who wanted the park closed (mainly white and middle class) and those who wanted it to remain open (predominantly black and Hispanic). No blood was drawn. Among the sectarian splinter groups present were the Schweitzerites, animal lovers who felt that the snake, as one of God's creatures, should not be hunted down but given free run of the park; a group of environmentalists petitioning for the razing of outlying slum areas for the purpose of creating a green belt; and a faction of welfare recipients demanding an immediate increase in their monthly payments.

The mayor, who had been known to venture out onto the steps of City Hall to address other assemblages on other occasions, did not make an appearance. Instead, he sent forth one of his young assistants, a man with a curly black beard and, although he was a graduate of an Ivy League college, a demotic New York accent that disarmed all but the most intransigent of crowds. Speaking with impeccable timing in the troughs between waves of boos and catcalls, he told the demonstrators that Hizzonner was unable to talk to them, much as he wished to, because he was on the phone to the president to ask for increased federal assistance to the city; he had made his connection and was on hold. The bearded man reminded the complainants that the police were at this very moment sweeping the park in force, under the stern instructions of the mayor to "find the snake, or I'll know the reason why." He shouted to them to "have faith," and then ran up the steps and into the building. People began drifting away. Others surrounded three pushcart vendors selling soft drinks and ice cream. A hard core, obviously the creatures of the opposition candidate, continued to call for the appearance of the mayor, but their ranks kept thinning. The demonstration was, to all intents and purposes, finished.

At 10:30 the police removed the barriers.

If I wanted to die of thirst, Police Officer Fleming

told himself, I would've joined the French Foreign Legion.

The only thing that was keeping him going was the promise of a lunch break once they had finished sweeping the area between the 79th and 85th Street transverses. He had been pouring sweat ever since the start. His uniform was soaked, his eyes smarted, his tongue felt like a slab of wood. So much sweat had run down into his shoes that he squished at every step. Still, he seemed to be holding up a lot better than most of the overweight cops. Funny, you'd think the fat ones had more schmaltz to burn, but it was the wiry types like himself who were doing the best.

He trudged on, thankful for small things, like not having to circumscribe the Belvedere Lake, like a lot of the others did, because of their position in the line. By now, Fleming was just more or less going through the paces. He kept his eyes on the ground, but mostly because it was too much trouble to keep his head up. As for looking up into trees, he had quit doing that when he had heard a Parks Department gardener say that there were over 100,000 trees in the park. Even with 500 cops that figured out to better than 200 trees per man!

By now, Fleming didn't give a shit whether they caught the snake or not. In fact, he was positive it was hopeless. He had stopped having that crawly feeling that started somewhere down in his sweating toes and worked itself up to the scrotum. Not that he was any less queasy about snakes but that he was just plain numb.

Nobody was talking to each other anymore. Earlier there had been a lot of fooling around and joking, but now nobody had the spirit for it. The mood had become sullen, morose, and Fleming was willing to bet that, in his thoughts, everybody was planning early retirement. How many had collapsed and been dragged off to the hospital with heat prostration or heat stroke? That stuff was dangerous, life-threatening. A few times already he had contemplated faking heat prostration so he could get off the line. He was sorry he hadn't done it, though now there was no point to it. Twenty minutes or so and they'd have their lunch break, and he was pretty sure they didn't serve beer in a hospital.

There were plenty of people in the park, some of them lying in the sun (dumbheads!) or playing ball (dumbheads!) and they moved slowly out of the way of the sweep when they bothered to move at all. Earlier, some Puries had scuffled with cops and been detained, but it was too much trouble to pull them in, so they had been turned loose and told to get the hell out of the park. Phony, snotty bunch of kids—they called that a religion? Now the cops weren't even bothering anymore. If somebody was laying down on the Great Lawn, let him be, it was a cinch he wasn't laying on top of the snake.

A loudspeaker blared, and the comfortable sonofabitch in the car said, "Okay, boys, we're finishing up this part of the park, and then it's lunch and all the beer you can drink—if you can afford it, ha-ha-ha. . . ."

Ha-ha-ha. Jerk. Fleming took a deep breath, put his head down, and plowed upward into an area full of trees and thick brush. It was the kind of terrain which, earlier, they had entered with great caution and checked with the utmost thoroughness. A low-hanging branch snapped across his face, and damn near give him a fit.. He wiped irrationally at his mouth as if the snake itself had brushed across his face. Christ, if this wasn't over soon he was gonna start screaming.

The snake was lying near the top of its tree when it first saw the approaching figure. As the figure came closer, the snake lost sight of it. The figure moved toward the tree and came into the snake's view again. The snake slithered downward, silent, swift, its fresh skin blending with the background of leaves and branches. Its flicking tongue picked up odor substances.

When the figure was directly below the tree it disturbed a low-handing branch. The snake anchored itself by its tail as the figure paused. It retracted the anterior portion of its body, mouth gaping, and tensed to strike downward.

The figure moved on.

The snake held its threatening posture, hissing softly, until the figure disappeared from sight. Then it climbed back up to the topmost branches.

The Reverend Sanctus Milanese stood motionless on his imposing doorstep, encircled by his security guard, Christ's Cohorts, uniformly tall, rangy, and fit. Despite the heat, or perhaps in defiance of it, the Reverend wore his long black cloak with its scarlet lining, and the small skullcap (scarlet with black lining) which had aroused indignation on the part of Catholics, who branded it a travesty of a cardinal's red calotte, and Jews, who claimed it was a mimicry of the yarmulke.

If the Reverend had called a press conference for any ordinary reason, he might have been ignored. But the announcement that he would issue an important policy statement defining the position of the Church of the Purification with respect to the snake in the park had intrigued the media. A blend of the snake and the unpredictable Puries represented a mix of volatile chemical elements certain to produce a satisfying explosion or, at the least, an interesting smell.

The Reverend Sanctus Milanese was a tall man with black eyes under strongly arched black eyebrows, iron-gray hair, a whisker growth so heavy that he was reputed to be obliged to shave no less than three times daily, thin lips, and a long unsmiling face. He did not move. His eyes, tilted upward to the heavens, did not blink. Although he had maintained this posture for more than ten minutes in the stifling heat, he showed no sign of stress or impatience. He was waiting for the TV crews to complete setting up their equipment.

In her notebook, Holly Markham wrote, *Made He man in his own image, question mark.*

It was a vice of Holly's that she was helpless to resist writing down observations which had little or nothing to do with objective reporting, and which never—well, hardly ever—found their way into her copy. She called them "snippets," and sometimes worried that they were the stigmata of a suppressed novelist.

Holly was part of a respectable number of newspaper, TV, and radio reporters massed on the sidewalk in front of Purity House, the Fifth Avenue mansion of the Reverend Sanctus Milanese. The building, in the style of a French château, had been built for his own use some eighty years before by a highly respected robber baron. It had remained in the original family until three years ago, when it had

been purchased, for cold cash raised by popular sub-
scription of the Reverend's followers, and presented
to him as a gift in celebration of his fiftieth birthday.
It thus became the third notable holding in the real
estate portfolio of the Church of the Purification.
The others were the Tabernacle, located in the East
Thirties, in the former church of a Greek Orthodox
sect which had prospered and built a new church; and
the former Dutchess County estate of a played-out
line of patroons, consisting of over a hundred acres
and seven buildings, including the forty-room main
house. This complex, called Eden Paradise, was used
as a training center for novitiate members of the
Church.

With the cameras in place and their sweating crews
at the ready, the Reverend Sanctus Milanese prepared to speak. He opened by bestowing his blessings
upon "my good friends of the media," and asking
the Lord to forgive them for sometimes writing igno-
rantly or invidiously of the Church of the Purification and its leader, which he had the humble good
fortune to be, unworthy as he was of the great honor.

Reminds me, Holly wrote, *of the preacher who
claimed that, when it came to humility, he was the
uncontested world's champion.*

"Speak the truth and shame the devil," the
Reverend Sanctus Milanese said sonorously, and his
voice won out over the noise of cars and buses rolling
down Fifth Avenue. "And I shall speak the truth."

His voice was booming-evangelical, which was to
say, Holly thought, a hard-sell voice. All evangels
were demagogues, selling promises. God loves you,
loves *you,* and if you love Him in return, heaven is
yours, in death for certain, and perhaps in life as
well.

"It has not been given to the police to uproot the serpent, for their mission was not blessed of God."

A reporter reminded the Reverend that the verdict of failure was premature. The sweep was not yet over.

Reverend turns piercing eyes on speaker, Holly wrote. *Evangelical eyes not worth a damn if they don't pierce. Cohorts turn eyes, too, not piercing but cold, bleak, inaccessible.*

"Now the serpent was more crafty than any beast of the field which the Lord God had made."

Scripture-quoting voice has special vibrato, Holly noted.

"Only God, who is all-seeing, knows where the serpent lurks. Shall He impart His knowledge to those who follow temporal sway?"

Holly raised her hand and called out, "To whom will He impart it, Reverend?" and thought, If I ever get bored with newspaper work I can always find a job as a straight woman.

"To those who walk in His ways."

A television reporter shouted, "Can we assume He has already passed the word on to you, Reverend?"

"He has instructed me as follows: Let your flock go into the park and their purity shall overcome the impurity of the evil serpent, and they shall find where it hides and then they shall destroy it."

That's it, Holly thought, that's the kernel of news in the shell of bombast. He's giving the police advance notice that he will defy them.

A reporter said, "City officials have warned the public not to search for the snake. Will you disregard this warning?"

The Reverend gave the speaker a pitying smile.

"Follow-up to an earlier question, Reverend. Will God tell you exactly where the snake is hiding?"

The Reverend Sanctus Milanese appeared pained by the crudity of the question. "Even disbelievers must understand that He moves in mysterious ways. He will not say, Here, go to this or that place. Instead, He will take the hand of one of us and lead us there."

"When will He do this—before or after somebody else is bitten?"

Cohorts give speaker death-ray looks.

"When, in His infinite wisdom, He sees fit."

"Your people will be taking chances. Suppose one of them gets bitten?"

"Then it is the Lord's will."

The Reverend Sanctus Milanese turned abruptly, with a theatrical swirl of his cape that displayed its scarlet lining, and strode on a direct collision course toward the massive, ornately carved door of his house. At the last moment the door opened from the inside, and he passed through it.

He makes a classy exit, Holly wrote, and shut her notebook.

Sweating copiously, Converse passed the afternoon in fitful catnaps and short, angry dreams. He had shut the air conditioner off on behalf of the python, and let it out of its cage so that it could crawl into the living room and bask in the patches of sunshine that came in through the south windows.

His dreams consisted of a series of tenuously connected situations in which he tongue-lashed the redhead cruelly, bringing her to the point of tears. The underlying theme was her duplicity; she had breached an honorable agreement by leaving a note behind her which contained her phone number and the message "Call me. Clare." Clare. He hadn't even known her name until he read it on the note.

He had picked her up at the Brentano's on University Place. Her husband was abroad on a business trip, and she had what she called an end-of-summer itch for a fugitive affair with an attractive partner. Strictly a one-night stand, and then goodbye. She happened to love her husband, or, at least, like him an awful lot. Besides, she could never be serious about an affair with a pickup, especially a man who went in for T-shirts with comic inscriptions. Her attitude had suited Converse perfectly, and they had made a compact which, besides being congenial to both of them, added a little erotic spice to the adventure: Like ships that passed in the night they would never see each other again, and, in fact, wouldn't even exchange names.

Her note had wantonly ruined a foolproof arrangement in which the danger of involvement would be taken out of his hands. It was his nature to be insanely susceptible to falling in love with the women he met. It was partially in an effort to cure himself of his affliction that he had quit his job at the zoo, which he liked very much, and signed on to hunt snakes in Australia. The Outback would offer few temptations. But the expedition had been delayed by a series of bureaucratic snags, and he had been left with almost two months with nothing to do. He had recognized his idleness as fallow ground for the forming of a liaison, and so, in self-defense, had imposed an iron celibacy upon himself. The nonidentification pact with Clare had seemed ideal, and then she had gone ahead and spoiled it, damn her.

He slept again, and a new and alarming com-

ponent invaded his dreams. Clare's body wore Holly
Markham's head. Waking, he mocked his dream.
Holly, the girl with the calm, unassertively confident
face? No sweat. Not his type. Nothing there to tempt
him. Then why had he looked for her in the crowd of
reporters before he left the park? No sweat. Just a
reflex; he turned toward good-looking women like a
flower turning toward the sun. Just a meaningless
tropism. Pretty? Not really, except when her face
opened up in its transforming smile.

As for Clare, forget it, he had torn up her note,
hadn't he? Well, actually, he had just crumpled it
and tossed it into the wastebasket. Should have
ripped it up and flushed it down the toilet. That's
what he would do, next time he got out of bed.

He fell asleep again and dreamed that Holly was
kissing him. He forced himself to wake up. He
thought of Captain Eastman. Why had he been tact-
less and made Eastman sore at him? Had he *wanted*
to alienate him so he could go out and catch the
snake himself, for reasons of vanity (succeed
singlehandedly where an army of cops had failed) or
reasons of humaneness (save an innocent snake's
life)?

The cat was spitting. Converse raised himself on an
elbow and saw the python twining up the lamp standard, where the cat was perching, back humped. The
cat wasn't showing any disposition to escape by jumping down to the floor. It looked determined to settle
the python's hash once and for all. Converse got out
of bed, picked up the python behind the head, and
tossed it wriggling into its cage.

He turned on the air conditioning, made himself a
drink, and switched on the television set in time for
the evening news. Almost immediately, Eastman's

face appeared, like a bad conscience. He was admitting to a smoothly persistent reporter that the sweep had failed and that he didn't know—"at this time"—what the next move would be. His face was eroded by fatigue and frustration, and he looked a great deal older than he had in the morning.

Converse got up from his chair and dug in the wastebasket until he found Clare's note. He smoothed out the sheet of paper and reread the note, then tore it up and flushed it down the toilet. When he came back, the herpetologist from the Museum of Natural History was on camera. Converse didn't hear what he was saying. He was listening to his own inner voice: If I hurry, I can run downstairs, open up a manhole, get into the sewer, catch the bits of paper. . . .

The phone rang. The bitch, he thought, she wasn't taking any chances, she wrote down my phone number. He picked up the telephone. It was Captain Eastman.

The police operation ended officially at 5:45, although its failure had been conceded long before the last few exhausted cops straggled out of the park into Cathedral Parkway. The mayor, who was known—and liked being known—as a "fighter," refused to acknowledge defeat until he had heard from the Police Commissioner himself, who phoned from his limousine, which was speeding southward to take him to the mayor's meeting.

The mayor, his staff, and several high officials of the city administration were gathered in the conference room. The mayor sat on the dais, between the colors of the United States and the orange and blue flag of the City of New York. Outside the room, the news media were waiting to be admitted for a promised press conference. With the arrival of the Police Commissioner, the mayor opened the meeting of what, depending on his varying mood, he referred to as "my official family" or "this pack of lazy, backbiting schleppers." He called upon the P.C. to report.

"In a nutshell," the P.C. said, "we didn't find the snake."

"Nuts are in nutshells," the mayor said. "I asked for a report."

The P.C. shrugged. "That's the good news, Mr. Mayor. The bad news is that there's been an unsportsmanlike upsurge of crime in those areas of the city where we pulled out personnel to try to find this fucking pagan snake. That there have been twenty-odd fires of suspicious origin. That there are traffic snarls around bridge and tunnel areas that won't be unsnarled until nine o'clock. That more than seventy-five cops ended up in the hospital, though all but a half-dozen were treated and released. That eight cops were hurt in scuffles in the park with citizens who refused to move out of the way of the police line when asked to do so. And that the PBA has threatened a job action because of what they call cruel and inhumane treatment of their membership."

"You don't have to say it with all that much relish," the mayor said. "That's the whole report?"

"The PBA is also going to demand my resignation."

The mayor made a gesture of dismissal. Such a demand was an old story.

"They accuse me of having forgotten my humble beginnings, when I was a cop on the beat. That hurts. I may sit behind a desk now, and ride in an air-conditioned limousine, but I have never forgotten my humble beginnings, and never will."

"Sit down, Francis," the mayor said. He turned to the meeting at large. "Gentlemen, we gave it everything we have, today, and now we're confronted with a very large problem—what to do for an encore?"

The staff, nodding, ad-libbed: "That's right— what do we do for an encore?" "That's certainly the problem." "Gave it all we had."

"I'm open for suggestions." The mayor surveyed the room. Nobody met his eyes. Everybody was frowning and stroking his chin. "Francis?"

The P.C. looked grim. "I got a meeting scheduled for later on with Plans and Operations, maybe some of those great thinkers will come up with something. But I'll tell you what we can't do—we can't mount another operation like today. I'll have a mutiny on my hands."

"Police work is no goddamn picnic," the mayor shouted. "Did they think it would be a picnic when they signed on? Forget I said that. They're the finest cops who ever trod a beat, and don't anybody ever forget it."

The mayor glared around the room. Everyone was still thinking hard and rubbing their chins. He could hear their whiskers rasping. The bearded young man who had addressed the crowd at City Hall in the morning was muttering.

"Speak up if you've got something to say," the mayor said.

"Okay. In my opinion, we should deal with first things first. What do we say to the press?"

"Well, what *do* I say to the press?"

"You praise the devotion and courage of the

police, cite some figures on how many of them were overcome by the heat, put in a good word for the P.C. After that, Your Honor, some bullshit about continuing to press the search relentlessly, every resource of the city thrown into the effort to apprehend the perpetrator—"

"We can do without your jokes," the mayor said.

"—no further sweeps on the scale of today's operation are under consideration at this time. Instead, stepped-up twenty-four-hour patrol of the park—"

He was interrupted by another aide. "Okay as far as it goes. But you know what the big question is going to be—are we planning to close the park?"

"Tell them it is still under intensive study."

"How many times can we keep saying that?"

"As many as I have to," the mayor said emphatically. "I'm never going to answer that question."

"It's a physical impossibility," the P.C. said. "I couldn't do it with ten thousand cops."

A voice said, "Emphasize that the rules about behavior in the park will be strengthened and stringently enforced, and that any citizen who disobeys will face immediate arrest."

"Careful, there," the black-bearded aide said, "or you'll have the Civil Liberties Union in the act."

Another voice said, "They're sure to quiz you about Milanese and his Puries."

There was a sudden shout from the president of the City Council, sitting in the rear of the room: "Those fucking bastards! They ought to be exterminated, especially that charlatan, that hypnotist, that so-called fucking so-called reverend."

The president of the City Council was a shattered

man. His only son was a Purie. Several months before, in desperation, he had had his son forcibly seized as he strolled on the grounds of Eden Paradise, and borne away to the family summer home in Lake George, where he was kept under twenty-four-hour guard and visited daily by a psychologist who sought, in the boy's words, to "brainwash" him. This virtual act of kidnapping was not the first such to be attempted by the distraught parent of a Purie, but it was the first by a prominent public figure. The incident had been widely publicized after the boy made a daring escape from the Lake George house and denounced his father as "a fascist member of a fascist regime." He had topped off his performance by gazing adoringly into the effortfully benign face of the Reverend Sanctus Milanese and declaring, "This great and holy man is my true father."

"Compose yourself, Larry," the mayor said. The president of the Council nodded grimly and subsided in his seat. After a moment the mayor said to the meeting at large, "What the hell are they mixing in this thing for? What are they bothering us for?"

The bearded aide replied. "They're looking for publicity. Their enrollment has been down lately, and they're falling behind in their mortgage payments. This is a convenient opportunity to get exposure on the tube and in the papers, and attract new recruits and money. That's what it's all about."

"Well, I don't like it," the mayor said.

"From the political point of view, it isn't all negative," the bearded aide said. "Automatically, anything the Puries are for, the recognized churches are against, so we'll pick up a large sympathy vote."

The mayor looked pleasantly surprised. The

remainder of the meeting was desultory. There were, Hizzonner said, other matters of moment to occupy them besides a lousy snake. Would anybody advance the claim, for instance, that dealing with those *momsers* in Washington and Albany wasn't of more moment than a lousy snake? Nobody advanced such a claim. The mayor, satisfied, adjourned the meeting and motioned to the bearded aide, who got up and went to the dais.

"Stick around, Seymour, and help out with the questions about the Puries, okay?" The bearded aide nodded. The mayor, sighing as he watched the reporters begin to file in, said, "Any other city, Seymour, if somebody got bitten by a snake, the public would blame the snake. Here they blame the mayor. Sometimes I wish the goddamn island would break loose and float down the river and out to sea, and attach itself to, let's say, the Azores or like that."

"Who can tell," the bearded aide said. "Maybe if you loosen it up at the bridges and the tunnels, it might happen. Shall I get my monkey wrench?"

NINE

THE CENTRAL PARK PRECINCT, formerly known as the 22nd, or Two-two, is located midway through the 85th Street transverse, on the south side of the road. Its appearance is far and away the most anomalous and distinctive of any police precinct in the city. It doesn't look like a police precinct (either the old fortresslike ones or the new, functionally modern ones), but a stable, which it was when it was built in 1871. It is an official landmark building, jealously protected against demolition; jealously protected also, as its officers suggest, against air conditioning.

The Central Park Precinct complex consists of a series of very low, two-storied, handsomely weathered red brick buildings built in a horseshoe shape around a central courtyard. The visitor who can close his eyes to the presence of police vehicles streaming in and out can readily imagine that he is in a charming old English mews.

Despite the serenity of its appearance, the Central Park Precinct is a functioning police station much like any other in the city. Its quaint brick buildings house a main precinct area, a shooting range, garages, an anti-crime unit, a fingerprint unit, a detective squad, administrative offices, a lab, a medical unit, a roll-call room, lockers, showers, an Old Records room containing blotters going back to the 1880s, and all the other facilities and appurtenances of a police station, including a detention cell on the ground floor near the entrance to the main precinct, a gloomy, dusty little room as grim as a medieval oubliette.

The Central Park Precinct is a unit of Manhattan North Task Force. Its jurisdiction is Central Park, "wall to wall," although one exigency or another does require it to wander out into the streets peripheral to the park. It is located in what is known, sometimes laughingly, as a "low crime area."

The taxi pulled off the transverse road and dropped Converse at the entrance to the precinct courtyard. A cop leaning out of a squad car window directed him to the main precinct entrance. Inside, fans moved hot air around, and there was a smell of age and, perhaps, of long dead horses. A heavily sweating policeman behind a long counter directed him down a narrow corridor lined with offices to the last room on the park side of the building. Converse knocked on the door and went in. Captain Eastman sat behind a desk in a round-shouldered slump.

"I thought your headquarters were in Flushing," Converse said.

"They are, but I'm on detached duty at this precinct for the duration. This is the office of the commander of the Two-two. He's on vacation, the lucky dog. Sit down.''

The office of the commander of the Two-two was tiny and cramped, and, although its window faced south, would be sunless on even the brightest of days. A fan buzzed away ineffectually at the window. Converse stood the Pilstrom tongs against the wall, and placed the pillowcase on the desk.

"It isn't much," Eastman said, "but it does have a bathroom and a locker room, and there's a cot stored away behind that door.''

His voice was thin, leeched of energy. He looked terrible, Converse thought. His face was dragged down in folds by fatigue, and his blue eyes were dull, their conjunctivas rimmed with red. He swiveled toward the window, then faced back again, and his face seemed to firm up, as though, Converse thought, in relief at his having dispensed with the small talk.

"I was a little fresh this morning," Converse said. "I'm sorry. But I knew you wouldn't find it, and it struck me as a pure waste of manpower.''

Eastman's lids fluttered tiredly. "How old are you?''

Converse was surprised. "Twenty-nine. Why?''

"I'm forty-eight. If I learned any one thing since I was your age, it was never to be sure about anything. There was always a chance, wasn't there?''

"What's more, I think *you* knew you wouldn't find it.''

"Another thing I learned is that being incorruptible isn't necessarily a virtue. We *had* to sweep the park today, whether we found the snake or not. We're dealing with people and their anxieties, you know, not a set of cold abstractions.''

"You underestimate people, like all bureaucrats do. Why don't you, just once, try telling people the truth?"

"Because they detest the sound of it as much as we dislike telling it. Every man is his own little bureaucrat. Can you imagine the reaction if we told the public the operation would probably fail?"

"The truth never hurts," Converse said doggedly.

"It does. Just take that on trust from an older man." Eastman's eyes darkened. "Yes, we put on a show, and it cost us. Aside from the cops that had to be treated for heat prostration, everybody else is all whacked out. A lot of them will be calling in to the sick desk tomorrow."

"You're not planning on doing the same thing tomorrow, I hope."

"I don't *know* what I'm going to do tomorrow. Maybe you'll find the snake for us tonight, so we don't have to worry about tomorrow."

Converse shook his head. "In one night? It isn't likely."

"You sounded a lot cockier this morning." Eastman pointed to the Pilstrom tongs. "Still, you brought your snake-catching gear along." Eastman's voice became urgent. "Mr. Converse, I'd like to find that snake before it bites anybody else."

So would I, Converse thought, but I have a problem: I can see this thing from all sides. Nobody else realizes that the snake is just as much a victim of circumstances as the people it bites. It had to be *brought* to the park, by somebody acting out of malice or ignorance or God knows what. Okay, but I mustn't let my feelings about snakes—do me something, I'm fond of them—get out of hand. The first priority is to save human lives. Death by snakebite is a horrible way to die. We can't have anybody else bitten, no matter *what* happens to the snake. But still, it keeps coming back to this, it's perfectly possible to save human lives without killing the snake. That's the truth of the matter, but Eastman would hit the ceiling if I said so. Not that I have to say it. Eastman is smart, he reads me very well.

He said, "You know, captain, it won't bite anybody who doesn't bother it."

Eastman's laugh was a bitter exhalation. "We keep getting reports from our patrols that the park is lousy with citizens hunting for the snake. In the dark, mind you, in the dangerous park after dark. Armed with forked sticks and crowbars and axes, and God knows what else. We're pulling some of them in to discourage them."

"Can you hold them legally?"

"No," Eastman said flatly. "It helps to scare them off. We escort them out of the park and warn them, and some go home, but others come right back in again through a different entrance, and take up where they left off, poking their sticks into bushes. They're all over the park."

"Well," Converse said, "they're going to make it so much harder for us to find the animal. It's going to be scared to come out."

"It hasn't struck me as being all that scary," Eastman said. He sighed. "We've also had our first hoaxter. Some jerk from Westchester drove in with a snake in a wicker basket. He was going to turn it loose in the park as a joke. Some joke."

"What kind of a snake?"

"A big long blacksnake. Harmless. Even I recognize that kind of a snake. A cop caught the guy about an hour ago just as he was about to turn it loose. We've got him in the detention cell and we're looking into seeing if there's some kind of charge we can prefer against him."

"Stupid bastard."

"Yes, well, that's what happens. There's going to be a lot more craziness, one kind or another, before we're finished." Eastman straightened up in his chair and made an effort at briskness. "Well, what are you going to do for us?"

"Try to find the snake. I wish to hell I knew what it was."

"Yeah, well, as the DI put it, you'll know when you find it. You don't think it's a cobra?"

"It's possible, of course, but I doubt it. Cobras chew when they bite. This one just makes a couple of neat little puncture holes. It's confident about how poisonous it is, so all it has to do is *inject* its venom."

"Do you know any snakes like that?"

"I know quite a few of them, but it's pointless trying to guess. There are twenty-five hundred different species of snakes, and maybe half of them are poisonous. In this case, we can eliminate those that secrete a hemotoxic venom, and those that *are* neurotoxic but whose venom is not so powerful, and those that are rear-fanged, and those that are small, since as a general rule large snakes distill a more powerful venom than small ones. . . ." He spread his hands. "And even when you rule out the ones that aren't aggressive it still leaves an awful lot of snakes."

Eastman nodded vaguely. He isn't interested in details, Converse thought. All he cares about is catching it, he doesn't care how the trick is done.

"Somebody said something about a mongoose," Eastman said without much conviction. "I saw one killing a snake in a nature film, once. Anything to it?"

"A mongoose can kill a snake, most times, and so can a hedgehog. Both of them are resistant to snake venom. But they're not natural enemies, and their tendency is to avoid each other. The fights you see are always staged. Men pit them and they fight to the death and the snake usually loses. Actually, the most efficient snake-killing animal is an African bird called the secretary bird. It's about four feet high with long taloned legs that it uses to stomp and gash a snake to death. In South Africa people sometimes tame them and keep them around the house for protection against snakes." He glanced across the desk at Eastman and laughed. "No, it isn't practical to put a secretary bird in Central Park."

"I guess not." Eastman's fleeting expression of hope disappeared. "You want to get started?"

"Might as well. There are two things we can try. We can shine a powerful flashlight beam around, and if the animal is nearby, the light bounces off its retina and you pick up the eye-shine. Trouble is, it's a local effect. You can't shine a light in the snake's eye if it's a block away."

Eastman grunted. "What's the other thing?"

"Stake out a watering place. Snakes are mostly, though not exclusively, nocturnal animals. If it wants a drink, it'll probably come out for it at night."

"You know how much water there is in the park?"

"You told me this morning—about a hundred and fifty acres. It's a very long shot, but there isn't much choice. The odds might be a little better tomorrow morning. Snakes are coldblooded, and have to lie in the sun to warm themselves up for an hour or so. Maybe less than that in this kind of weather, because they don't lose too much heat during the night. They like to bask early in the morning, and they like lying on a rock if there's one around."

"You know how many rocks there are in the park?"

"It's a problem. But if you give me a week or so, I'll guarantee to turn it up."

"Look," Eastman said, "you're the expert and I have a lot of confidence in you. But it didn't take those two guys who got bitten any week to turn it up, did it? Both of them found it inside of twenty-four hours of each other."

"Yeah, well," Converse said, "they were just lucky. It was pure dumb luck."

Converse decided to stake out the Belvedere Lake because it was there, or near there, that Roddy Bamberger had been bitten. For all anyone knew, the snake might have been going to or coming from a drink when Bamberger had run across it.

"But it could have drunk in a lot of places." He tapped his fingers on Eastman's police department map of the park. "The Lake to the south, the Conservatory Water to the southeast, or even here. . . ." With a broad sweep of his palm he covered the Receiving Reservoir that ran almost the entire width of the park between the 85th and 97th Street transverses.

"It's long odds," Eastman said. "Why don't we use some manpower and stake out *all* of the possible watering holes?"

"Because there's only one of me," Converse said, "and your cops would probably miss it or else step on it in the dark and get bitten."

Eastman said, "We'd better go back over your contract and include a breach of modesty clause." He covered a yawn with his hand. "We know the snake was around the Belvedere Lake a couple of night ago. Is it their custom to hang around in one place?"

"Again, it depends on the species. As a rule, snakes aren't all that territorial except when they're breeding, so it could be anywhere in the park. But at least it's a starting place."

"We're not going to find it, right?"

"It isn't likely," Converse said. "We need time."

"We haven't got any," Eastman said.

They left the precinct around nine in a squad car driven by a patrolman who took them out of the park into Central Park West, then brought them back in again at the Hunter's Gate and drove on the pedestrian walks past the Swedish Schoolhouse, the Shakespeare Garden, and the darkened Delacorte Theatre. Except for one group of half a dozen young men and women whom they took to be Puries, there was no evidence that citizens were still at large in the park searching for the snake.

"At least I hope that's the case," Eastman said. "Muggers don't take kindly to having crowds of people wandering around in their park after dark."

The police car pulled over to one side of the walkway and parked. Converse and Eastman got out and walked down the embankment to the lake.

"This is as good as anyplace else. We might as well sit down."

"Suppose it comes along," Eastman said. "I mean, sitting down, we'd be sitting ducks, wouldn't we?"

"Of course, if it comes down for a drink on the other side of the lake we won't see it. But it was near here that that fellow was bitten."

"You're *sure* it's okay to sit down?"

"Sure. That way there's no chance of our stepping on it."

"If you say so." Eastman touched the Pilstrom tongs. "I know what this stick is for. The pillowcase—I remember you putting that rattlesnake into some kind of a yellow bag."

"It was a yellow pillowcase. Listen, captain, it would be better if we didn't talk. Okay?"

"I thought snakes were deaf."

"They are. I'm not. I want to be able to hear it if it comes."

Eastman fell silent. Behind them, the driver had turned off the car's motor and lights. Converse could see him behind the wheel. Above them, the sky seemed to be pressing down, as if it bore a tangible weight of clouds. It was the color of lead, except where it was tinged with red from the upfling of neons in the center of the city. The oppressiveness of the heat seemed worse than ever. The park was quiet in the still air, except for the occasional sound of an auto horn or a noisy transmission as a car accelerated.

Eastman was sitting motionless with his head bowed, his hands clasped on the grass between his legs. He was probably terrific on stakeouts, Converse thought, a man who knew how to do that most difficult of things, wait. If the snake came along, Eastman wouldn't give them away. Not that there was much chance of it. Even if it was still in the area, even if it did come to the lake for a drink, it would be next to impossible to detect unless it practically ran into them.

He shifted his position slightly and dabbed at his sweaty face with a corner of the pillowcase. Eastman hadn't moved, not even to scratch his nose or mop up sweat. His breathing was regular, and Converse realized that he was asleep. He smiled in the darkness, and settled himself into a more comfortable position. But he kept his head raised, peering through the gloom for something that might never come and, if it did, might come and go unseen and unheard. He felt something on the back of his hand. A raindrop.

The snake curved in its flowing S-movement, propelling its great length forward swiftly toward the water it had drunk from on the previous nights. From time to time it paused to taste the air with its darting tongue. When it felt the first drops of rain it stopped. It raised its head high, tongue testing. Then the rain came down in a sudden torrent. The snake slid into a coil as the downpour pelted it. It lowered its head to within an inch or two of the ground, and moved from side to side in an almost dancelike rhythm.

The downpour beat against its body, colder than it liked. The rain was so heavy it bounced off the parched ground, and quickly formed puddles. The snake uncoiled and slid forward again toward the lake. Then it stopped, dipped its head, and drank from a puddle. Afterwards, it returned to its tree.

After the first warning drop or two the rain fell out of the sky in sheets. In a few seconds, Converse was soaked to the skin. Nevertheless, Eastman continued to sleep through it. Converse shook him awake.

"Christ," Eastman said. "Where did this come from?"

"Let's go."

Converse held out his hand, and Eastman came to his feet awkwardly and with some effort. With the rain soaking him he looked old and bedraggled. They ran to the squad car and jammed into the front seat beside the driver.

"Now what?" Eastman said.

"Maybe it'll cool off the weather," the driver said.

"Now we can go home," Converse said.

"Can't we sit here and watch from the car?"

Converse shook his head. "It won't come tonight, not now."

TEN

HIS TECHNIQUE WAS DEPLORABLE, but his stamina was prodigious, and he was sweet in a dumb kind of way. Stamina and sweetness normally ranked well down on Jane Redpath's scale of masculine virtues, so it remained an open question in her mind as to whether or not she would have gone to bed with him if he hadn't offered to go to the menagerie with her. At this point the matter was purely academic.

"This point" was 3:30 in the morning. The alarm clock was clamoring, and here he was again, looming over her, undepleted and eager, broaching her sore pussy with a miraculous erection. She opened to him, halfway between weariness and helplessness, and wondered if she couldn't catch a catnap in the few minutes until he was done. But instead she responded with enthusiasm to his thrust, and finished up squealing with pain and delight.

While she was showering, he parted the curtain

139

and stepped in with her. She felt him against her, and realized, incredible as it might seem, that he was prepared for another assault, so she turned on the cold water full force, and even his Phoenix-like member wasn't up to coping with such a deterrent. He dwindled, and then she had to put up only with his cavorting and hollering and pounding his chest and spitting streams of water and a few other locker-room antics. Finally she turned off the water and jumped out of the shower stall, and before he could rouse himself again, without bothering to dry herself thoroughly, put on her jeans and T-shirt. He tried to take them off again, but she fended him off and chivied him into getting dressed. She diverted him while they drank coffee by praising him for his courage in offering to accompany her to the park. She told him that he was the ballsiest man—in the sense of being gutsy, she added quickly—she had ever met. His chest—and nothing else, she noted thankfully—swelled with pride.

It was probably true, she thought, as he sipped his hot coffee and made a thoroughly unconvincing disclaimer of his bravery. He was not only one of the bravest men she had ever known, but incontestably the stupidest. The stupidest *girl* she had ever met was Jane Redpath.

They prepared to leave. She gathered up her tripod and slung her Hasselblad over her shoulder. Jeff stuck a hefty tire iron in his belt, picked up a forked wooden stick and a burlap bag, and they were ready. She thought the tire iron was a pretty good idea, but she wasn't so sure about the forked stick and bag. They reminded her that there *was* a snake in the park. She had given it some thought earlier, but rationalized her fears in terms of the enormous size of the park. Still, the knowledge of the snake's presence had made her squirm, and she might very well have postponed the expedition if her paper hadn't already been badly overdue.

She warned Jeff that she didn't want him to do anything silly like going off on his own to hunt for the snake. He said the stick was just a precaution, and relax, baby, relax.

In the taxi that took them downtown through deserted streets, he groped her, naturally, and she tried to divert him by being serious and unsexy. She went on about her photographic project, which was to constitute the thesis for her Physiology M.A., but it didn't slow him down.

"God, I love your apples," he said fervently, with his hand inside her T-shirt.

"Whenever people think of sleep problems," she said in what she hoped was a pedantic, sedative voice, "they tend to think exclusively in terms of human beings. But it's obvious that we can learn much from animals. . . ."

He was nuzzling her neck with his handsomely broken athlete's nose. The cab driver, who drove with his left hand extended through the window, as if to cool his fingers, kept turning his head around at intervals to check the activity in the back of the car.

"Jeff," she whispered. "Stop it, everybody's looking at us."

He placed his hand between her legs. "I can't get enough. You know?"

"How could I not know?" She tried to pin his hand down, but realized that he would take it as a playful test of strength, so she stopped. "Look, in case we meet that snake . . . I mean, it's not too likely and all, but . . . I'm scared, Jeff."

It was a fresh effort to distract him, and it succeeded. He didn't remove his hand, nothing as definitive as that, but he stopped trying to poke into her.

"No sweat, baby. If we run across it, we'll just catch it, and that's that."

She gave him an only partly feigned shiver. "It's dangerous. I'm so scared. How are you going to catch it?"

He had already told her how, in detail. He had spent the previous summer in the Southwest on some kind of archeological dig, and in the evenings, in his free time, had gone out catching rattlers with his colleagues. "Great sport" was how he had described it. But he didn't mind repeating himself.

"It's simple. All you need is a forked stick. You spear them just behind the head with the stick, then you grab them there with your hand—behind the head, so they can't nip you—and just pop 'em in a bag. Nothing to it. I hope we run into the one in the park so I can show you."

"But it isn't a rattler. They think it might be a cobra."

"No difference. A snake is a snake. What you have to keep in mind is that snakes have a very low I.Q. When they're threatened, and can't run away, they attack. Well, they have this low intelligence rating, and all they can think of is that they have to bite something. So you give them the stick, and they bite *that*."

In his enthusiasm he removed his hand from her crotch to gesture, and forgot to put it back. For this relief, much thanks. "They bite the stick?" She tried to put an enormous amount of curiosity and wonderment in her voice. "And then what?"

"Then you shake them off the stick and pin them down. It's easy."

"Easy." She strove for a tone combining skepticism and admiration.

"Anything's easy, if you really know what you're doing."

He prattled on with earnest enthusiasm as the driver entered the 97th Street transverse and headed eastward through the park. All she had to do was keep him going for another five minutes. The trip back was another matter, but maybe she would be able to think of something.

The snake glided onto the pavement, dry again since the cloudburst. It moved slowly, cautiously, as its tongue brought in the mingled odor-substances of many animals.

Once or twice it lifted its head high and peered into a cage. Even when the cages were empty, the odor-substances were strong.

In one cage, two lions were asleep; their powerful smell was familiar to the snake and disturbing. One of the lions twitched uneasily in its sleep before the snake moved on.

The cab driver dropped them at Fifth Avenue and 65th Street. They entered the park through the Children's Gate, and walked toward the Arsenal, ivy-covered red brick, where the park's administrative offices were housed. It was dark, except for a modest floodlight over the steps, and a faint reflection at a downstairs window from lights somewhere in the interior of the building.

Now that they were actually here, Jane felt nervous. If Jeff had any fears or qualms, he didn't show them. Well, that was the wrong way to put it. He didn't show them because he hadn't any. He was fully tooled up for the venture: tire iron in his belt for disposing of muggers, forked stick over his shoulder to deal with snakes. And if there was a night watchman, he would undoubtedly disarm him with sheer ebullience.

They skirted the Arsenal to the left, walking softly on their sneakered feet, circled to their right, and came into the menagerie. It was still an hour or so before dawn, and the menagerie was dark and shadowy except for the thin spread of light from the spaced lampposts. Behind them, on Fifth Avenue, the buildings loomed blackly, except for an isolated light at a window here and there, where, she thought, some despairing soul waited for the dawn or the resolution needed to end his life.

"Okay," Jeff said. "Where do we start?"

He spoke in his normal voice, and in the nighttime hush it echoed like a gunshot.

"*Shsh. Quiet.* You'll wake everything up."

He surprised her by lowering his voice to a creditable whisper. "You're gonna wake them all up anyway with your flash."

"I'm not using a flash. I'm doing a time exposure with a very fast film. ASA 400. It should work with the light from the streetlamps."

Something was moving to her right. She turned quickly and saw two points of light. She gasped, and clung to Jeff, and then realized that an animal was watching her through the bars of its cage. It was a shadowy gray bulk, and she couldn't make out what it was.

"Jesus!" Trembling, she rested her head on his chest. "It scared the shit out of me."

"Relax, you're with Jeff, okay?" His voice was soft, he was a terrific whisperer, an ace, better than she was herself, and he was patting her ass caressingly. "I like *these* apples, too."

"Please, not in front of the animals." She pushed him away, took a deep breath, and decided that she had herself together again. "Let's go to work."

She moved on to the next cage. The plaque read: BARBARY SHEEP. She peered inside. At first the cage seemed to be empty, but when her eyes became accustomed to the gloom she could make out the sheep. There were two of them, lying toward the back of the cage, tan animals with strongly curved horns. Both were motionless, asleep.

"I'm going to get these. Please keep quiet."

He watched as she opened the telescoped metal legs of the tripod and fitted the Hasselblad to it. She adjusted the settings, sighted through the finder, then decided to make an adjustment. Behind her, Jeff gave a tiny cluck of impatience and breathed heavily on the back of her neck. She sensed that he was about to pat her ass again, too.

She said, "You're making me nervous. Go take a walk, okay?" He grunted and looked surly; he didn't like being dismissed. He didn't like standing around and doing nothing, either. He needed something to do, even if it was nothing more than a brush with a mugger. "What I mean—check out the other cages, see what I can shoot next. Okay?"

"Okay."

He strode off to the south end of the line of cages. She sighted on the sheep and felt for the shutter release. Before she could press it there was a sudden outcry, shrill, panicky (or so it seemed to her), and then pandemonium. From nearby cages and from within the animal houses she could hear the roar of big cats, the chatter of monkeys, indefinable screams, whines, snarls, even the barking of the seals in their pool.

Through the finder she saw the sheep bound to their feet, bleating. He's done it, she thought, the clumsy oaf somehow startled them and woke up the whole fucking zoo. She whirled, catching up the camera and tripod, and started toward him angrily. Then she stopped dead. He was crouched, his back to her, facing a snake, the longest and lithest-looking she had ever seen or even imagined. Its head was high off the ground, its mouth was agape.

She let out a cry of terror, and knew in that instant that her reaction was no different from that of the other animals. The urge to turn away and run was overwhelming, but she knew she couldn't desert Jeff. The snake horrified her, but there was something thrilling in the way Jeff faced it—in the knotted back muscles standing out against his damp T-shirt, the alertness of his posture, the athlete's grace and self-confidence.

He was moving the forked stick toward the snake and whispering softly, encouragingly, laughing a little at himself: "Toro. Ho, toro, make your move."

The snake was erect, tensed, threatening, hissing hollowly. Its body seemed incredibly long and slender, the neck swelling on a vertical axis, the eyes wide and menacing. Barely aware of what she was doing, she planted the tripod and put her eye to the finder. She placed her finger on the shutter release. Peering through the finder, holding her breath, she saw Jeff extend the stick at full length. She pressed the shutter release almost by reflex, and it seemed to trigger off movement. The picture in the finder became unfrozen. The snake and the stick seemed to meet, and then Jeff dropped the stick with a clatter. He cried out. She shut her eyes, shaking with fear. Jeff's voice came from directly in front of her. "The bugger ran up the stick and bit me."

She opened her eyes. His left hand was clasped over his right forearm and he seemed flushed, but he was calm. "Oh my God!"

"It's okay," Jeff said. "It's gone. It ran away."

He lifted his left hand from his arm and she saw two small spots of oozing blood an inch below the crook of his elbow.

"Oh, Jeff, Jeff, what can we do? We have to get you to a hospital."

He slipped his belt out of his trousers, looped it around his arm just below the biceps, and pulled it very tight. "The thing of it is," he said quietly, "the thing is to keep calm, because if you get excited the heart pumps quicker and the poison circulates that much faster. So everybody concerned has to relax, okay?"

Behind her, a voice called out roughly, and she turned, her heart thumping. A figure was moving toward them hulkingly out of the shadows. A brilliant light came on and blinded her.

For a brief time, Jane Redpath had company in the waiting room, a middle-aged black man with a deep laceration under his right eye that seeped sluggishly into his bloody handerchief. He was naked to the waist above a pair of blue jeans and bed slippers, and he chatted amiably while he waited to be tended to. He had actually been on his way into the emergency room when they had come in—she and Jeff and the two cops—but he held no resentment at being superseded. The cops had been called by the menagerie night watchman, the man who had flashed his light at them after Jeff was bitten. At first he had been more concerned with their trespassing than with getting help, but he had moved quickly when Jane had screamed at him in a hysterical rage. Jeff had quieted her, and apologized to the watchman.

The police car had responded quickly, and driven them to East Side Hospital, where Jeff was rushed into the emergency ward at once. They had not allowed her to accompany him. He had walked in under his own power, smiling at her and telling her not to worry, and to go home and catch some sleep. He'd give her a ring later on.

The man with the injured eye told her that his wound had been inflicted by his wife, wielding a high-heeled shoe. They had quarreled, and she waited until he was asleep before hitting him.

"But she was real sorry, you know," the man said. "She didn't mean to hit me in no eye, but only in the head. But in the dark, she aimed bad."

Jane murmured something, sitting on the edge of a soft chair and wishing that she smoked. The nurse at the desk was busy writing up reports, and she would frown at them from time to time, as though the man's soft voice interfered with her concentration.

"She would not have hit me in the eye on purpose," the man said. "She know where her bread is buttered. I am a jeweler, and with this hurt eye it will be trouble putting the loupe in the eye. You understand?"

But you can use it in the left eye, Jane thought dully.

"You might say I could use the loupe in the left

eye," the man said, "but I never could use the left eye for that. You understand?"

"Habit," Jane said.

"Habit," the man said with satisfaction. He examined his bloody handerchief and then returned it to his eye. "That's what it is, Miss, just old habit."

The telephone rang. Jane watched as the nurse answered it briefly. The nurse told the man with the injured eye to go into Room E. The man nodded politely to Jane and went into the emergency ward. Jane got up and walked to the reception desk. The nurse looked up from her papers, frowning.

Jane said, "Can you find out how he is?"

"I can't disturb them now," the nurse said. "There's a whole team in there working on your. . . ." She paused.

"Friend," Jane said. "We're awfully close friends."

"The best thing is to sit down and compose yourself. They're doing everything they can in there to help him."

Jane went back to her seat. She shut her eyes and cried inwardly, without tears. When she opened her eyes a man in a white jacket was standing over her.

"I'm Dr. Moran."

"Yes." She couldn't say any more. The doctor looked grave.

"We've administered a polyvalent serum, he seems to be responding moderately well. He's remarkably calm, and that helps."

"Then he's going to be all right?"

The doctor made an ambiguous movement of his head that was neither affirmation nor denial. "He wasn't able to describe what the snake looked like with any certainty. Did you get a good look at—"

"Oh my God!" Jane said. "I left it in the police car! My camera. I took a picture of it."

Dr. Moran was sprinting toward the emergency ward entrance.

Within ten minutes of receipt of the report from the RMP car that had brought Jeff to the hospital, the police put two Emergency Service Unit trucks and every man and vehicle the Two-two could muster into a broad area surrounding the menagerie. In the darkness, the park glittered with the rays of flashlights and the powerful searchlight beams mounted on the ESU trucks.

The police were to work into the daylight hours before their fruitless search was called off.

Fumbling for the phone in the darkness, Converse knew with certainty that it would be Eastman, and it was.

"Sorry again. We have another victim of the snake." Eastman paused, as if to allow him to say something, perhaps to echo his, Eastman's, own grimness, but he was silent, and Eastman went on. "I'm at East Side Hospital. We have a picture of the snake. It's being developed. Can you come over?"

"Right away."

He hung up, and was already on his feet, groping for his clothing, when he realized that he had not even inquired about the victim, asked whether he was alive or dead. But, then, Eastman hadn't mentioned it, either.

When the snake left the menagerie area it did not return to its tree but ranged far afield from it, questing, as it had been ever since the rain had stopped, driven once again by an age-old imperative of its species.

It ran northward, to the more uncultivated section of the park. Its movements were swift, with a quality of urgency. It did not move in a straight line, but quartered an area, delving into wild places, squirming into heavily overgrown patches, probing with its small head.

It was already light when it came upon a burrow concealed under a fallen tree in a tangle of heavy growth. Its previous occupant was a small animal, perhaps a family of small animals, but the faintness of the odors analyzed by the Jacobson's organ indicated that the burrow had been vacant for some time.

The snake cautiously broached the entrance to the burrow with its head, careful not to disturb the brush that covered it. It slid downward a short distance to make certain it was uninhabited (if there was an animal inside, it would leave in panic at the first appearance of the head), that it was large enough to accommodate the snake's length, that it had at least one additional exit.

The burrow fulfilled the snake's requirements in every way. It slid all the way inside. It tried the second exit hole, again careful not to dislodge the brush that hid the opening but would not obstruct a quick escape if one became necessary.

The snake coiled its long body comfortably inside the burrow and went to sleep.

A few minutes after Dr. Moran had left her, one of the cops who had driven them to the hospital came running in with Jane's Hasselblad. He went straight through into the emergency ward. He came out a

short while later, and stopped when he recognized
her.

"Be okay, honey, be okay."

"Did you see him?"

"Just for a second."

She wanted to ask if he was in pain, but instead she
said, "Did he say anything?"

"No. I mean, not that I heard. He might have been
talking, but I wasn't there long enough. They just
took the camera and I came out."

"Yes. Well. Thanks, officer. For everything."

"Be okay. You'll see."

He touched the bill of his cap to her and left. A
moment later a heavy-set, ruddy-faced man came
hurrying in. He was wearing slacks and a mesh shirt,
and she heard him tell the nurse that he was Captain
Something-or-other before going through the
emergency ward entrance. Presently, the black man
came out, wearing a T-shirt which someone must
have given him. There was a neat bandage under his
eye, very white against his skin. He came over to
where she sat.

"See? Never hold the loupe with this thing on."

"I hope you'll be all right," Jane said.

"Be all right, all right," the man said. "But have
to lay off a few weeks, because I can't use the loupe
in the other eye." He grinned. "Wife hear that she
gonna get mad all over again. Make her wish she
done hit me in the other eye."

After he had gone, Jane tried to catch the nurse's
eye, but the nurse kept plugging away at her reports.
Some nurse. An accountant. Jane looked at her
watch: 5:30. It was probably beginning to get light
out by now, but you couldn't tell in this windowless

room. Dr. Moran appeared in the doorway, smiled at her, then snapped his fingers and went back into the emergency ward.

She conjured up an image of Jeff. He was lying on his back on a table, speaking to the doctors surrounding him. "Keep calm, fellers, and we'll all pull together and get this thing whipped. Teamwork and calm —right?" Her eyes filled with tears. Jeff—such a dumb shit of a jock, all muscle and cock and an empty attic. Right? Wrong! He was a goddamn angel!

She remembered how he had calmed her down, and then calmed the watchman and persuaded him to go for help. While the watchman was gone he had told her that he was going to lie down, and that she mustn't get alarmed, that lying down was best for slowing up the action of the venom. He stretched out on the pavement, holding his tourniquet tight with his left hand, and when she asked him if it hurt he said it didn't, all he felt was just a kind of pins-and-needles effect. . . .

A young man came loping into the reception room from outside. He spoke to the nurse, who picked up her telephone. The young man waited impatiently. He was dressed in a torn T-shirt inscribed: *Coxswain, Venice Gondola Crew*. The nurse nodded to him and he charged through the emergency ward door just as Dr. Moran came out again.

Dr. Moran sat down in a facing chair. His knees made soft contact with hers. He had great dark Irish eyes, and he brought them very close to her. It made her dizzy to look at them. He told her that Jeff was holding his own, and that if they were able to identify the snake they would then probably inject him with the *specific* antidotal serum. . . .

He spoke in a soothing, warm voice, meanwhile bearing down on her with those luminous bedroom eyes. She began to sob again. Dr. Moran tilted his head solicitously and patted her shoulder. Then she felt his hand slip down and touch her breast.

"There now," Dr. Moran said, "there now." His thumb was caressing the rim of her breast. Therapy, right? "Would you like me to give you something to calm you down?"

Give *yourself* something, she thought, give yourself something to calm your pecker down. She stopped crying and said, "No, I don't need anything. I'm okay."

In fact, she thought, I'm better than okay. I'm quite calm, and if he doesn't take his finger away I'll break it off for him. I'm calm, she thought, because that's the way to honor Jeff, that terrific, courageous, wonderful fucking machine. You're too honest and simple to die, Jeff, she thought, and moved back in her chair, removing her breast from the gently palpating thumb of Dr. Moran, of the deep velvet eyes, the shitty eyes. . . .

"Feeling a little better?" Dr. Moran said.

"Much better," she said calmly. Boy, she was so calm she could taste it. "And instead of sitting here and trying to feel me up, doctor, why don't you go back in there and see if you can't help save my Jeff's life?"

The picture had been enlarged to five by nine, and it was still wet. It had been placed on a table in an empty room in the emergency ward, and Captain Eastman was studying it from a distance, with a mingled expression of revulsion and fascination. The picture was surprisingly sharp and well defined, considering the meager light it had been shot in. The anterior portion of the snake was curled upward on the stick, and its mouth was gaped wide open over Jeff's arm, whether a moment before biting or just afterwards, Eastman couldn't tell. The snake's posterior section trailed off at the bottom of the stick, long and tensile, strongly curved, as if to brace itself against the pavement for the drive up the stick.

The phone rang. The receptionist said that Converse had arrived.

"Send him right in." He went out into the corridor and beckoned to Converse when he came through the door. Converse ran toward him. "Thanks for getting here so quick." He led the way into the room.

"How is the patient?" Converse said.

"Not too bad. He's young and strong, so. . . ."

Converse had spotted the picture and brushed by him. He bent over the table and let out a low whistle.

"You recognize it?" Eastman said.

"It's a black mamba." Converse leaned over the picture for another look. He straightened up and said, almost reverently, "God, it's beautiful."

Converse was on the telephone, trying to raise a nightman at the Bronx Zoo. He told Eastman that, although the black mamba was of the genus Dendroaspis, which was covered by the polyvalent antivenin, the zoo had a specific black mamba serum in the refrigerator in the reptile house; he would ask to have it rushed down to the hospital.

Eastman said, "I'll find another phone and call the precinct up in that area, I think it's the Four-eight, and ask them to shoot the stuff down in a squad car.

After that, I'd like you to come out to the menagerie with me.''

"Okay. But don't bet that it's hanging around there. Black mambas are very wide-ranging snakes, and they move like something shot out of a gun. It could be a couple of miles away from the menagerie by now."

Eastman went out into the corridor to look for a telephone. He paused by the open door of Room D, where the Code Blue team was working on Jeff.

"Oh, Christ."

The team of a half-dozen doctors and nurses was gone. There were only two figures beside the table. One was Dr. Shapiro, with a cigarette in his mouth. The other was a nurse. Shapiro, with his hands at his sides, was looking down at the patient. The nurse was attaching a tag to the patient's big toe.

Eastman went into the room. "What happened?" he said to Shapiro. The figure on the table was very still.

"We lost him," Shapiro said. He didn't look at Eastman. "We thought he was going to make it, and then he just went out, he simply blinked out on us."

"Damn," Eastman said.

"When he began to go out it took us by surprise. We had thought he was going to pull out of it. Somebody got the bright idea of turning him over, and we saw the hives on his back." Shapiro struck his thigh with his fist. "If they had appeared on the front of him, as they usually do, we'd have been able to shoot some adrenalin into him."

"What did the hives mean?"

"Anaphylactic shock. Antivenin is extracted from the blood sera of horses that have been injected with dosages of snake poison. There's a class of people who are profoundly allergic to horse serum and go into anaphylactic shock if they're given it. It can be fatal if it's not treated."

Eastman nodded. "I've heard of that. But I thought there was a way of testing it beforehand."

"There is." Shapiro's voice was weighted with fatigue, and Eastman thought, Everybody is bone tired, all the good guys are weary, and only the snake is full of energy. "But you don't stop to test for allergic reaction when somebody is dying of snakebite. You have to hurry. In other circumstances we'd have recognized the symptoms of anaphylactic shock right off the bat. The trouble is, they're very similar to the symptoms of neurotoxic poisoning from snakebite, so we couldn't tell." Cigarette smoke was curling up around his eyes, and he blinked. "The hives were something else, but they were on his back and we didn't see them until it was too late." He turned to face Eastman fully for the first time. "I'm getting disgusted with people being killed by that snake."

Eastman said, "I thought doctors didn't smoke."

Shapiro looked at the cigarette in his hand. "I thought so myself. It's that damn snake. It has me doing things I don't do."

"Yeah," Eastman said. "Can you spare one of those?"

Shapiro gave him the cigarette. "Take this one. I don't smoke."

Eastman took a deep puff. The filter end was wet. "Has anybody told that girl out there yet?"

"I'm going right out there to tell her."

"I'll do it. I'm used to it."

"Well, if it comes to that, I'm used to it, too."

Eastman started toward the door. "I'm sorry, doc."

"Tell it to *him*." Shapiro inclined his head toward the figure on the table.

As Eastman left the room he saw Converse turn out into the corridor. "I got through to the zoo," Converse said. "You got hold of the police up there?"

"Not yet."

Converse frowned. "Let's go, captain, that serum could make a big difference."

"Not really," Eastman said.

ELEVEN

CONVERSE SAID, "The name of the snake is black mamba."

A reporter in the front row said, "Mamba? That's a dance, isn't it?"

"Mamba," Converse said, "from the Kaffir word *m'namba*. The black mamba is the largest poisonous snake in Africa and the deadliest."

It was 8:30, and Jeff had been dead for almost two hours. Converse was sitting behind a scarred oak desk in the shooting range of the Central Park Precinct, flanked by Captain Eastman at his right and Deputy Inspector Scott at his left. The press was facing him, sitting in chairs that had been hastily collected from various offices in the precinct. The desk was cluttered with radio and television microphones. TV cameramen roamed the long room with handheld cameras. There were no special lights;

the DI had refused to allow them to be brought in. A trace of cordite lingered in the air.

Everyone smelled of coffee except the DI, who smelled of anger and frustration.

They had driven from East Side Hospital to the precinct in the DI's car. The DI had spoken only once: "Haven't you got anything else to wear but that stupid shirt?"

"Sorry," Converse said, "my tails are at the cleaners."

Eastman gave him a warning look. The DI curled his upper lip in an expressive sneer. Later, while they were waiting for the press to assemble, the DI, in a voice resonant with passion, had declared that he despised newsmen, that they were "parasites living off the carrion of tragedy." The unexpectedly dramatic turn of phrase made Converse aware, for the first time, that the DI, with his hollow, attenuated face and the dark, brooding intensity of his eyes, presented the classic image, bordering on travesty, of an old-fashioned Shakespearian actor.

The DI had opened the press conference with a flat announcement to the effect that the perpetrator had been identified, and that Whatsisname would provide background information and answer questions.

Holly Markham was sitting halfway back in the row of chairs. She looked up from her notebook and smiled. Converse frowned and said, "The black mamba is not actually black at all, but dark olive on top and whitish underneath. But in bright sunlight it has the appearance of being black, hence the name."

He was surprised to see how many reporters had shown up; after all, there were only three daily papers in the city. But, besides the radio and TV people, there was representation from the wire services, New Jersey, Connecticut, and suburban New York papers, and a few stringers from metropolitan newspapers as far away as California.

Someone asked, "What part of Africa does this mamba come from?"

"It's distributed throughout most of Africa, coast to coast, except for the northernmost parts. Incidentally, it's misleading to call it just 'mamba.' There are three different kinds of mambas—the black; green, which is found in savannah country and riverine forests and is exclusively arboreal; and Jameson's, which is a rain forest snake. All three are slender, with a small, coffin-sided head and a prehensile tail."

"From the picture, how big do you judge our snake to be?"

"At least ten feet, maybe as much as eleven. It's a superb specimen."

The DI muttered impatiently. Converse looked at him questioningly, then went on.

"The black mamba has a legendary reputation in Africa. It's feared, respected, in fact it's held in awe, much as a tiger or lion might be. Some of the stories you hear about it are exaggerations, especially its speed on the ground. For example, there's a persistent claim that it can overtake a galloping horse."

"Can it?"

"It's unlikely. Estimates of its speed vary between seven and twenty miles per hour. My guess would be about ten miles an hour."

One of the reporters sounded disappointed. "That's all?"

"It's a hell of lot if you're crawling on your belly. It's undoubtedly the swiftest snake in the world. I saw a few black mambas in Africa when I was a student. I can tell you that it's a genuinely intimidating sight to see an irritated black mamba racing across the ground with its head a foot and a half in the air and its mouth gaped wide open. A rabbit doing ten miles an hour is one thing. Being chased by an extremely venomous and aggressive snake at that speed is the stuff nightmares are made of.''

The man who had made the joke about mamba being a dance made derisive sounds. Converse recognized the professional skeptic. Every audience he had ever addressed had one, varying only in degree of belligerency. Except for kids, of course. This one didn't look like a fire-eater—a thin gray-blond man wearing gold-rimmed eyeglasses.

The man spoke up. "Whether I could outrun your snake or not is beside the point. It's pure myth that snakes chase people."

"For the most part that's true," Converse said equably. "But some snakes—the king cobra or hamadryad, the black mamba, some others—will sometimes take out after somebody, usually on their breeding grounds during the mating season, but often on other occasions when they're highly irritated. And if a black mamba was chasing *you,* sir, I'd bet on the snake."

The DI gave him a black look. Eastman cleared his throat, a sound of warning.

"You'd probably cheer the slimy thing on, too." The man's nondescript face had a capability for scowling.

"As most educated people know by now," Converse said mildly, "snakes aren't the least bit slimy, they're dry and rather pleasant to the touch."

The man screwed his features into an exaggerated

expression of disgust. "Slitheriness to one side, how do you feel about the fact that they poison people, sometimes fatally?"

"A great many more snakes are poisoned by man than the other way around. Smokestacks, auto emissions, industrial wastes, insect control poisons—"

"Fine," the man said. "Exterminate them. They're not good for anything, anyway."

"Then how come man eats them, turns them into leather goods, exhibits them in zoos, exploits them in various forms of entertainment? If you're looking for a villain, blame the man who turned that black mamba loose in the park. He's the one to hate, not the snake."

The man waved his hand in a gesture of dismissal. Holly Markham stood up. "Will it help you to find the snake now that you've identified it?"

Her question was to the point, and the assemblage, which had been tense during the exchange with the previous speaker, relaxed. Converse said, "It defines the problem without simplifying it. So far as its habits go, the black mamba is an all-purpose snake. It's arboreal part of the time—it likes to lie in the low branches of trees or even in bushes to take birds, and it may bask on a treetop, too, though, like most snakes, it likes a rock better. But most of the time it's terrestrial. It hides in bushes, in thickets, under rocks, in hollow trees, and very often in a well-concealed burrow."

After an interlude of note-taking, a TV reporter asked if the black mamba was as dangerous as a cobra.

"In my opinion, much more so. It's a lot more aggressive, and it doesn't have to go into a set striking posture before it bites. In fact, it can strike with extreme effectiveness in any direction while it's running at top speed. The cobra strikes inaccurately in daylight. The black mamba is equally deadly by day or night. Taking everything into account, I'm inclined to think it's the most dangerous snake in the world.''

"You mean the most poisonous?"

"It's not the most poisonous, although two tiny drops are sufficient to kill a man in as little as twenty minutes." He paused. The DI was examining his fingernails with undisguised boredom. Eastman's expression was studiedly neutral. The rest of the audience seemed impressed. "There are three elements that make a snake dangerous: the potency of its venom, the position of its fangs, and its aggressiveness or disposition to bite. The black mamba rates high on all counts."

Someone called out, "What do you mean by the position of the fangs?"

"Some species have fangs that are situated at the rear of the mouth. So it's harder for them to bite accurately and efficiently. The venom of the boomslang of Africa, for example, is terrifically potent, but because it's rear-fanged it doesn't deliver its venom as effectively as the black mamba, whose fangs are in the front, practically under the animal's nose."

A small man with a wisp of white hair asked what the most poisonous snake known was.

"The king cobra, the largest of all poisonous snakes, can kill in fifteen minutes. The Australian death adder and taipan, the Asiatic saw-scaled viper, the South American cascabel—they're all about equal, and probably slightly more potent than the black mamba. But after a while, in highly venomous snakes, the exact degree of potency doesn't make much difference. They all kill, and kill very quickly if antivenin isn't administered in a short time after the bite. Incidentally, the cobra and the black mamba are both of the family Elapidae, and are related. The black mamba also spreads a hood when it's irritated, but vertically rather than laterally as the cobra does, and nothing like as showy."

Holly spoke up, asking him to define aggressiveness more fully.

"In simplest terms, willingness to bite when threatened or irritated. There are some deadly snakes which just won't bite at all, except for food. The green mamba, for example. In Africa, boys shinny up palm trees for coconuts even though the trees are swarming with green mambas. The greens just get out of the way. Sea snakes are among the most poisonous known to man, but when fishermen bring them in in their nets, they just pick them up and throw them back into the water, and rarely seem to get bitten. . . ."

The DI was stirring restlessly. Converse, warming to his subject, ignored him.

"There's a very poisonous snake called the blue-banded krait. It's absolutely deadly at night, but simply can't be made to bite during the daylight hours. Children play with them, manhandle them, in the villages. People have been known to beat them with a stick, nail them to a board, subject them to torture—even to the point of death—without being bitten."

He paused for a flurry of note-taking, and observed that even the DI seemed mildly interested. Holly Markham was wearing a yellow silk blouse that went beautifully with her black hair. Big deal, black goes with yellow—so what?

Someone called out, asking what the black mamba ate, and with what frequency.

"Small mammals," Converse said. "Mainly rodents. As to frequency, snakes are erratic eaters. They can go for long periods, months, without eating. It's largely a matter of opportunity, if food is around they'll eat fairly often."

The joker in the gold-rimmed eyeglasses said, "What was this snake in the menagerie for—to eat an elephant?"

Converse said, "It's possible it chased a rodent into the area."

"Doesn't that mean that its lair, or whatever you call it, is somewhere in the neighborhood of the menagerie?"

"Not necessarily. Black mambas range over a very wide area. They cover ground at a tremendous speed, don't forget."

A hand rose in the rear of the room. "Why is this snake biting all these people? Why doesn't it just run away and hide, the way snakes are supposed to do?"

"In the first two deaths, I can only make a guess. Somehow, whether they knew it or not, these people posed a threat to the snake. Maybe, in the dark, they stepped on it. Step on a snake and it will bite." He shrugged. "In the latest case, the provocation is obvious. The guy was trying to catch it. A black mamba that's cornered will attack without hesitation."

A television reporter specializing in violent city news, a semi-famous face, said, "What about the old wives' tale about snakes not dying until sundown?"

"There's a fair amount of truth to it. Chop a snake's head off, and the body will continue to writhe for several hours. And a poisonous snake can inflict a fatal bite up to forty minutes after its head has been severed from the body.''

There were exclamations all around the room, ranging from horror to wonderment, and a good deal of note-taking. That's what they want, Converse thought, the exotic, sensational details. They don't give a damn about what makes snakes tick.

"Young man?" The speaker was a middle-aged man with a white moustache. "How many more people is this snake of yours going to bite before you kill it?"

"Why kill it? Why not capture it and put it in a zoo?"

The DI was on his feet. Unmindful of the microphones, he shouted, "Zoo, my ass. We're going to kill the shit out of that fucking snake. Okay, Whatsyername, move over."

The DI motioned imperiously. Converse changed seats with him. Eastman hitched his chair closer to the DI's. Together, they began to grapple with questions about the police search of the menagerie area (no luck, task force withdrawn), whether another sweep of the park in force was contemplated (not at this time), what additional steps would be taken to protect the public (the Commissioner's office is working on the problem), whether or not these steps might include closing the park (we're just working cops, we don't make that kind of decision). . . .

Converse sat erect in his chair so that he could see Holly. He caught her eye and she gave him a quick smile before she turned her attention back to the DI and Eastman. He continued to stare at her, compelling her to look at him. She did. She stared back. Their eyes locked and held. Liberated woman, giving

back as good as she got from male chauvinist? But
there was no defiance in her gaze. Eyes uplooking.
He felt lightheaded, giddy. Their eyes remained
locked. An indefinable (but familiar) sensation began
in his legs, paused at his groin, swept upward to his
head, and made him giddier than before.

Suddenly, he remembered a movie he had seen at
the Museum of Modern Art a few months before. It
was about Catherine the Great, a very old flick, made
about two hundred years ago. Elisabeth Bergner was
Catherine, Douglas Fairbanks Jr. was some kind of
duke or other. Their eyes met across a large candlelit
room filled with courtiers. They stared at each other.
No expression on their faces, but presently the flame
on the candle in front of each of them began to waver
slightly as their breathing became shallower and
quicker. They kept staring. The candle flames began
to waver with increased speed, more strongly, then
faster still, more intensely, orgasmically. . . .

Groaning, he forced his eyes away from Holly.
Douglas Fairbanks Jr., Godssake, he must be as old
as the picture, two hundred give or take a decade. His
gaze, out of control, turned back to her and coupled.
He listened to his breathing. Fast and shallow, would
make a candle flame dance with passion. And he was
getting lighter headed all the time. Rest of the room
blurring, voices fading. Knowing his weakness, he
knew himself to be in serious trouble.

Captain Eastman's voice, coming as from a great
distance, tugged at his attention. ". . . unless Mr.
Converse has anything else to add?"

He looked at Eastman. Thank God for Eastman,
the evil spell broken. He shook his head. Eastman
adjourned the press conference. Get out of the room

fast, Converse told himself, eyes to the front, full speed ahead.

He threaded his way between the rows of chairs with swaying hips, like a broken field runner, making for the door. From the corner of his eye he saw Holly getting to her feet. He stopped abruptly. "Can I buy you a cup of coffee?"

Each time the frown appeared on the woman's face she would read on another sentence or two before raising her eyes from her paperback book. Then she would say, "Peggy, remember what I said about staying on the pavement," or "That's far enough, come back here now."

The child ignored her within the permissible limits she had established in her twenty-two-month-old mind. She was sitting on the pavement and crooning softly and pleasurably to herself. She was plump, with long silky brown hair and violet eyes.

The woman would continue to watch the child for a brief time, then return to her book, the frown erased except for a barely perceptible remnant, some external tic of anxiety. In another minute or two the frown would reappear and she would look at the child again.

She was sitting on a bench in the shade, a short distance inside the park from the Boys Gate at Central Park West and 100th Street. The snake in the park was not the proximate cause of her frown, although it did contribute to her alertness. Her more immediate, and ongoing, concern was the large number of Hispanics who frequented the park in this area (but what was she to do, if she lived at 96th Street?). The snake was an exotic peril, distanced by its prominence in the media; the Hispanics—with their boisterous voices and passions throbbing just below the surface—were a familiar threat that existed right under one's nose.

"Peggy, I don't want you lying on the dirty pavement and getting yourself all filthy. Get up at once."

The child paid no attention to her. Her cheek brushed the pavement as she bent forward from her sitting position in that miraculous boneless way of small children. She was following the progress of a tiny ant that was climbing over her tanned leg. It tickled her skin and made her laugh.

The mother said, "Peggy," and, sighing, turned back to her book.

The ant descended from the child's leg. Effortlessly, the child rocked up onto her knees, and crawled after the ant. She found it, and cupped her hand over it. The ant crept out from under her hand and ran off. The child chased after it, crawling rapidly on her hands and knees. Near the edge of the pavement she lost it. She stopped, her eyes close to the ground. When she lifted her head she saw the snake. It was on the far side of the railing that edged the pavement, its head visible through a tangle of brush. The child clapped her hands together in surprise and delight.

The snake watched the child, hissing softly. Its tongue probed the air. The child was not moving, it was not an imminent threat, but the snake was wary. The child clapped her hands again, and crawled closer to the railing. The snake tensed. Its hissing became harsher, it opened its mouth wide.

The mother looked up. "Peggy, what are you doing there? Get back here at once!"

The child paused, looked at her mother, then crawled forward again.

"Peggy! Damn that child."

She put her book down on the bench and got up and started down the walkway toward the child, her mouth thinned with annoyance, her frown settled deeply between her eyes.

The snake's length was concealed by the brush. Only its head and the erect portion of its anterior were visible. When the child stood up and moved forward, its eyes were almost on exactly the same level as the snake's. The snake hissed harshly, its mouth gaped widely.

When it felt the vibrations of the woman's footsteps in the substrate, it turned away from the child. The appearance of this fast-moving new threat confused it momentarily, and then it turned its attention back to the child, who was now well within striking distance.

The woman bore down on the child from behind and swept her up in her arms angrily.

"Didn't I tell you to stay near me? Bad girl."

The child struggled and tried to slip down out of her mother's hold, her arms stretched outward to the snake. The child almost plunged forward out of her mother's grip. But the mother held on to an arm, and used it as a lever to lift her off the ground. She shifted the child to her hip, and, scolding, fending off flailing arms and legs, carried her back to the bench. The child screamed with rage.

The snake watched vigilantly until they had disappeared from view. It stopped hissing and closed its mouth, although it still remained poised in striking posture. Its tongue darted out. After a moment it turned in a looping circle and crawled back into the brush.

The coffee shop was crowded with second-breakfast eaters, and they shared a table with a pair of West Side merchants who debated the merits of Hispanics as customers: tremendous buyers but irresponsible payers. No candles wavered, even though Converse and Holly did some staring across the table. The auspices were all wrong—she had to rush back to her office to do her story, the merchants were loud and diverting, hot coffee was an antiromantic beverage. And, finally, there was a constraint between them, as if, Converse thought, they were both regretful of their unpremeditated passion at the press conference.

They came out of the cool coffee shop onto the baked pavements of Broadway and awkwardly avoided looking at each other.

"Well," Holly said.

"Well," Converse said. He was feeling a sense of deprivation, of something unaccountably lost. "You ever see an old flick about Catherine the Great? Douglas Fairbanks Jr.? It's about two hundred years old."

She nodded. "Elisabeth Bergner was Catherine. It's considered a classic of sorts. Why do you ask?"

He shrugged. "It just popped into my head. Before. I mean during the press conference."

"Oh." She gave him a quick, up-looking, candle-flame-wavering glance, then turned her eyes down and said, "Better get back to work."

"See you around."

"See you."

"Thanks for the coffee."

Maybe they both wanted to linger, Converse thought, and maybe that was why neither of them did. He walked softly so that he could hear her footsteps, and resisted looking back until just before he turned a corner to head eastward toward the park. She was nowhere in sight. No declaration of any kind, no exchange of phone numbers. Just "see you" and "thanks for the coffee." All for the best. If he thrilled to the sound of footsteps, could a disastrous involvement be far behind?

At Amsterdam Avenue, a *New York Post* truck hurled a pile of papers in the direction of a stationery store. The bundle just missed taking him off his feet. He read the headline:

SNAKE THREE, PEOPLE ZERO

TWELVE

THE POLICEMAN AT the desk in the Central Park Precinct recognized Converse and waved him on toward the Commander's office at the end of the corridor. Captain Eastman, stripped to his shorts, was lying on his back on a cot. There was no ease in his sleep, Converse thought. He lay heavily on the thin mattress, as if at the mercy of the downward pull of gravity, or his problems, or perhaps his age. The hair on his chest was white, matted with sweat.

Converse shut the door softly and went back through the corridor. In a small office opposite the desk, four hoods were polluting the air with cigarette smoke. They were dressed in dirty jeans, wisps of shirts that exposed their chests, studded leather belts, beards, gunfighter moustaches, long unkempt hair. They were a part of the Central Park Precinct's anticrime unit.

Converse stopped. "You guys know the park," he

said. "Where's the best place to hide? The least people, the most wild areas?"

Three of the detectives turned to the fourth, and one of them said, "Ask Sergeant Paschik. He's our first whip, and he's been here at the Two-two a little over a hundred years."

Sergeant Paschik was in his forties but, with his unshaven face and drooping, two-toned, gray-and-black mandarin moustache, he looked no less raffish than his younger colleagues.

"Sergeant?" Converse said.

"Uptown. North of 96th Street. It's a fact that about ninety percent of the people use the park below 85th Street. The Receiving Reservoir takes up most of the space between 86th and 96th, so I would concentrate on the area north of 96th."

"Is it less manicured up there?"

Paschik nodded. "It's real wild up there. You could get lost in some parts if you didn't know your way around."

"Or don't speak Spanish," one of the detectives said.

Paschik said, "It's a fact that above 96th the population, east side and west side both, is mostly Spanish. Naturally, they use the park near their own neighborhood. So it's a fact that it's not as safe there as in the southern part."

One of the detectives said, "I thought the snake was biting people around 80th, around there."

"Was," Converse said. "But its instinct would be to find a wilder and less frequented territory."

He thanked the anticrime squad, and they wished him luck. He went home, fed the python and the cat, and went to bed to catch up on his sleep. He dreamed of Catherine the Great, Empress of all the Russias.

• • •

The handout from the office of Hizzonner the mayor read: "I profoundly regret the tragic death of this fine young man to whose athletic prowess we thrilled so many times in the past." Jeff had been a second-string pulling guard on the Columbia football team. "Yet, even in this moment of tragedy I cannot pass up the observation that he was foolhardy. If he had not tried to catch the snake, but had merely retreated, no harm would have befallen him.

"And so I take this opportunity once again to urge the public, with all my heart, to exercise the utmost caution. Above all, do not attempt to take matters into your own hands. The police, with the help of experts, are redoubling their efforts. Do not hinder or hamper them in their work. Do not endanger your own life. Please cooperate.

The Reverend Sanctus Milanese, the solicitation of whose views had by now become a regular item on the itinerary of the media, said: "The members of the Church of the Purification are conscripted in the army of God to destroy the personification of evil. Can soldiers sit on the sidelines while this messenger of Satan crushes the city in its oily toils? The police are powerless, for it is not given to a temporal force to overcome the Devil. Only the godly are sanctioned for this work, for only they are blessed by Divine guidance. They shall prevail who are pure."

"You're going to continue to search for the snake in defiance of the orders of the police and the mayor's instructions?"

"We respond to only one Authority, and His name is God. We will continue our search as before, and there may be new initiatives as God proposes them."

The Police Commissioner, told about the

Reverend's statement, said that the police would not tolerate vigilantism in any form or for any reason. Whoever disobeyed the police directives would be dealt with sternly.

Jane Redpath refused to be interviewed for television. She said, "I know how much you bastards like to have people weep on camera for the entertainment of your audience, and I realize I'm being unsporting, but you can all go fuck yourselves."

With Jeff's death, the city turned a corner. It became euphoric. The snake in the park became a jewel in the crown of the city's obsession with its own eccentricity. The public reasserted its prideful conviction that it inhabited the most put-upon city in the whole world. When bigger and better and more unendurable disasters were contrived, they were visited justly upon the city that matched them in stature; which was to say, the city that was superlatively dirty, declining, expensive, crime-ridden, unmanageable, and glamorously unlivable beyond any other city in the world. By lunchtime, gallows humor jokes were already epidemic. And never mind that most of them were retreads of stale ethnic jokes; they worked surprisingly well with the mere substitution of the word "snake" for "Italian" or "Polish."

Manufacturers of novelties, famous for their opportunism and dazzling speed of production, succeeded by late afternoon in flooding the city with snake buttons, snake decals for auto bumpers, stuffed snakes of many lengths, designs, and colors. Not long afterward, strikingly realistic, battery-powered snakes of great technical sophistication were to appear. There was a run on canned rattlesnake fillets in gourmet specialty stores, and the brave people who ate them inevitably compared their taste to that of chicken, only better.

Four Hollywood film companies filed notice of intent to make a movie about a snake in Central Park; by nightfall, one of them had brought a lawsuit against another, charging infringement of its title, "Black Mamba." The news division of all three television networks patched together half-hour films about snakes for presentation following the eleven o'clock news, with full commercial sponsorship. A porno film, in which a young woman performed the sex act with a squirming and unhappy snake, was revived and did turn-away business at the box office. A nightclub introduced a snake-charming act: a man in a turban playing a flute for a cobra so lethargic from being refrigerated that it could barely spread its hood. Educational paperback books dealing with reptiles flooded the newsstands and bookstores. Herpetologists and zoo curators were at a premium for guest appearances on television talk shows. Snakeskin shoes, jackets, handbags, ties, and belts were snapped up in clothing and department stores. Sheets, pillowcases, and window drapes with a serpentine motif appeared almost overnight.

Comedians on television, at hotels, in nightclubs, and even in a Broadway show here and there, introduced snake jokes. These ranged from the innocent and simpleminded ("Goodness snakes alive!", "It's me, Snake, I mean Jake") to the dirty and simpleminded ("What's eleven feet long and stands up when it's irritated? Sorry to disappoint you, baby, it's a black mamba").

The reptile houses at the Bronx and Staten Island zoos were so packed with spectators that it was almost impossible for any but those in the front ranks to see the exhibits. When a man visiting the Staten Island Zoo used a hammer to smash the glass of a cage containing a sand viper and then attacked the snake with a breadknife, the police were called in to clear the snake house for the rest of the day. The next morning, crowds were kept back five feet from the cages by barriers, and special guards were on hand to protect the snakes from further assassination attempts.

A well-known showman made the front page of two of the city's three daily newspapers with his offer of $20,000 for the snake in the park, alive.

Throughout the day, alternating between the claustrophobic office of the Commander of the Two-two and the desk up front, where he hovered nervously around the teletype, Captain Eastman had been logging reports from the park. Good news and bad news. Good: there were many fewer people in the park than the day before, whether because they were paying heed to the mayor's plea or simply because of the heat, which had touched 99 degrees at three o'clock, there was no way of telling. Bad: lots of Puries out, neatly dressed, barely seeming to sweat (maybe they *did* have an in with God, Eastman thought), methodically checking out likely areas where the snake might be hiding. There had been several minor scuffles with the police who ordered them back onto the walkways, and one serious one. Two members of the Christ's Cohorts, the Purie security guard, had engaged in a slugging match with a cop. It was only with the arrival of reinforcements that the Puries had been subdued. They had been booked at the Two-two and been held in detention for several hours before it was time to take them to night court, where they were charged with disorderly conduct, assault, and resisting arrest.

The cop who had fought with the Christ's Cohorts had lost a tooth. What had impressed him, aside from the fact that they were handy with their fists, was their lack of emotion. "I've never seen guys fight like that," he had told Eastman. "No swearing, no hollering, not even a mad expression on their face. I swear, it gave me the creeps."

Technically, Eastman was "coordinating" the police effort in the park. Although he had been desk-bound for several years, he had never really become accustomed to it. He thought of it as "sitting on his ass," when he should be "doing something." He would have much preferred being out in the field with one of the ESU trucks. Near ten o'clock there was a bit of gruesome comic relief. A grinning cop reported that he and his partner had come upon a Purie wandering through the park, dazed, battered, completely naked, and had taken him to West Side Hospital. He had been snake-hunting in the Ramble, according to his story, when he had been set upon and beaten by a half-dozen men. The cop, winking, describing the Purie as "one of *them*," said that he had obviously been gang-shagged.

Converse arrived with his stick and pillowcase, looking so refreshed and rested that Eastman almost hated him for it. Youth. But the prospect of getting out of the precinct house and "doing something" palliated his sourness.

"Godssake," Converse said. "It looks like a mob scene."

The driver had taken them into the park through the Engineer's Gate at 90th and Fifth Avenue, and was following the East Drive around the perimeter of the Receiving Reservoir. The park seemed to be twinkling with lights, and they could make out shadowy figures, some of whom must have been police personnel, others, Puries. Driving, they were almost blinded by the brilliant sweeping floodlight of an ESU truck.

"Where do you want to stop?" Eastman said.

"Noplace," Converse said. "What black mamba in its right mind would turn up with all this going on? Those lights? Those people clumping around everywhere? Forget it. It's going to hole up and stay hidden until everybody goes away."

Eastman's definition of "doing something" did not include riding around in a police car. "How the hell can you hope to find it if you don't get out and look for it?"

"No way," Converse said. "If I knew all this crap was going on I would have stayed home. Remember what I told you about a snake having to be found by stealth?"

"Certainly I remember," Eastman said. "I make it a point never to forget anything you tell me. Then what the hell are we going to do?"

"It's hopeless," Converse said, "and there's no sense getting sore, Captain. You want to get out, I'll keep you company. But it's a pure waste of time."

Eastman was silent. He sat hunched against the window of the car, glowering.

Converse said, "Anyway, our best chance is to catch it basking. It's one of the few times a snake stays put. I'll be out here tomorrow morning just before first light."

The car rode on between the huge North Meadow at their left and the small East Meadow to the right.

The driver slowed down. "What do we do, captain?"

"Shit, I don't know. It's a lovely night for a spin around the park. What do you say, Hortense?"

Converse shrugged. "I'm sorry, captain."

Eastman sighed. "I guess you're right. Tomorrow morning—you going to pick me up?"

"I could," Converse said. But. . . ." His voice trailed off.

"But you'd rather not?"

Converse nodded. "It's really a one man job. You'd simply be trailing along."

He's probably right, Eastman thought, and I can use the sleep. Then a suspicion stirred in his mind. "Look, are you afraid I'll shoot it or something?"

"If I find it," Converse said with a grin, "I'll turn it over to the Lost Property Clerk."

Eastman told the driver to find someplace where he could turn around. "Get a fix on one of the floodlights and drop me off by one of the ESU trucks. Then take Mr. Converse here to somplace where he can catch a bus home."

Converse said, "Don't waste your time, captain."

"Waste of time or not, I'll be doing something."

"Instead," Converse said, "let me buy you a beer."

"I don't drink on duty."

"When are you *off* duty?"

"That's it," Eastman said. "Never."

Near 115th Street, a rat jumped out of an over-turned garbage can. It stopped right in the middle of the sidewalk and looked at him. It was an ugly old bastard, with a scrunch-up face and a long wormy tail and red eyes. Its fur was a mangy gray, same like the color of morning before the sun over the East

River would get high enough to clear the tenements and throw a little light around.

Alvis Parkins said softly, "Shitface, I'm gonna waste you."

The rat was watching. It was a smart old rat, and Alvis knew that if he made a sudden move it would take off. So, smiling and talking sweet to it, he began to ruffle up the bottom of his shirt, slow and easy. Gently do it. Slip the piece out quiet, cock it, level it, and then boom, blow old rat away.

He had the piece in his hand when the rat suddenly took off, scuttering off the curb and racing for the other side of the street. Alvis steadied the piece with both hands, squinting down the short barrel, tracking old rat until he had it right where he wanted it. But he didn't pull the trigger. He lowered the gun abruptly, shoved it back under his belt, and pulled his shirt over it.

Dumb shit, he thought, watching the rat disappear in an alley between two buildings, dumb shit, you came near fucking up. Dumb nigger shit, all you need was make a gunshot noise so somebody call the cops and they pick you up for just being in the streets this time of morning, and they spread you up against a wall and find the piece on you. What make it worse, that piece wouldn't never have shoot straight enough to hit something, especially a old gray running rat. Maybe couldn't even hit it with a professional piece, a hundred- two-hundred-dollar piece, so how was he ever gonna hit it with a little old twelve-dollar hunk of junk iron. Forget it. Besides, why should he go exterminate a rat in Spanish Harlem? Let the spics kill they own goddamn rats.

The good feeling he got when he first spotted the rat went away and he began to feel sour again.

Walking on south, he swore out loud whenever a car
or truck went by on Seventh Avenue. Mean as he felt,
better not let nobody fuck around with him. One bad
look and he would burn somebody. Saturday Night
Special couldn't hit no rat halfway across the street,
but point blank up against somebody it would blow
half their ugly face off. The sun was lighting up the
sky, though it was still gray down below as he crossed
Cathedral Parkway, sauntering, ignoring a couple of
trucks, making them blow their horns at him, making
them hit their brakes. Screw them. Street belong to
me every much as it do to them. He went into the
park through the Warriors Gate. Still pretty cool,
though in a few minutes the sun would start hotting it
up. Remembering the heat and stink of the apartment, he was glad he had that ruckus with his aunt, it
give him a good excuse to split. Get away from heat
and old Uncle Tom aunt at one and the same time.

Silly old bitch didn't know the score. Thought
dope was bad, thought chicks was bad, thought
school was good, thought church was good. Knew he
had the gun, she would probably call the cops in.
Mostly he didn't pay no attention to her, but tonight
she was waiting up for him, and her jaw just go like a
express train—fifteen-year-old boy have no call to
come in four-thirty in the morning, and et cetera. He
sassed her and sassed her, and finally old auntie get
mad and take a swing at him. When he like to fall
down laughing at her, she come on with the big black
skillet, and could have bust his arm if it land. So he
dodge around the kitchen, and finally get around
back of her and take it away and smash the table with
it, and then run out the door.

Have to get something going for hisself and split
for good. Too old for living with old auntie and the

rest of the kids. Needed a pad anyway, tired of balling chicks on rooftops. Come to think of it, in his whole life never had no chick in a bed. High time. Have to promote hisself some bread. Meanwhile, shit, what he doing in this dumb park? What he care about grass and trees and such shit? And don't forget old snake. Old black mamba. Old nigger mamba. Didn't scare him. Old snake come dancing along, he pull his piece and blow old snake's head away. He laughed at the image of a headless snake.

He ran up a hill, and looked down the Meer to the east, with sun on the water now, and straight ahead of him the long stretch of the North Meadow. He raced down the far side of the hill, sliding on his sneakered feet, grabbing at branches as he went. His momentum carried him down onto a walkway, and he had to put on the brakes or run right into the railing and bust his balls.

At the West Drive, a car came along, with its headlights still on. As it went by, a red face under a hard hat poked out and shouted jeeringly at him.

"Honkies," he shouted back, "motherfuckers, shit-eaters."

The car slowed, and a muscular arm hung out of the window, feeling for the door handle. Alvis's heart began to thump. He reached under his shirt for the hard blunt shape of the piece. If they got out of the car he would gun the mothers down! The car picked up speed and went on. The beefy red face was hanging out the window, mouthing words that were lost in the sound of the accelerating car. Alvis shouted, "Pink-face! Shit-face! Motherfucker!"

The car disappeared around a curve.

He grinned, and crossed the roadway jauntily, forcing another car to squeal its brakes. He smiled, feeling good, and ignored the shouts that drifted back from the car.

At the Reservoir, the early-bird joggers were out, most of them dressed in white shorts and T-shirts and expensive sneakers. Dudes were soaked in sweat, red in the face, and sucking air like they was gonna die very next step. One was a pretty young chick with silky blond hair flying behind her and little tits that bounced like crazy under her T-shirt.

"Hey baby," he yelled at her, "how you like some *real* exercise?"

After that, he started jiving most of the joggers. "Look, dads, you too old, you gonna have a heart attack." "Hey, man, you look like a busted-down hoss." "Look at the great tits on you, mister." A young black man came sailing along, slim and high-kicking, barechested, wearing a yellow sweat band around his forehead. "Show them honkies how to do it, brother," Alvis yelled.

Alvis decided to run, and he began to breeze past the joggers, giving them a little grin as he went by. But after one circuit he quit. Too hot, man. He started back to the north, going off the walkways and climbing up a hill whenever he saw one. It was a good feeling being up high. He liked it even better when there was also a lot of trees and bushes, like being hid out in a jungle. He hacked his way out of a jungle, came down into the open, and then ran at a big steep sloping rock. Hey, man, watch this move, up the rock like a fly climb a wall. His sneakers gripped and his momentum carried him to the top. And there, stretched out about a mile long, was a big mother of a snake.

• • •

The stone struck the rock in front of the snake, and skittered away. The snake's long body stirred into movement at once, gliding over the rock, taking up its own slack. Its head rose upward on a taut column, and its tongue flicked out. When a second stone landed just in front of it it recoiled for a moment, and then its head rose higher. Its eyes picked up the flight of the third stone while it was still in the air. The stone fell, and almost hit the snake in the arc of its bounce. The snake turned and crawled down the slope of the rock, its scutes pushing back against the irregularities, pressing the long body forward in a powerful twisting movement off the face of the rock and into the underbrush.

Alvis could hardly believe the speed of the snake. It moved like it had a revved-up engine. With a yell, he came out of concealment and ran up the side of the rock. He stopped for a second and took out his piece, then ran down the outer side of the rock in the path the snake had taken. He stopped again at the bottom and peered into the tangle of brush.

At first he didn't see anything, and then he picked up the snake's movement, and saw it wriggling down under the brush. Got me these great eyes, he thought. He leveled the piece downward at the snake, but it was too tough a shot. Still, it felt good, pointing the piece, and it kept him from getting scared. He tracked the snake with the piece, and then, suddenly, it disappeared. He stared at the brush where he had last seen it. Not there. Nor was any of the brush moving.

"Be fucked."

He picked up a stone and tossed it down where he had last seen the snake, in a mess of dead branches, vines, last year's brown leaves, the trunk of a rotten tree. The stone landed where he wanted it to, and he watched good, but there wasn't no movement.

"Be fucked."

He thought about it for a second, then edged forward real easy into the brush, moving sidewards, so that if old snake came at him he could swivel around and hightail it for the rock. He had this funny feeling in his feet, but he wasn't gonna let no snake bluff him out. He held the piece pointed downward, with his finger on the trigger. He took a little jump onto the fallen tree trunk. He hunkered down on the tree for a good look all around, but he couldn't see no sign of the snake. Then, just when he was about to stand up, he spotted the hole. It was under the tree, and twigs and like that all around it. No wonder nobody could find old snake. Well, he thought proudly, they don't none of them have the good eyes like Alvis. He laughed gleefully, then clapped his hand over his mouth. Didn't want snake to hear him.

"Gonna ice you, snake."

He stepped down from the tree trunk, one foot at a time, slow, not making a sound. Then he crouched to one side of the hole, and slowly reached around with the piece, curving his arm so the muzzle was pointing right into the hole. He felt real cool, but playing it safe in case old snake decided to pop out suddenly. Laughing softly to himself, he steadied the piece and slowly flexed his finger against the resistance of the trigger.

In the hole, the snake hissed harshly as the light at the entrance to the burrow darkened. Its tongue brought in a strong odor of threat. It pushed forward

in a sudden powerful thrust, and surged out through
the exit hole. It struck twice, in rapid succession.

The piece fired into the hole and recoiled, and at
the same moment Alvis felt a sharp sting on his neck,
and then another sting, and the second time he saw
the snake, the head up tall and the mouth wide open.
He jumped up and ran backwards a few steps. The
snake was watching him, hissing and swaying. He
clapped his hand to his neck, and saw there was a
little smear of blood on it. Sonofabitch had done bit
him, crept out through another hole, and done bit
him. Motherfucking snake! Shouting, swearing,
Alvis backed up a few more feet, raised his piece, and
fired twice before the piece jammed. He saw the slugs
hit the ground and raise dust and bits of leaves, and
he knew he had missed. The snake started to crawl
toward him, coming like an express train. He
wheeled around and ran for the rock, and he went up
it like a fly up a wall. No time to put no fancy moves
on. Just keep running or he would get catched up.

The snake pursued as far as the rock and stopped.
It held its posture of threat for a while after the figure
disappeared over the top of the rock. Then it returned to the burrow. Its tongue at the opening
brought in a disquieting smell, sharp and acrid. The
snake didn't enter until the smell grew lighter. It went
in cautiously, and didn't relax its tension for a long
time.

Got to get me to a hospital, Alvis thought, but not
to no honky hospital. You black, they treat you like
shit in them places. One time, some kid on the block

OD'd, and they kept him waiting so long that when they got around to him the poor fucker was dead. Uptown, the patients were black, and so were some of the doctors.

So he ran northward through the park, sometimes touching his neck, and feeling okay because it wasn't bleeding no more.

He wasn't running real good, feeling some tired, but he reckoned he wasn't gonna die because he was young, not old like them other ones. He wasn't breathing too good, but shit, you wanna feel great if you bitten by a mile-long crawler?

He stuck to the walkways. They wound around a lot, but it was easier to run on the flat surface. Chest felt funny, and legs going heavy, but he kept running, kept putting 'em down one after another. He could hear the sound of his sneakers slapping down on the pavement. Old sun was up hot now. He felt sleepy and like to lay down. He ran around the Cliff, and tried to turn on more speed. Almost out now. Then the wall was coming up in front of him. He had some trouble getting over it. Legs heavy, heavy. But finally he cleared it, and was out of the park.

He started to cross Cathedral Parkway and began to stagger. Car coming down at him, have to turn on the speed. But his legs was folding up under him. He heard the car screeching its brakes, coming on big as a house. At the last second he tried to put on a move, but his legs was noplace, and the car hit him and tossed him, and he was dead when he came down.

Converse stood in the center of the North Meadow, facing east. The invisible presence of the sun, hidden beneath the rooftops of Fifth Avenue, backlit the buildings and turned them into cut-out silhouettes. On the Meadow, the parched grass looked gray. Above, the sky was a mottled gray; to the west, it was still dark.

The approach of daylight was reassuring, and it evaporated the remnants of uneasiness Converse had felt when he had entered the park from Central Park West and begun to walk along the eerily deserted walkways. Although he wasn't a particularly scary type, he was aware of the city's legendary perils, and he kept his nerve up kiddingly by imagining himself making a nice move with the Pilstrom tongs, ringing a mugger around the throat, and popping him into the pillowcase. Being careful, of course, not to get bitten.

The tongs and pillowcase were well on the optimistic side, considering the intimidating size of the area he had to cover. Already, in his short walk, he had seen half a dozen heavily overgrown sites that might suit a black mamba as a hiding place. The question was where to start. At the moment, with the rim of the sun just beginning to appear over the buildings, he simply didn't know. The vastness of the park made it all seem hopeless.

No. He shook his head, as if to reprove himself. He was a good herpetologist, he knew snakes, and he would turn up the black mamba no matter how much territory he had to scour. The real problem was that everyone was in such a bloody hurry. Well, there wasn't any way to do it in a hurry. The watchword was patience.

The sun was a whitish watery semicircle above the rooftops, and already he was beginning to feel its heat. And so would the black mamba. At this very moment it might be moving, in its swift elegant glide, toward the rock it would bask on. Maybe. In this

alien terrain it might feel safer climbing into the top
branches of a tall tree, basking, and then swinging
back down to shade in the thick foliage below. The
green mambas did that as a matter of course, and so
did the blacks when they were so inclined.

He hoped its inclination would be otherwise; it
would be very difficult to spot in a tree. As a general
rule, black mambas weren't all that shy. They were
secure in the knowledge of their speed and the potency of their bite, and since this one was obviously a
highly aggressive specimen, it was reasonable to expect that it would choose to bask on a luxurious rock.

Okay, Converse told himself firmly, so much for
pure reason. Let's get organized. No point trying to
check out any rocks today, too random, not likely to
produce any results. The sun was already up, and
climbing fast. The snake wouldn't require much exposure; in this heat it wouldn't lose much body temperature through the night. Best idea would be to ex-
plore the whole northern sector, east to west, from
the 97th Street transverse to the end of the park,
marking out likely places for closer examination.

There were lots of likely places—wild, untended
areas with heavy tangled brush, fallen trees, piles of
leaves and dead branches. More of the city's poverty;
no money available to the Parks Department to hire
enough groundsmen to prune and chop and clear and
haul away. He moved slowly and methodically,
resisting the impulse to look at this or that rock, to
plunge into an inviting thicket.

When he heard a patter of footsteps he was taken
by surprise. It was a black kid, running—the first
human being he had seen since he had entered the
park. Soon there would be others. He watched the
kid for a moment. He himself was a jogger and, com-

pared to his own stride, this kid's was sloppy and disjointed. He watched until the kid disappeared behind a rise, heading toward the north end of the park.

Aside from a single crumpled dollar bill, a few coins, a pack of cigarettes, and a condom tucked away in a packet of book matches, Alvis Parkins's pockets were empty. There was nothing to identify him.

Together with his effects, he was taken to the morgue, where he was tagged and assigned to a chilled drawer. Among other injuries, his neck was broken and badly lacerated, and the fang marks were obliterated. Not that anyone would have looked for them on the body of the victim of an auto accident.

The police began a routine effort to find his survivors. But there were no fingerprints on record, and nobody made a missing persons inquiry. His aunt, the only one who might have done so, was accustomed to the boy being absent for days at a time. Eventually, the Medical Examiner's postmortem examination would turn up evidence that Alvis had been bitten by the snake in the park, but it would be ten days before the autopsy was performed, due to a heavy work load and the fact that several autopsists were on vacation. Since the cause of his death seemed clearly evident, Alvis Parkins was a low-priority case.

THIRTEEN

WITHIN THIRTY-SIX HOURS after Jeff's well-publicized death, the mood of the public had taken a sour turn—from ruefully amused acceptance of the snake as an appropriate symbol of their city's magnetic genius for attracting disaster to something approaching mass neurosis. Much of it was hysterical and self-hypnotic. People began to talk about "that crawly feeling in the legs." Some, before sitting down in a restaurant, would lift a tablecloth to look under the table; others would leave a play or concert or film before it was finished because they kept imagining snakes crawling around their feet in the darkness. The worst were those who began to suspect their own apartments, hesitating to enter a dark room for fear a snake might be lurking there, looking under their beds, shaking out their blankets. Some conjured up snakes curled up on the floorboards under their feet when they drove their cars. Some went so far as to check their pockets or handbags before venturing in for a handkerchief or a coin. All over the city, people took to sitting in chairs with their feet tucked under them.

The new mood was nourished by the almost daily occurrence of what the newspapers took to calling "snake-associated" deaths. These events dulled all but the most insatiable appetites for sensation.

The first incident took place in an apartment on Third Avenue, in the Seventies. A man, returning home in the evening, tiptoed toward his balcony, where his wife was watering her plants, and tossed a large kapok-filled novelty snake at her feet, at the same time screaming a warning. The woman whirled around, saw the snake almost under her foot, and recoiled from it in a spasm of revulsion. She struck the guard rail of the balcony with both feet off the ground, and with such force that she somersaulted backward, and fell to the street twenty floors below.

Another man planted a similar snake in his wife's bed. She got under the cover, felt something odd, and turned on her bed lamp. (Many suggestible people, these nights, were turning on their bed lamps, only to discover that the "snake" was their own sweat trickling down their legs.) The woman leaped out of bed when she saw the snake, screamed, staggered toward the bedroom door, and fell dead of heart failure.

In a crowded movie house near Bloomingdale's, a voice (whether female or a male screaming in falsetto was never established) called out, "Snake! The snake is here!" A few people rose reflexively, and then the

entire audience was on its feet. In the panicky rush
toward the exits people were injured badly enough to
be hospitalized, and a young man who was trampled
underfoot died when fragments of his shattered
eyeglasses were driven into his brain. After the
theater was emptied the police searched the house but
found no snake.

In the incident at Macy's department store, two
people died, and more than a hundred and fifty were
injured. This time, there was a live snake involved. It
appeared suddenly in the aisles on the main floor,
one of the busiest and most crowded in the huge
store. Several women saw it at the same time and ut-
tered piercing screams. The snake scudded over the
floor in a panic of its own, then disappeared behind a
counter. It was a long snake with a slender body and
a small head. When it was found, after the entire
floor had been cleared, and the casualties had been
taken away in ambulances, it was identified by a
Museum of Natural History herpetologist as a black
racer, a thoroughly harmless snake but one which
superficially resembled a black mamba. This
suggested that the release of the racer in the store was
the work of a sophisticated and sinister intelligence.
The perpetrator was never found, although the police
checked patiently and doggedly into the stories of
several witnesses who claimed to have seen a shifty-
eyed man carrying a wicker basket.

On a Friday, at a few minutes past three o'clock in
the morning, two couples—well-dressed, in their
early forties, suburbanites, as it turned out, winding
up a night on the town—emerged from a nightclub in
the East Fifties. While the doorman went off to find
a cab, the two couples, almost anachronistically

dressed in evening clothes, waited under the lighted marquee. At that hour, the rest of the street was dark.

Suddenly, one of the women let out a prolonged, piercing scream of terror. The others, shocked and startled, followed her pointing finger to a snake crawling toward them out of the darkness. The men pushed the women, both of them now screaming, toward the door of the nightclub. The second man, a burly six-footer, stood his ground, and, as the snake came close to him, leaped into the air and landed on it with both feet. The man jumped back. He heard wild laughter somewhere in the darkness up the street, and realized that the snake was made of metal, covered by plastic painted to simulate a snake's skin; it moved on a tread that gave it both its forward thrust and its articulated serpentine motion.

The bulky man began to run up the street, shouting, toward the continuing sound of laughter. The other man and the two women came out of the club. They heard the pounding footsteps and shouts of the bulky man diminishing. Then the footsteps stopped, and they heard a scuffling sound. There were more shouts, a series of thuds, a cry of pain. The second man shook himself out of his daze and ran up the street after his friend.

He found his friend stamping repeatedly on the already bloody and mashed face of another man, and it took all his strength to pull his friend away, meanwhile shouting, "Charlie, that's enough, you'll kill him. Charlie, for God's sake, you're killing him."

In the event, it turned out that the trickster, who, as the autopsy later showed, had been drinking heavily, was already dead, his neck broken before the stomping had begun. When the police arrived, they were noncommittal, but at least three people among the crowd that had gathered on the scene said, with almost the identical phrasing, "There ain't a jury in the whole city that would convict him."

By the end of the third day, Converse had covered about sixty percent of the area between 97th Street and the north end of the park. He had divided the area into quadrants on an imaginary perpendicular drawn from 102nd Street east to west, bisected by another perpendicular drawn from the midway point of the 97th Street transverse to the Farmers Gate at Cathedral Parkway. For no particular reason except that he had to start somewhere, he began his search in the southwest quadrant, which took in the North Meadow, the Pool, the Cascade and a promising sector near the Springbanks Arch. Then he moved on to the southeast quadrant, which went fairly quickly because much of it was taken up by a portion of the North Meadow and the whole of the East Meadow.

He would arrive at the park before dawn, and position himself where he could watch a likely rock. When he had convinced himself that the snake was not going to appear, he would try a second rock. By that time the sun would have been up for a couple of hours, and the snake, wherever it was, would have been finished basking. He would then starting checking out trees, top to bottom, foot by foot, and then back again until he was satisfied that the snake was not there; its olive coloration would make it difficult to spot in the shadow-dappled foliage. He would finish up by wading through heavily overgrown patches, with particular attention to places where the black mamba might have found a burrow.

By ten o'clock, exhausted, he would call it quits. By then, anyway, there were too many people around—amateur herpetologists (averaging about fourteen years of age), uniformed officers and detectives of the Central Park Precinct, Emergency Service Unit cops, and, of course, the omnipresent Puries. Eastman had accompanied him on the second morning, drawn with fatigue, coughing uncontrollably in the sodden predawn air. Eastman had wanted to know why he choose to stake out one particular rock of a number that seemed equally promising, and he had replied that he had a "feeling" about it. Shortly after 8:30 Eastman had returned to the precinct house.

This morning, when Converse walked into the office of the Commander of the Two-two, Eastman looked alert, as though he had caught up on some sleep. But his face sagged wearily when he saw the empty pillowcase.

"No headway," Eastman said. It was not a question but a flat statement.

"I didn't find the black mamba," Converse said primly, "but I've eliminated another sector, and the way I look at it, that's progress."

"Yeah, I guess so, I guess you could call it progress."

"Count your blessings, captain. Since that fellow was bitten in the menagerie, nobody else has been bitten. Maybe it's dead."

"You believe that?"

Converse shook his head. "No."

"It hasn't bitten anybody else, but it's still a threat

to bite somebody. Anyway, even if it is dead, that won't be the end of it unless we can prove it. You been reading the papers? You know how many people have died because of that snake?''

Converse nodded. "They're all crazy in this city. They're killing each *other*. That's not the snake's fault." He got to his feet. "Maybe I'll find it tomorrow."

"Sure."

"I'll find it," Converse said.

Eastman said, "Well, let's hope it's real soon, so that our citizens can go back to killing each other for conventional reasons, and we can get that fucking Reverend off our backs, and that fucking DI off *my* back, and so the fucking mayor can win the fucking election and stop bugging the P.C., who bugs his deputy, who bugs . . . and the bug stops here."

Converse went out of the office. He felt depressed.

And he was still depressed hours later, after he had slept, and eaten, and watched the television set—not the news, but a police drama in which all the undercover cops looked exactly like the members of the anticrime squad of the Two-two, right down to their stylized moustaches and beards. The depression remained. He felt awful.

At 11:30 he phoned Holly Markham. He had decided to call her at 8:30, though he didn't admit it to himself. All he really wanted to do was satisfy a purely idle curiosity about where she lived. He looked her up in the Manhattan phone directory. She lived on East 85th Street. He shut the phone book. He watched some more television, had something to eat, played with the python, played with the cat, damn near played with himself. He took a cold shower, chilled himself thoroughly, and decided to go to sleep. He got into bed, got out, drank water, peed, got into bed again, got up, drank a straight shot of bourbon, got into bed, got out, put on the light, and dialed her number from memory.

"Yes?" Her voice was tentative, wary.

He said, "I'm sorry. This is Mark Converse."

"Why are you calling at this hour?"

Her voice had changed. He couldn't tell whether she was glad to hear from him or just relieved that she didn't have to cope with a heavy breather.

He said, "I'm calling because I'm Douglas Fairbanks Jr., and you're Catherine the Great, Empress of all the Russias."

He heard her make a little sound of surprise, and then she said, "Listen, I have to get to sleep."

He said, "I have a very strong feeling for you."

"Well, I have a very strong feeling for you, too, but that's no reason to call up in the middle of the night, not a little thing like that."

"Tell me to go away, okay. But don't make a joke out of it."

"I'm not joking, Mark. That's the joke, you know, I'm not joking. Yours truly, Catherine, Empress of all the Russias."

"You're not joking?"

"No, I'm not." There was apprehension in her voice, it quavered.

"Oh, Christ. Look, I've got to see you. I can't stand it. I need you very badly. Can I come to your place? Will you come down here?"

After a long silence she said, "What you really mean is that you *want* me. That's honorable, but it's different from needing me. If you ever need me, really need me, call me and I'll come right over. Okay?"

He hung up the phone without answering. He went to bed, and lay on his back with his head resting on his folded arms, and ran the conversation over and over again in his mind, the way one did with a misplayed poker hand, haunted by nuance and regret. In the end, he vowed never to call her again, and to stop loving her at once.

The snake no longer came out of its burrow during the daylight hours, except for a brief period each morning to bask on a nearby rock.

On this night, as it had on several previous nights, it drank from the Loch, lying midway between the East and West drives. On the way back to its burrow it surprised a squirrel on the ground. The squirrel leaped for the base of a tree and began to scramble up, but the snake, its head already reared high, launched an upward strike and sank its fangs into the squirrel's haunch, just above its bushy tail. The squirrel squealed, and slipped back momentarily, but recovered and scampered upward.

The snake did not pursue the squirrel up the tree. It waited below, coiled, staring up into the shadowed branches. Its sharp eyes picked up the squirrel when it began to fall, and followed its descent to the ground. After eating the squirrel, the snake returned to its burrow. The process of digestion, already begun by the injection of venom, would take approximately six hours.

FOURTEEN

HOLLY SHOWED HER press card and a tall, muscular, aloofly courteous Purie wearing the armband of a member of Christ's Cohorts led her down an aisle of the Tabernacle to the front row. The man sitting next to her was a city news reporter from the Associated Press. The rest of the row reserved for the press was empty.

The A.P. man said good morning, and in an ambiguous tone that mixed gallantry and resentment, complimented her on looking so fresh and dewy at the unearthly hour of 9:30 A.M.

She acknowledged with an ambiguous smile of her own. Was it her fault that it took a full week before she began to show the stigmata of fatigue? Well, not that it was any of the A.P. man's business, but she had spent most of the night awake, agonizing over whether or not to rush downtown to Mark Converse's place and cradle his head against her breast.

Want, need, what was she, a blue-ribbon semanticist? But last night the distinction had seemed important, and so she had remained in her bed and paid for it with hours of sleeplessness.

The Reverend's recruitment meeting had drawn a full house. Every seat in the Tabernacle was taken, and there were dozens of standees at the rear and against the side walls. The crowd, young, mostly in its early twenties, was hushed and expectant. Holly looked at the flyer she had been given at the door. It was an application form for membership in the Church of the Purification. No selling copy, no hype, just a chaste logo that read "Church of the Purification" and a few dotted lines for name, address, age, present religious affiliation.

"They're getting members," the A.P. man said. "According to our church news man, they've been signing up in droves, the usual white kids from good families."

The Purie membership was overwhelmingly middle class, with access to money through their parents, no matter how much the parents were opposed to their joining. Whatever else you said about the Reverend, Holly thought, he was shrewd. He read the public mind—at least that segment of it that was likely to respond to his primitive appeal—with great accuracy. Latching on to the issue of the snake, however blatantly opportunistic it might seem to be, looked certain to pay off in enlarged membership and increased revenue to contribute to the support of his various real estate holdings, not to mention fuel for his gas-eating limousines, the cost of expensive red silk linings for his cloaks, the salary of his personal French chef. . . .

The organ played a sudden monitory chord in a

minor key. A dazzling white spotlight settled on a white door at the side of the stage. The organ repeated the chord, held it in a trembling vibrato. The door opened and the Reverend Sanctus Milanese strode toward the podium. The spotlight accompanied him, focusing on the brilliant scarlet of his calotte, leaving his face in shadows.

"The footlights are dimmed, the curtain is up, the star has appeared," the A.P. man said, "and that magical moment before the performance begins is at hand. I hope to hell it's a good show."

But it wasn't really, Holly thought. Not that it was bad, either, just that it wasn't new. Her notes read: Star in fine fettle, but material old hat. Usual burning eyes, evangelical tones, well-timed swirl of cape to show red lining, for which I would willingly become Purie if he would give me a bolt so I could make a seductive housecoat. Rings same old changes on established theme. Snake is Satan's messenger. Can be captured only by the pure in heart—guess who? The location of the lair in which the evil serpent lurks will soon be vouchsafed to us by Him. All in good time, however, for He moves in mysterious ways His miracles, etc. Drama trite, leading man terrific. Give it one star.

Nevertheless, the audience was eating it up. Not a muscle twitching, barely breathing, eyes glued to the figure on the dais.

The A.P. man whispered, "Same old crap." He was obviously disappointed—as she herself was —that the meeting was not producing any dramatic news.

The Reverend was expounding on the villainous role the snake had played throughout the history of man and religion. The symbol of Evil from time immemorial. Ever the servant of the Devil, eager to do his most heinous bidding. From time *im-mem-morial.* The serpent in the Garden of Eden, traducer of Eve. . . . Now if he had said seducer, Holly thought, we might have had a flashy bit of revisionist theology.

The A.P. man said, "I was half hoping he would come up with something wild—like the Chinese thing."

A year earlier, for some fancied slight, he had had his adherents try to set fire to the Chinese Consulate on 65th Street.

Somebody behind them shshed the A.P. man. They didn't want to miss a word of the Reverend's wisdom. Well, it was their privilege. Holly let the sound of his voice wash over her. She had really been glad that Mark Converse had phoned her, and not terribly surprised, either. Douglas Fairbanks Jr. and the Empress of all the Russias. She had really wanted to go to him, and only the intervention of her guardian angel, who checked in whenever she became too susceptible to her emotions, had prevented it. Right on, guardian angel, mustn't be all that biddable, chaps lose respect for a girl who's that available. Right? Bullshit. Better to follow where the heart —and loins—led.

The Reverend was driving hard into his peroration, making his pitch for recruits. Come to us, come to Purity, offer God a sign that you long to be purified, enlist in the legions of the pure, who shall inherit the earth more surely than the meek, step forward in purity into the presence of the Lord. . . .

With an operatic swirl of his cape, red and black mingling richly, the Reverend walked off attended by the faithful white spotlight.

Holly said goodbye to the A.P. man and started up the aisle. At the door, a wooden box was beginning to overflow with membership applications. The Reverend was on the beam, Holly thought, he was riding the snake's tail to glory.

The event that came to be known as the Day of the Dog was inspired by a "name withheld" letter to the *Daily News* suggesting that dogs, which were constantly turning up snakes (often when they were least wanted), were better equipped to sniff out the snake in the park than cops with a degenerated human smelling apparatus. The writer added that, if the police refused to employ the Department's own dogs for this purpose, individual dog owners should organize their own posse.

The idea became an instant success. Before the day was over, hundreds of dog owners began to bombard the special police line; others, accompanied by their pets, picketed police stations. What was a more or less spontaneous, unorganized movement suddenly solidified with the fortuitous ascendancy of a Mrs. Reginald Campbell, who, finding herself singled out by a television interviewer at the scene of a picketing, announced that there was no time to lose, that the very next day was none too soon. She exhorted all dog lovers within the sound of her voice to appear at the park tomorrow in the forenoon with their animals, which would then be unleashed and, having located the snake, bark loudly and reveal its hiding place.

Thereupon, a police lieutenant who had come out of the precinct to watch the proceedings issued a warning to the effect that the city ordinance pertaining to unleashed dogs, and the fine appertaining thereto, would be strictly enforced.

He was barely heard over the roars of approval for Mrs. Reginald Campbell and the barking of the assembled dogs.

But Mrs. Campbell herself responded to this threat later in the evening when she was interviewed for television at her home. Photographed in her living room, surrounded by her standard poodle, her Airedale, her two German shepherds, and her miniature schnauzer, she offered the following stratagem: "If a policeman attempts to hand you a summons, simply say, 'Sorry, officer, my dog accidentally slipped its leash.' "

When Mrs. Campbell's remarks were brought to the attention of a police official, he said, "The law doesn't make any distinction between dogs that are deliberately set free and dogs that become free by accident. All owners of dogs that are off the leash will receive summonses."

The following day, at eleven o'clock in the morning, some four hundred people and six hundred dogs of the most diverse breeds had gathered at the Bowling Greens. Holding her standard poodle, her Airedale, her two German shepherds, and her miniature schnauzer on a five-leashed rein, lifting her voice above a concerted din of barking, whining, snarling, snorting, and whimpering dogs. Mrs. Campbell offered her salutatory address.

"Welcome, dog lovers of the City of New York. I am deeply touched by this tremendous response to my television appeal. I know that you share with me the conviction that our beloved pets, left to their own devices, will generously ferret out the slimy creature which has made our beloved park an unsafe haven in this most trying time for all of us. . . ."

She paused as a phalanx of policemen, led by a

lieutenant, pushed their way toward her through the crowd. The lieutenant spoke to her, but his words were inaudible because of the booing of the crowd, which also served to incite a fresh outburst from the dogs. The lieutenant addressed the crowd, which overrode his voice with even louder booing. The lieutenant spoke to Mrs. Campbell, who nodded graciously and held up her hand to the crowd, which presently fell quiet.

"Dear friends," Mrs. Campbell said. "The officer has asked me if he might be permitted to say a few words to you."

The booing started up again, interspersed with shouts of "No! No!" One of Mrs. Campbell's shepherds mounted her miniature schnauzer. The schnauzer snapped at the shepherd and forced it to dismount. Mrs. Campbell yanked at her reins, and her five dogs were pulled off balance into a struggling bunch.

"In the true spirit of democracy we will allow the lieutenant to have a few words," she shouted, "and then we will go about our business as if he had not spoken."

Wild cheers from the crowd. A toy poodle jumped out of its owner's arms and ran madly through the crowd, yipping in a shrill, excited voice. The owner set out after it, calling its name, which was Mon Trésor. The poodle swerved sharply and took off in the direction of the Sheep Meadow.

Mrs. Campbell kept her hand in the air until she had comparative silence. The lieutenant cleared his throat.

"I realize that you are all acting with the best of intentions. . . ." The crowd jeered. The lieutenant, sweating visibly, went on. "We of the police are duty-bound to uphold the law. I therefore advise you that if your dog is off its leash, you will receive—''

The crowd burst out into laughter and shouts. The lieutenant stopped speaking and appealed to Mrs. Campbell. She shook her head firmly, indicating to the lieutenant that he had had his day in court. The crowd applauded. The lieutenant moved off and joined his fellow officers. Mrs. Campbell held up her hand for quiet.

"Dog lovers, unleash your animals!"

In the course of the next few hours the police issued a summons to everyone holding a dogless leash. Most of the summonses were torn up and thrown away.

In the aftermath of the Day of the Dog, the police estimated there were at least twenty-five dog fights in which blood was drawn, and perhaps eighty more that were broken off by mutual consent or interrupted by owners, several of whom were bitten in the process, some by their own dogs. There were thirty mountings leading to consummated intercourse. Three squirrels were killed. Six children sustained bites.

One dog suffered a broken rib when it was kicked by a man it had snapped at. Two dogs died of coronary occlusion. Thirty-five dogs collapsed with heat prostration. Four dogs were run over and killed by cars. Damage to shrubs and other plants was called ''catastrophic'' by the Parks Department. Nineteen dogs were lost; of this number, fourteen were reclaimed by their owners, many of whom were obliged to pay a reward; five, perhaps the victims of kidnapping, were never recovered.

By three o'clock, all dogs were leashed and most had been taken from the park. Shortly thereafter,

Mrs. Campbell departed following a brief statement for the television cameras.

"I blame the failure of our pets to find the snake on police harassment. Now, if you will excuse me, I must go to the vet." She held up the bloody left paw of her Airedale for inspection. "Checkers—I named him after Mr. Nixon's wonderful dog of yesteryear—cut his pad on broken glass. Instead of harassing dog owners, the police should keep vandals who break glass in this once-lovely park out of this once-lovely park."

A television reporter said, "There were hundreds of dogs running free out here today. Yet, not one of them found the snake's trail. How do you explain it?"

"It's not whether you win or lose," Mrs. Campbell said, "but how you play the game."

If three years as a reporter of city news had taught Holly Markham anything at all, it was to take nothing on faith. And so, late in the afternoon, she went around to the Public Library and, sitting in the North Reading Room with a pile of books, compiled notes on the relationship of snake and man from "time immemorial." Her findings not only refuted much of the Reverend's sweeping claim, but overturned a few conceptions of her own.

Rev's assertion (she wrote in her racing shorthand) that snake "symbol of Evil from time immemorial" is pure nonsense. Actually such is case only a lousy two thousand years, and even then only in *Western* theologies. Fact is, from "time immemorial" man's reaction to snake highly contradictory: worshipped, feared, hated, admired, etc.

Many civilizations, both primitive and advanced,

held snake to be deity or semi-deity, e.g.—Australian bushmen regarded (still regard?—check out) snakes as sort of water god, make rain fall, help find springs, etc. Ditto, Hopi Indians, used snakes as go-betweens to plead with rain gods to make rain.

More snake worship: pythons in Africa; king cobra in Burma. Cobra also venerated in India; in old days, Dravidians believed headmen reincarnated as cobras. Mexico: famous Quetzalcoatl, feathered serpent, combination snake and bird, god of civilization, inventor of agriculture, metallurgy, patron of all the arts. The Poo-bah of animals!

Beginning to sweat, Rev?

More: Babylon: snake symbol for Ishtar, goddess of sexual love. Okay, snake obvious phallic symbol, ancients knew it before Freud. And not just symbolic, either—in many early pics, snakes shown diddling women. Greeks and Romans: both used to regard snakes as sacred creatures. Household pets in Old Rome, everyone who was anyone kept one around the house. Check out if poisonous. Marc Antony referred to Cleopatra, respectfully, as "serpent of the old Nile." Egyptians supposed to have kept snakes in home, too—tamed asps. Check with M. Converse, can poisonous snakes be tamed? *Don't* check with M. Converse, ulterior motive involved—right?

Sweden: as recently as sixteenth century, Swedes worshipped snakes as household gods, and snakes not to be killed under any circumstances. Notion later spread to other European countries.

Ancient Greece: snake regarded as healer. *Vide* Aesculapius, god of Greek medicine. Caduceus, staff wreathed with two snakes, carried by Hermes, and still familiar emblem of physicians and medicine. Go fight the AMA, Reverend!

But Reverend has his innings with coming of Christianity, where snake firmly established as symbol of evil. Christians opposed idea of snake worship (one God, right?), so fingered it as epitome of evil. Snake's big caper: tricked Adam and Eve into original sin and expulsion from Eden. Said God: "Henceforth be enmity between serpent and man," and turned it into a belly-crawler. Church put shoulder to wheel, selling idea of snake as symbol of evil. Put it across, too—credit where credit due. Medieval artists (dependent on church for patronage) used snake as symbol of evil. In old drawings, Devil's penis snakelike, sinuous, sometimes forked, resembling snake's tongue. Sounds interesting.

Modern times: in Abruzzi region of Italy, snake-handling feature of religious festival taking place every May; in church in Kentucky, twenty-five years ago, handling of snakes—diamondback and timber rattlers—used to be regular occurrence. Hopis (see above) do snake dance in Arizona, priests take heads in mouth. Ugh!

Fact: although people die of snakebite (most in Asia, Australia, Africa, fewest in Europe, U.S.A.), number comparatively small. As M. Converse (what, again?) said, many more humans poison snakes than other way around. Most common—sprays used to kill insects, insects swallowed by snakes, accumulate in liver, liver swells until snake dies painful death. No snakes eat humans, but humans eat snakes. Large constrictors most sought-after delicacy. Australian aborigines eat practically anything that crawls, but not poisonous ones. But Japanese eat sea snakes,

which *are* poisonous. In Hong Kong, discerning
diners eat poison kraits and cobras. U.S.A.—rattlers
on menus used to be known as "prairie eel."

Theories on why people hate snakes: they prefer
upright animals, reflecting own image. Bears, cats,
dogs, penguins, all get up on hind legs. Same sense,
people like expressiveness in animals, particularly
dogs, unlike snakes, which are stony-eyed because
have no way of closing eyes. Probably not
poisonousness of snakes that fills humans with
revulsion so much as slitheriness. Also, they're
sneaky—hard to see, *vide* snake in grass. But
children two and three years old like to play with
snakes. Around four, though, begin to develop aver-
sion. Proves no *innate* fear of snakes, but instead
brainwashing by parents?

Snakes as medicine: snakeskins used to cure
everything from lumbago to hot flashes. In U.S., in
more innocent times, hustlers sold "snake oil" as
panacea. Years ago, Italian ladies would eat vipers to
make complexion smooth. What price beauty! Hip-
pocrates devised pessary of snake's fat and bull's fat.
Pliny (the Elder, the Younger, who cares?)
prescribed snake fat to cure baldness. Central
American Indians drank rattlesnake venom as
aphrodisiac. In some American Indian tribes,
pregnant women ate powdered rattlesnake to shorten
labor, as follows: child in womb hears rattle and
hurries to get born, figuring snake is coming after
him if he doesn't get out. Contradiction here,
suggesting fear of snakes is prenatal? No. It's adult
assigning own fears to unborn child.

Tidbits: man in California (where else?) committed
suicide by jumping into rattlesnake pit. Hannibal

supposed to have catapulted pots of snakes into Roman ships, causing panic. American Indians used to shoot at U.S. Cavalry with arrows dipped in snake venom. Didn't work.

Talk to editor about using some of this stuff as shirttail piece to Reverend story? Remember bits and pieces to show M. Converse how terrifically knowledgeable I am?

The snake cornered a rat near the retaining wall along Central Park West, but the surprise was not complete. The rat heard the slight sound of the snake's movements, and, before the snake could strike, ran away along the base of the wall. Where the wall broke for an opening to the street the rat stopped and turned and saw that the snake was pursuing it. It ran again, rounding the wall into the 4 A.M. stillness of Central Park West. It paused briefly at the curb, its fur tinging from green to red with the change of a traffic light. When the snake slid around the wall onto the pavement the rat fled across the street.

Halfway up the street the rat tired, and the snake gained on it. The rat darted suddenly to its left, scampered behind a brownstone stoop, and hopped through the bars in front of an open window leading into a basement apartment.

The snake crawled past the stoop to the window. It inserted its head and neck through the bars, sinuous, swaying, then slid forward onto a table standing against the wall beneath the window. Without stopping, without waiting for its posterior to clear the bars, it began to wind down the table leg to the floor.

It paused, with its long wet tongue flicking, then

glided through an open doorway into another room. It paused again, and now its flicking tongue tasted other odors than those of the rat.

Webster McPeek would never truly know whether he heard the snake or was simply awakened by some atavistic instinct. He sat upright in bed, and saw the snake almost at once and very clearly, in a fling of light from the streetlamp outside. Its head was up, its tongue was darting in and out. McPeek shouted, loud and hoarse, his voice clogged by fear. His wife awoke in panic, and, when she saw the snake, screamed. The snake started to curl its long slender body into forward motion, and when McPeek realized that it was heading toward the children's bedroom he leaped out of bed, and ran after it toward the open door.

But the children, aroused by the shouting and screaming, were out of bed, and they appeared wide-eyed and frightened in the doorway. The snake was between McPeek and the children. He tried to wave them back into their room, but instead they ran toward him, arms outstretched, and the snake's head leaped forward and the children screamed. He ran toward them blindly, with his wife just behind him.

In the darkness, the snake struck out in a panic at the threshing legs, the stamping feet that threatened it. It struck several times, until the feet and legs retreated, and then it turned in a tight arc and glided swiftly back the way it had come, its head still high, its mouth open. It didn't pause, but pushed itself toward the table. It wound up the leg in a continuous motion, and slid through the bars over the window.

The snake ran down the street toward the park.

But when it started to cross, a brightness bore down on it, moving very quickly, intensifying as it came closer. Pressing down hard with its scutes, throwing its body into powerful curves, the snake produced a surge of speed that carried it safely past the huge oncoming brightness. It ran along the base of the retaining wall until it found the opening it had come through in pursuit of the rat. In the park, it slid off the pavement into the concealment of grass and brush.

Hyman Closs, cruising north on Central Park West after dropping a fare at 96th and Amsterdam, spotted the snake when he was a block away from it. At first he didn't believe it was real; it was one of those crazy fakes that were all over town. But when it slid down off the curb he knew it was no fake, it was *the* snake. He clammed his foot down on the accelerator and bore down on it. He braced himself queasily for the impact of his wheels bumping over it, but to his astonishment it outran him, and crawled up onto the sidewalk.

He braked, and looked behind him. It was gone. The *speed* of it! Tingling with excitement, he made a U-turn and headed downtown. He considered stopping at a phone booth, but he didn't want to get out on the street at 4:30 in the morning, so he decided to go to the precinct in the 85th Street transverse.

Racing southward, cheating on lights, he still couldn't believe how fast the thing had crawled. A shame he had missed it. What a hero he would have become! Still, he would have quite a story to tell Florence in the morning. In fact, he couldn't wait to tell the cops. But at 94th Street a man and woman flagged him, and before he knew what he was doing, he screeched to a stop. Pure instinct, right? He would have pulled away, but the man was already tugging at the door handle, and he had to let them get in. They gave him an address near Gramercy Park.

He asked them if they would mind if he stopped at the precinct first—it would only take a couple of minutes, and he would raise the flag, no charge—but they were smooching back there, and didn't even hear him. He did sixty all the way downtown, but then they decided to go to an all-night joint in the Village, and he had to take them there. He dropped them, finally, and raced over to the 9th Precinct on East Fifth Street, but by then the police knew all about it. They asked him some questions and made a couple of notes, and then told him that he would have to move his cab because he was blocking the street.

FIFTEEN

WEST SIDE HOSPITAL, although it was accustomed to the presence of the police, had never known such a convocation of high brass as it now had in its waiting room. It was 5:30 in the morning, and such was the haste with which the group had gathered that most were unshaved and wearing yesterday's shirt. Captain Eastman had convened the meeting, or, rather, made the call that set it in motion. As soon as the report came in, he had phoned the DI, who had in his turn called the Deputy Chief in charge of SOD, parent organization of the Emergency Service Unit. The Deputy Chief had phoned the Borough Commander, and so it had gone, upward through the ranks, to the Commissioner himself. No one had objected to being wakened in view of the gravity of the occurrence, and only the P.C., who was being murdered by a hangover, failed to show up at West Side Hospital.

Inside, in the emergency ward, an augmented Emercrit Group (West Side's equivalent of East Side's Code Blue Team) was working to save the lives of Webster McPeek, his wife Emily, and the two McPeek children, Webster Junior, nine years old, and Charlene, six. Only ten-month-old Parker McPeek, who had slept through everything in his crib, had not been bitten. The victims had been administered black mamba antivenin immediately upon arrival at West Side but their present condition varied. The two males seemed to be responding well, but Mrs. McPeek and young Charlene were, in the words of one of the Emercrit Group, "touch-and-go."

The police brass, centered about a Deputy Commissioner at one end of the waiting room, were deep in conference. DI Scott and Captain Eastman, the two lowest ranks, had not been invited to join. They stood a little way off, smoking. Presently, the Deputy Chief in charge of SOD separated himself from the group, and beckoned DI Scott to one side.

"The heat's on," the DC said. "You've been given forty-eight hours to get that snake. When it starts biting people outside the park, it's going too far. You know who those people are?"

"What people, sir?"

"The family that got bitten. They're from Trinidad. She's a social worker, and he works as a warehouse man for a supermarket chain in the daytime and goes to law school at night. These aren't any of your welfare blacks, but a fine wonderful family. You get the point?"

"Yes sir. There's going to be a public outcry."

The DC nodded. "Your ass is on the line, Vincent. You've got forty-eight hours to get the snake. After that, you'll be reassigned to someplace dirty.

Nobody's fooling around, now. This comes straight from the top."

The DC went back to join his peers, and DI Scott gave Eastman the gist of his conversation with the DC. "No question about it, this is a bullet straight from the P.C., bless his aching head. I'm telling you flat out, Tom, that if I go to Siberia you're coming with me."

"Look," Eastman said patiently, "we've been doing our best, robbing men from everywhere to put them in the park, even some old desk-duty cops who are practically crippled by arthritis. Our ESU trucks and personnel are out there all day long. And Converse has been going out every morning, like I told you, trying to find it sunning itself—"

"He hasn't produced any results," the DI said flatly.

"Maybe not. But he knows what he's doing. Sure, the brass shoots an ultimatum at us, but it's still going to take time. It's a process of elimination."

"Well," the DI said, "our asses are on the line, and I think I just thought of a process that will eliminate the whole process of elimination."

As the DI finished speaking to Eastman, Converse's alarm clock went off. He sipped a cup of instant coffee while he shaved and dressed, and turned off the air conditioner before he left. He found a cab cruising on Hudson Street. Its driver was a kid with a beard who confessed that he was lost in the Village and would welcome guidance. He took notice of the Pilstrom tongs.

"You gonna take a chance at catching that snake?"

Converse nodded.

"I don't believe in killing things," the driver said earnestly. "Like Schweitzer? I mean, the snake has a right to life. It's a part of the ecology."

Eighth Avenue was dark and squalid. In a half hour, Converse thought, it would be *light* and squalid.

"You know," the driver said, "Schweitzer would go out of his way to avoid stepping on an ant?"

"Some snakes *eat* ants."

"Ah," the driver said, "eating is different from killing. Eating is *ecology.*"

Converse got out at 100th Street and Central Park West, near the Boys Gate. There were only a few cars going by on the street, mostly cabs with the off-duty signs lit. To the east, the sky was lightening, but the sun was not yet up. It was the eleventh or twelfth day of the heat wave—he had lost count—and this was going to be another ninety-plus day. He shifted the Pilstrom tongs to his shoulder and headed into the park.

He ambled eastward along the walkways, dreaming about Holly Markham, Empress of all the Russias, and it wasn't until a ray of sunlight struck his eyes that he realized that he had been dawdling. He began to trot, holding the tongs in front of him now, like a soldier on a bayonet charge. By the time he reached his first target area of the day, not far from the short road (CLOSED TO THE PUBLIC—POLICE ONLY) that connects the East and West drives, the sun, white and aqueous, was starting to clear the buildings on Fifth Avenue.

The site was a hollow in a heavily wooded, overrun area, dense with undergrowth, fallen leaves, a tangle of bushes, ground creeper, weeds, a couple of fallen trees; and, above it, a large flat plateau of rock. It was a beautifully convenient rock, Converse thought, in the perfect neighborhood for a black mamba's home. But that had been the case, to be sure, in a dozen previous sites he had checked out.

Moving cautiously, he edged toward a position that would bring him up to eye level with the table of the rock. He inched forward, careful to avoid making vibrations that a snake might "hear," and took cover behind a thick bush where, if he didn't move about unduly, he wouldn't be likely to be spotted by a snake's sharp eyes.

A long bar of sunlight appeared on a margin of the rock, toning its color down to a warm gray; as Converse watched, the strip broadened visibly. In a few minutes it would cover the entire surface and provide an irresistible basking place for a black mamba. He shut his eyes against the brightness, and when he next opened them, the rock was bathed in sunshine. He shaded his eyes with his palm and stared outward at the rock.

When he first heard the sound—or *thought* he heard it; it might have been wishful thinking—he pushed his head forward, straining. Nothing. Silence. Then he heard it again, a mere whisper of sound, but continuous now, and his heartbeat accelerated with an almost painful abruptness. Not daring to move, he listened with terrific intensity, and presently he was sure of it, certain that it was the sound he had been waiting to hear for all those long mornings in the park.

It wasn't much of a sound, and an untrained person might not have heard it at all, or, hearing it, might have dismissed it as of no consequence. But to a herpetologist it was unique and unmistakable—an

innocent-enough rustle, much like the sound of a
jump rope being drawn through the grass. His heart
was thumping so hard that for a moment he en-
tertained the ludicrous notion that it was straining
the thin material of his T-shirt.

As the sound came perceptibly closer beneath the
rock, he thought joyously, *My God, Converse,
you're a lucky man,* then shook his head as if to
rebuke himself. Not luck; it wasn't luck at all, but a
reward. He had been doing all the right things, he
had been patient and painstaking, and sooner or later
it was inevitable that he would find it.

The sound had become louder and more distinct.
Converse, tingling with excitement, looked out un-
blinkingly over the flat sunbathed surface of the rock
and knew that in just another short moment he
would see it: a small head would appear over the rim
of the rock, swaying on a sinuous neck, a tongue
would flick in and out, in and out, alert dark eyes
would probe for danger, and finally, the black
mamba would insinuate its great curving length up
onto the rock.

The rope-dragging sound intensified, and Converse braced himself for his first sight of the snake.

Then the sound stopped.

The snake felt the vibrations first at a distance. It
paused below the rock and raised its head warily. It
could see nothing threatening. But the vibrations
continued, and they were disturbing. It darted its
tongue and swiveled its eyes. Then, all at once, the
ground became active, it began to shake, leaves and
small stones flew, and there was a great wind. The
snake whipped around in a swift turn and slithered
into the brush. Even here, down below, leaves were

blowing about, fragments of twigs were stinging its flanks. It broached the entrance to the burrow, pushed past the debris which had piled up around the entrance, and slid inside to safety.

Later, Converse was to realize that he should have heard it long before he did—perhaps *did* hear it, but only with his ears, not his brain, because he was so intensely concentrated on the top of the rock and the sound of dragging rope.

When the leaves and small stones stung his legs, and the trees and bushes began swaying, the sound crashed in on him with a roar. He looked upward just as the helicopter passed over him, so low that it barely seemed to clear the treetops. It was painted blue and white, there was a number on the fuselage, and, in large letters, POLICE. No longer cautious, he came out of his hiding place and leaped up onto the flat shelf of the rock. He shook his fist up at the helicopter and screamed, "You bastards! You dumb, stupid, fucking saboteurs!"

The courtyard of the Central Park Precinct was seething with activity when Converse got out of his taxi. Cars were pouring out of the underground garage, cops were piling into the ESU trucks, and still others were lined up in platoon formation. Inside the main precinct building there was more turmoil, with additional cops and plainclothesmen crowded around the desk. Nobody paid any attention to him as he went down the corridor to the Commander's office. Eastman barely glanced at him. He was speaking on the phone, which he held tucked in between his shoulder and chin, and at the same time shuffling papers on his desk. He was unshaved, his clothes were rumpled, his blue eyes were puffy and slitted.

By the time Eastman finished his phone call, and took several others, all of which seemed to concern the deployment of police from other precincts to duty in the park, Converse's anger had simmered down. Nevertheless, the first words he said to Eastman were, "Well, you fucked it up, captain."

Eastman's reddened eyes looked startled, but he didn't say anything. He held up his hand warningly, as if to indicate, Converse thought, that he wasn't yet ready for anger, that he adjusted gradually to the unexpected these days where he would have leaped into its face twenty years ago.

"A helicopter," Converse said. "It would have been cheaper to call it up on the telephone and warn it to take cover. I swear, captain, it made me sick."

Eastman nodded, as if, at last, he was on familiar ground; there was always, inevitably, something that made someone sick.

"Why didn't somebody ask me about it? I could have told you it wouldn't work. You promised to give me time."

"Time ran out a few hours ago," Eastman said. He took note of Converse's puzzlement. "You didn't hear about it?"

Converse shook his head, and Eastman told him about the McPeek family, his face blank, as though, Converse thought, he had exhausted pity and anger.

"The little girl died a few hours ago. The wife is still on the critical list."

"Oh, Christ."

It was the kind of accident that occurred from time to time in Africa, when a black mamba would pursue a rodent into a house. In India, as well, where a cobra might enter through a ventilating duct. His eyes welled with tears.

"So we have no more time for the scientific approach," Eastman said. "We're putting every policeman we can spare into the park, and we're going through the houses on the street where the family was bitten. And that's why we put the helicopter in the air."

"It's awful," Converse said. "It's a great pity." He brushed at his eyes. "But you won't be helping them or anybody else by using a helicopter." Remembering how the ground had trembled, and the storm of stones and vegetation, Converse's indignation returned. "That damn stupid machine, just when the snake . . . might have been coming out to bask."

He had almost given himself away. Had Eastman detected the slight hesitation when he had caught himself up? He gazed past Eastman's head to the window.

"What happened when the helicopter came over this morning?" Eastman's voice was heavy with suspicion. "Were you on its trail?"

"If I was on its trail, I'd have picked it up after the helicopter was gone, wouldn't I?"

And so he should have done. He should have waded into that hollow that he was so sure was the black mamba's home and turned it over until he found the snake. But he had been carried away by anger.

"Because," Eastman said, "if I find out that you found it, and aren't telling, so help me, I'll beat the living shit out of you."

The captain's eyes were ice and fire at the same time. This is how he must have been, Converse thought, when he was younger. Maybe I'm doing him a favor, rejuvenating him.

He said calmly, "Relax, captain, you're beginning to sound like an old-fashioned ass-kicking cop. I know you're not but—"

The hand that closed on the back of his neck was like a steel clamp.

He wrenched himself free of it and whirled around.

"Get the fuck out of here," DI Scott said, "and don't come back."

Converse had breakfast at the same coffee shop where he had gone with Holly. He ate slowly, touching his neck tenderly from time to time. Nobody had manhandled him that way since he was a kid, but his indignation was tempered by the thought that he had lied to Eastman. He liked Eastman. Eastman was a good man. But, like everybody else, Eastman wanted to kill the snake.

He drank a second cup of coffee. There was no hurry. After a while he would return to the park, go down into that hollow, and stay there until he found the black mamba. He would catch it, bag it, and . . . and then what? Sneak it up to the Bronx Zoo and give it to his old boss for safekeeping? Turn it over to that showman and collect his twenty thousand dollars? What he would really like to do was shove it down DI Scott's shirt collar.

He walked slowly northward along Central Park West, resting on a bench now and then, fighting off the temptation to doze. There were five police cars parked near the Boys Gate, and a lot of cops inside the park. As he walked eastward he passed a group of Puries being herded by some cops. The Puries looked disheveled, and one of them had a bloody lip. The cops were grim-faced. He turned and watched the cops shove the Puries into patrol cars. More work for the Reverend's lawyer, who had been kept busy the last few days bailing out the Reverend's flock.

Two cops, carrying shotguns, were standing beside the thicket that led up to the rock overlooking the black mamba's hollow. Converse stopped and swore silently. Keep going, he thought, come back later. He nodded to the cops and sauntered by them, then stopped again. While there was only a small chance that they would find the snake, suppose *it* found *them*, and attacked?

He turned and went back to the cops. One of them recognized him and said hello. "It's the snake guy," he said to his partner.

Converse said conversationally, "You fellas got a lead of some kind?"

The cop who had spoken first said, "We're looking, that's all. Christ, we never stop looking."

The other cop gestured toward the thicket with his shotgun. "Come on, Charlie, let's get it over with."

"I hate this duty," Charlie said. "Ask me to kick a door in with a perpetrator inside and I'll do it, but snakes. . . ." He shuddered.

"You can save yourself the trouble," Converse said. "It's not in there."

"You checked it out?" Charlie said.

"Yesterday. It's not there."

"He's the snake guy," Charlie said to his partner, "so there's no point to going in there."

Converse nodded. "Waste of time."

The second cop seemed doubtful. "The sergeant finds out we dogged it, we're in trouble."

Charlie said, "You *want* to go in there?"

The second cop said, "That sergeant is a bitch."

The stubborn sonofabitch, Converse thought, he's going to win out, and I'm going to have to go in there with them to protect them, and if the snake does show up they'll repay me by blasting it to bits.

"Ah, what the hell," the second cop said, "let's forget it. Sergeant beefs, we'll tell him the snake guy says it ain't there, right?"

Concealing his relief, Converse nodded and said, "See you, fellas," and walked away. A dozen paces on he looked over his shoulder. The two cops were heading away from the thicket, walking toward their squad car, drawn up on the grass. Satisfied that they had given up, he headed toward Central Park West. He would come back later, toward morning, after the police had cleared out of the park, and bag the black mamba.

He left through the Boys Gate and caught a bus. The man beside him had a newspaper. The headline announced the death of Mrs. Emily McPeek. Converse wept. The man moved to another seat.

The attack on the McPeek family affected the city as no previous event had done. Reflexively, spontaneously, people began to gather at City Hall. It started near noon and gradually, throughout the day, increased in numbers and intensity. Many came from other boroughs—Brooklyn, Queens, the Bronx—to voice their shock and horror. The fact that the snake had invaded a victim's living quarters created a new level of terror.

Nevertheless, the gathering was quiet. There were some concerted, rhythmic calls for the mayor to appear, but for the most part the crowd was orderly. A change of mood took place with the arrival in the afternoon of organized groups representing several unions, welfare recipients, P.T.A. mothers and the unemployed. The emotions of the crowd, worked on by these experienced demonstrators, began to heat up. The crowd became noisy, then unruly. The mayor's bearded aide made three separate appearances on the steps, but the crowd refused to be satisfied with anything less than the presence of the mayor himself. At length, near 5 o'clock, when the size of the crowd had been swelled by home-going workers, the mayor was at last persuaded to show himself.

An hour later, still somewhat shaken, Hizzonner phoned the Police Commissioner. "I want to tell you," he said, "that although I am no stranger to harassment by the public, this is by far the worst I have ever gone through."

"I know," the P.C. said, "I've been going over the reports. They're bad."

"Bad is not the word for it. Do you know that some character took a punch at me? I almost got *hit*."

"You're right. Bad certainly isn't the word for *that*."

"My staff, they said, 'Show yourself, that's all they want. Show yourself and they'll be happy.' So I stepped out onto the steps, and this guy ran past your cops and took a swing at me."

"I'm looking into it," the P.C. said, "and I'm going to ride some asses. Also I'm issuing instructions to beef up the force at the Hall."

"What bothers me is that it might catch on, and that the *level* of violence might escalate." The mayor's voice lowered to a whisper. "They might try something with a *gun*."

"Oh, no," the P.C. said, "that just isn't done."

"A thing like that could change overnight. It worries me."

"Well, I'm not a psychologist, your Honor, but for some reason, they like to go right to the top. The president, yes, everybody wants to shoot the president, because he's the top man, that's what seems to appeal to these nuts and their ambitions."

"It has been said—and by God, it's the truth—that being mayor of New York City is the second most important job in the United States after president. Well, suppose you get some nut who isn't as ambitious as the others, who maybe is content to knock off the *second* most important man in the country?"

"I don't think anybody hates you that much, Mr. Mayor."

The mayor laughed bitterly. "We won't go into that. Let's get to the point. The snake. It's driving this city crazy. It's making national and even international news. The hotels and restaurants and theaters and airlines are driving me crazy. Even the overseas airlines. Hundreds of cancellations. We need those tourists, Francis. Destroy that snake before it destroys *us.*"

SIXTEEN

THE LORD IS MY SHEPHERD.

Graham Black stood on the flat rock and stared down into the tangled thickets of the hollow. It was deeply shadowed with the dark of evening and the overhanging miasma of evil. The Lord is my shepherd, and He has led me. Down there lurked the beast, the messenger of Satan, upon whom the beloved Reverend Sanctus Milanese had declared holy war. And under his inspired generalship I, Graham Black, humble soldier in the army of the Church of the Purification, have been directed to the lair of the enemy. Thank you, Lord.

If Graham Black had been capable of detachment, he might have recognized that his afflatus was familiar, that he experienced it anew each day, each time he explored another possible hiding place; and that the litany of faith had never altered or wavered in all the days he had spent scouring his assigned sec-

tor of the park. But Graham Black did not question
himself. He knew only certainty. Why else was he
returning to a place he had already searched
thoroughly once before? Was that not a Sign in itself?

The Lord is my shepherd.

The revelation had come earlier in the day, and,
dizzy with joy, he had wanted to rush to the evil
place, but God had blessed him with caution as well
as wisdom. There were many police in the area, and
they would have beset him and hindered him in doing
the Lord's work. So he had waited until the approach
of darkness, when the police had given up and gone
away. And then he had come straight to this place.

As he started off the rock and down into the
shadows, he felt himself trembling. Not in fear but in
expectation. God is my buckler and my shield, He
will allow no harm to befall me. I feel His presence
all about me, an invisible cordon of security and
love.

He ducked his head and swept aside the low-
hanging branches of a tree, and entered into the fetid
place of the messenger of Satan.

Now, responding to another of the imperatives
that directed its behavior, the snake had defined the
perimeters of its territory and would defend them
jealously and aggressively. It would be more than
usually watchful of encroachment, more than usually
alert to threat, more than usually irritable and willing
to bite. So that, when it felt the impact of the footsteps on the substrate, it did not withdraw into its
burrow, but instead began to hiss harshly, its head inclined forward, its mouth gaped wide, its body tensed
to strike.

• • •

Gazing at Evil, its mouth open to an astonishing width, swaying, hissing, Graham Black felt a shiver of fear. But God was his shield, and he felt comforted, and his fear was vanquished and he felt a great suffusion of strength flow through him. Joyful of his new courage, he wondered if he might not advance upon the beast, seize its terrible head in his hands and throttle it. But the Reverend Sanctus had forbidden such a course of action. "Do not attempt to deal with the serpent yourself. Only note where it hides, and then justice will be done. Anything else is vanity."

Perhaps it was as well. The serpent was truly horrifying, and, looking into its terrible staring eyes, he felt fear again, and was shamed by it. But would it not be vanity, also, not to feel fear for this powerful agent of evil, this monstrous embodiment of the Antichrist?

His mission was accomplished, with God's help he had found out the serpent. But the snake's wide stare was compelling, hypnotic, and he lingered. Then, just as he turned to leave, the snake began to move toward him, gliding over the leaves and brushy debris, and its speed was terrifying. But he remembered being told that a snake only rarely pursued a man and that, in the event that it did, a man could easily outdistance it.

He put his back to the advancing snake and, lifting his feet high to clear the underbrush, began to run. The play of his muscles and his surefootedness exhilarated him. When he began to climb upward from the hollow toward the rock, he turned for a look over his shoulder, certain that the serpent would be far behind him, if it had not abandoned the chase

altogether. But it was still pursuing, and it had closed
the gap between them, its head high on a forward
slant, the long slender body curving behind.

Graham Black did not look behind him again,
straining as he pushed upward toward the rock, and
he had almost reached it when he felt a blow against
the calf of his right leg.

Captain Eastman arrived at East Side Hospital in a
dead heat with the television crews. A reporter
wearing a backpack pushed a microphone in his face.
He brushed it aside and went into the reception
room. It was heavy with smoke and crowded with
reporters. His I.D. got him past the security man
guarding the entrance to the emergency ward, but no
farther. The guard posted at the door of the room
where the Code Blue team was working on the victim
wouldn't budge.

Eastman lost his temper and tried to force his way
past the guard and got into an undignified shouting
and pushing match with him. The door opened and
Dr. Shapiro came out, looking angry.

"What the hell is going on out here?" He stared at
Eastman. "What are you trying to do, captain?"

"I'm sorry." Eastman made a gesture of apology
to the guard. "How is he, doc?"

"You ought to know better, captain." Shapiro
frowned and hesitated and then said, "He's responding to the antivenin. We think he's going to
make it. Thank God."

"Thank God," Eastman said. "He can tell us
where the snake is. Can I go in and talk to him?"

Shapiro shook his head. "No. Anyway, he won't
talk to you."

"He's *able* to talk?"

"Yes. But he won't even talk to *us*. He flatly refuses to say a word to anybody but the Reverend Sanctus Milanese."

The Reverend Milanese's gleaming black Rolls-Royce (custom built at a cost of $125,000) turned into the Emergency Ward driveway, and was surrounded by reporters before it had come to a full stop. The press of bodies made it impossible for the doors to be opened. Cameras focused through the windows on the back seat of the car, where the Reverend's Milanese's saturnine face, shrouded in the stiff collar of his cloak, could barely be discerned.

The stalemate was ended when a second car, a more modest Mercedes-Benz, pulled in behind the limousine. Four Christ's Cohorts got out, formed a wedge, and opened a path to the Rolls-Royce, roughly displacing the reporters. The rear door opened, and the Reverend Milanese emerged with a flash of scarlet cape lining. Another three Christ's Cohorts got out, and, with the four from the Mercedes, formed another wedge. With the Reverend Milanese in their center, using their shoulders and elbows, they pushed through the crowd to the entrance. Inside, they swept on into the emergency ward, carrying the protesting security guard with them.

Presently, those in the reception room heard shouts and the sound of scuffling through the door. Later, the guard posted in front of the room where Graham Black was being treated told the reporters that the Puries had forced their way into the room and roughed him up in the process. He exhibited a welt on his right cheekbone, and said that he would bring suit against the Church of the Purification for aggravated assault.

In the hospital cafeteria, Captain Eastman drank his coffee, grimacing, as though it was medicine. Which, in a way, it was—an antisleep potion. Yet more than once, in the past week, it had occurred to him that he couldn't have made less headway in the search for the snake if he had just allowed himself to drift off to sleep. He looked at the phone sitting at the cashier's elbow. Dr. Shapiro had promised to call him as soon as the Reverend arrived, the estimable, fucking, phony Reverend Sanctus Milanese.

He had no patience for the Puries or their religion, with its arrogant insistence that God was *their* God. But didn't his own religion make the same claim of being specially chosen? And the Jews and the Moslems and what-all-not? One God, but everybody had an exclusive on Him. He thought of the Purie lying upstairs in the emergency room. He was glad he was going to recover, but it was inevitable, the way the Puries had been roaming through the park, that one of them would get killed.

And now what? If they had been a pain in the ass before, what would they be like now? There was a real fanaticism about those clean-necked young people, and wheresoever their Reverend led they would follow. What idiocy would the Reverend dream up to harass an already overworked police force? Manpower was being stretched to the limits as it was, especially in problem areas like Harlem and Bed-Stuy and the South Bronx, where people were exacerbated by the heat and demanding blood in arguments which, in cooler weather, would have ended with just a blow or even a few angry words.

When the telephone rang he reached across the counter and took it out from under the cashier's hand. The Reverend Milanese had just left the emergency room. . . .

Eastman yelled, *"Left?"* and slammed the phone down furiously. He ran up the stairs to the reception room. The Reverend, surrounded by his bodyguard, stood in the center of a clot of newsmen, his face turned upward, his eyes shut, his sallow lips moving. The reporters were shouting questions at him: "Did you speak to him?" "What did he tell you?" "Do you know where the snake is?"

The Reverend lowered his head. He held his hand out, palm up, for silence. "I have seen Graham Black and I have prayed with him."

Eastman had to restrain himself from joining the chorus of questions. Inwardly, he framed one of his own: "You mean you wasted your time praying when you could have asked him where it happened?"

"Is that all? Didn't he say anything about the snake?"

The Reverend faced the speaker. "Graham Black beseeched me to carry on the task that God has imposed upon us, namely, to exterminate the messenger of Satan and so purify the tainted city. Needless to say, I rededicated myself to the effort in the name of the Lord God, and pledged new initiatives to destroy the wicked serpent."

A voice, louder than the other, caught the Reverend's attention. "Did he tell you where to look?"

The Reverend's black eyes glittered. "What I said to him, and he to me, was the private conversation of priest and communicant. Would you wish me to violate that confidentiality?"

A few voices shouted, "Yes, yes," and the Reverend's lip curled. There was a volley of questions: "You spoke of new initiatives. What are they? Be specific, Reverend." "Will you tell the police what you were told by Graham Black?" "Are you going to defy the Police Commissioner's warning about vigilante actions?"

" 'The Lord went before them by day in a pillar of cloud, to lead them the way; and by night in a pillar of fire.' We shall do God's bidding in the way that He prescribes. We obey His laws, not the Police Commissioner's."

The Reverend nodded to his guards, who began to push against the crowd toward the exit. The reporters followed, still shouting questions. A TV newsman reached in with his microphone. "Reverend, tell us how soon we can expect this new initiative of yours to start."

The Reverend, after a moment's hesitation, said, "Armageddon is tomorrow. Tomorrow, the emissary of the devil will be extirpated."

The Reverend's guard swept through the door into the courtyard, and the reporters piled out after them. Eastman crossed the almost empty reception room and went into the emergency ward. Shapiro was in the corridor, sitting on a stretcher, his legs dangling.

"You promised to call me when he got here," Eastman said. Shapiro looked up with a bitter smile. "They manhandled us. Those goddamn goons charged in and shoved us all to one corner of the room, so they could talk to each other without being overheard. I had no way of calling you, I was under *restraint*."

"Was he asking questions? Did it look as if he was interrogating the patient?"

Shapiro nodded. "At one point he showed the kid a sheet of paper, cardboard, maybe a map, and the kid looked at it and pointed at it, touched it."

"You couldn't make out *anything* they were saying?"

"Not a word. They were whispering, and we were off in the corner with those fascist bastards glowering at us. I swear, you could *smell* the violence in them. In a hospital. In a *hospital*. I'll tell you something—if I could have gotten my hands on a scalpel I would have killed one of them."

"You can press charges against them if you'd like."

"I was ready for murder," Shapiro said. "I was ready to cause death. Me, a healer."

"Will you let me talk to him now?"

Shapiro shrugged. "Why not? I'll give you two minutes. But you won't get anything out of it. He won't talk to you."

For all of the time Eastman was in the room bending over the table, Graham Black looked up at the ceiling and moved his lips in prayer. He gave no indication that he knew Eastman was speaking to him, or even that he was there in the room.

Shapiro told Eastman his time was up, and escorted him from the room. "I'm sorry," Shapiro said, "but I told you."

"Yeah," Eastman said. "Tell me, doc, you got some medicine for being middle-aged?"

"If I did, I'd take it myself." He anticipated Eastman's question. "I'm thirty-one. It hits some people early."

SEVENTEEN

IF A DAY that started out badly kept on getting worse, it could turn out to be memorable. When Holly still hadn't shown up by 7:45 for a 7:00 date, Converse knew that the day—which had begun with the helicopter, and gone on with his being fired by the DI and having his neck squeezed, and had continued with his waking up sour and out of sorts from an afternoon nap—was going to be one of those red-starred calamities that one could look back on in the future with awe and a sort of inverse pride.

For a while, he was sure he was going to turn the day around. He had phoned Holly at her newspaper, where three people, speaking brusquely against a background of clacking typewriters, had asked him to hold on. When he heard her voice he said, "This is Mark Converse. Can I see you tonight?"

"Yes, of course."

"I don't think you could classify it as a case of actual need. I just want to see you."

"I want to see you, too."

She had named the time and the place. The place was a five-minute walk from his apartment on Charles Street, and was called, for no reason of decor, or anything else that he could fathom, the Blue Griffin. Earlier, before she was forty-five minutes late, he had sat at the bar and amused himself by trying to think of more appropriate names. The one that seemed most successful was The First Person Singular. It fit the clientele a lot better than the Blue Griffin.

The clientele were, as she had told him—*warned* him—writers who lived in the Village, plus an occasional uptown editor paying a visit to a resident author. Converse had heard of the Blue Griffin, but had always passed it by. Writers didn't interest him; not before Holly, at any rate. Now, based on his forty-five minutes at the bar, he had concluded that writers were a misnomer. Talkers—that was the right word.

At 7:30 he decided to leave. Half an hour late was already too much leeway, it bespoke indifference, at the very least. But he ordered another drink, to delay broaching the heat outside for another little while, and also to see if two writers who were upstaging each other's books might eventually come to blows. He doubted it, even though they shouted fiercely, but in this weather you couldn't tell.

He became aware that someone was calling out his name. He responded, and was told there was a phone call for him. He took his drink with him and edged between the two writers, who had by now abandoned scalpel wit and taken up bludgeons: "You're a prick." "Look, you mother-fucker. . . ." He found the phone booth in the deeper recesses of the room. It was Holly.

" . . . trying to get you, but the damn phone there was busy. They talk a lot. Had you noticed? I looked for you at the hospital. . . . What did you say?"

He had groaned.

She said, "You don't know? Didn't Captain Eastman call you?"

"Dead?"

"He's going to recover. He's a Purie. Why didn't they tell you?"

"I got fired this morning. Was he able to talk?"

"Fired?" The syllable was sharp, brittle. "What's that all about?"

"Where are you, Holly?"

"At the office. I'm finishing up my story. I'll leave in five minutes and take a cab down." She spoke hurriedly, as though to get the nonessentials out of the way. "What do you mean you were fired? How did it happen?"

"Finish your story," he said, "and come down here and I'll tell you."

"Tell me now. It belongs in the story."

"No."

"Why not?"

Because it's unimportant, he thought, because the only thing that matters is your getting here as soon as possible. He said nothing.

"If you won't tell me yourself I'll have to phone Captain Eastman and ask him about it."

"What do you mean *have* to?"

"And then it'll take longer, and I won't be able to leave in five minutes. But if you tell me now—"

"It's a question of priorities, right?" He was deliberately sloshing his drink around, taking some sort of odd pleasure in its running over and wetting his fingers. She was silent. "Is that right?"

"Don't be unreasonable."

"Unreasonable. Unreasonable is what it's all about, isn't it?" He waited. "Well, isn't it?" The line hummed between them. "You're a dumb bitch."

He hung up.

Converse stood at the bedroom window of his floor-through apartment, which faced the backs of the buildings on Perry Street and their postage-stamp-size backyards. Directly across the way, a handsome, nearly naked couple was broiling meat on a hibachi.

It was stifling in the room. He had turned off the air conditioner, partially to restore a little animation to the python, partially to punish himself, to make his body feel as miserable as his spirits. The bad day had gotten worse, but he was about to put a limit to it. He would take a leaf from his boyhood when, on disaster-filled days, his mother would pop him into bed early. She had understood that the only cure was to retire from the day by imposing an end upon it. That was what he could do. Declare the day finished, by edict, by going to sleep at 8:30.

Tomorrow morning—a new, unsullied day—he would go to the park, descend into that hollow, and catch that damn snake once and for all. It was, he thought, quite a snake, even for a black mamba. How many had it killed already—four, five? He had heard of a black mamba in Africa that had killed some eleven people before it was taken. The herpetologist who had told him about it had characterized it as a "rogue." Well, he was inclined to give the snake in the park the benefit of the doubt. Irritable, yes, but with good reason, what with being in an alien terrain and under the constant strain of being threatened. But whether it was a rogue or simply a snake instinctively defending itself, it was sure as hell an aggressive individual of an aggressive species.

He heard the cat spitting, and turned around. The python was crawling toward the cat, which stood its ground, back humped, eyes glowing. He grabbed up the python an instant before the cat leaped. The snake coiled around his arm. He unwound it and put it into its glass cage. He turned on the air conditioner and placated the cat with a bowl of milk. Then he evened matters out by feeding the python a live mouse.

He went back to the window to see how the couple was making out with their cooking. Hibachi, hot coals, and steak were lying in the dust, and the obvious culprit, a red setter, was groveling with guilt. On any ordinary day, the scene would have been good for a laugh. But not on a bad day. With masochistic zeal, he totted up the disasters: helicopter, DI squeezing neck, getting fired, Holly's clay feet, and—why had he put it out of mind?—the biting of the Purie. If he had gone down into the hollow after the helicopter incident, instead of screaming at Eastman like a piqued adolescent, he would have deprived the Purie of the opportunity of getting bitten. It had never once occurred to him that someone else would find the snake's hiding place.

"Converse," he said aloud, "you're a murderer and a shit."

The self-accusation was exaggerated. The Purie

was alive, thank God. Nevertheless, he had behaved badly. And so, as he did whenever he was forced to admit that he was somewhat less than perfect, he became extremely drowsy. He watched moodily as the python began to ingest its mouse, then fell into bed and went to sleep.

He woke with the ringing of the doorbell. He got out of bed and felt his way through the darkness to the living room. Without bothering to ask who was there—that basic first line of defense against intruders—he opened the door. Holly. She was wearing tailored yellow slacks and some kind of a slip-over blouse. He was wearing artfully ragged denim shorts.

He said, "Sorry, no comment. I'm not talking to the press today."

She said, "I went to the Blue Griffin first, thinking you might still be there. Can I come in?"

"Don't waste your time—my lips are sealed."

"Please?"

He stepped aside to let her in. She walked halfway across the dim room. He stood near the door and watched. She turned to face him.

She said, "You could use some light in this room. Can I have a drink?"

"I don't give drinks to reporters." He heard his own voice with a feeling of surprise. It was small and pinched.

She said, "I do believe you care," and walked back across the room toward him, smiling.

Captain Eastman lay on the damp sheets of the cot in the office of the Commander of the Two-two, and slept intermittently and poorly. Earlier, he had attended a meeting at the Borough Commander's office on East 21st Street. The Borough Commander had said that there was no doubt that the Puries knew the whereabouts of the snake, and that they would go after it tomorrow, as their Reverend had promised. Therefore, the park would be saturated with police beginning an hour before dawn. Just to be on the safe side, there were augmented patrols out tonight, with orders to pick up anybody on foot and run them out of the park.

There was no question, the Borough Commander said, but that the Puries were cooking up something. Their headquarters were under surveillance, and dozens of Puries had been coming and going ever since the Reverend's return from the hospital. They would stay for an hour or so and then leave.

"They all look alike. Cleancut kids, short hair, neat clothing. I never thought I would put down white, short-haired, cleanly dressed kids, but they make me sweat more than any black militant or bearded desperado I ever saw."

Eastman dozed briefly and woke, remembering his telephone conversation with Holly Markham, who wanted to know why Converse had been told off. He had tried double-talking, but she kept pressing him, and finally, in a mood of exasperation he went beyond the scope of her questions and blurted out that *he* was pissed off because Converse knew where the snake was hiding. But when she kept after him, insisting that he ought to tell her what evidence he had to back up his statement, he retreated and said that there wasn't any evidence, that it was just a hunch.

"How do you know that in Converse's case it isn't just a hunch, too?"

He recognized, as much from the tone of her voice

as what she had said, that she had suddenly changed her tack; that she had stopped being a newspaper woman and become an advocate. He had felt a deep pang of envy for Converse, for his youth, for the pretty, desirable girl who had sprung to his defense. . . .

But he knew that he was right, that Converse *did* know. And the longer he thought of it, tossing on the lumpy mattress, the angrier he became. What I should do, he said, half aloud, is go down there and beat on him until he tells me where it is.

Outside, there was a sudden gust of laughter, and Eastman glared at the shut door, thinking, It's not funny, nothing is funny anymore.

Converse said, "I want to pay you a compliment. I hope you won't take it the wrong way and get your feminist hackles up."

She shook her head from side to side on the pillow and smiled.

She had an infinite variety of smiles, all bewitching; this one was a half-smile, and it was at the same time mysterious and tender. The sheet they had covered themselves with in an initial shyness was crumpled beneath her. Her slender thighs and long legs were beautifully shaped. So were her breasts, so was her chin. As though in self-defense, he searched for a flaw, and could find none.

He said, "You're even better-looking naked than with your clothes on."

She frowned.

"That's just a sudden thought that occurred to me. It isn't a compliment. The compliment is that you're the brightest girl I ever had."

"Had?"

"I guess I have trouble expressing myself. Well, you know, fucked."

Her frown deepened, then smoothed away in laughter. She drew his head down and kissed him lightly. They exchanged playful kisses until suddenly the pressure of her hands on his back turned urgent. With some effort, he resisted the pressure.

He said, "When I said on the phone that you were a dumb bitch, it was because I thought you cared more about your lousy scoop than you did about me."

"Scoop. We don't allow scoops on my paper." Her hand trailed lightly down his chest. "My friend, there's a time for talking and a time for fucking. You know what I mean?"

Her legs parted, and she pulled him down and into her. Later, with the sheet drawn up to their waists, they slept a little. When she woke he was faced toward her, and speaking seriously, even anxiously.

"Eastman?" She tried to wake herself to his question. "Eastman. He said you blew your stack about the helicopter this morning, and his boss walked in. . . ." She trailed off, shrugging, and her breasts quivered beguilingly. "He's been looking for another herp."

Converse nodded. "There are some good ones in town. *Very* good ones." He looked away from her. "But a new herp won't know where the snake is."

"But you do. Eastman said you did."

"I could have caught it this morning, even after the helicopter, but I didn't. So that Purie found it and got bitten. I'm responsible for him getting bitten. Is that what Eastman said?"

"He wouldn't go any further, for attribution, than that he had a *hunch* you knew where it was."

"Did you write it up—what he said?"

"I tried to get him to come out and state it flatly. It's my job, Mark, you know. But he wouldn't, so I couldn't use it."

"Well, *I'm* telling you. I know exactly where that black mamba is."

"Okay, thanks. But it's a hard-and-fast rule of mine that anything I hear in bed is off the record."

"That's nice to know."

She assessed the tension in his voice and laughed and kissed him. "I just made that up. I've never been to bed with a news source before."

"It was wrong not to have picked the snake up this morning—right?"

She hesitated before saying, "Right, it was wrong."

"And the Puries are going after it tomorrow, and someone else might get bitten, maybe even tonight. Right?"

"Mark, I can't help you assess your guilt, you've got to do that by yourself. But not *now,* darling."

He rolled out of bed. He seemed to disappear in the darkness, but then she saw him straighten up from the floor. He started to pull on his jeans.

"What are you doing?"

"I'm going to catch the black mamba. Before it bites anybody else."

"Oh no. Don't go now. Please?"

He sat down on the edge of the bed and slipped on his shoes.

He wants to expiate his sin of omission, she thought. "Mark, I don't want you to leave me, I really don't. Besides, it's dangerous at night, isn't it?" He shook his head. "Listen, come here a minute." He started to pull a T-shirt on, and when his head emerged he shook it again. She whispered, "Come back to bed. I want you. Right this second."

In the other room a buzzer sounded. Converse said, "Chrisesake." He went out to the living room and opened the window and looked out. He said, "Chrisesake" again, and called out, "I'll be right down." He shut the window and returned to the bedroom. "It's Eastman."

Her body gleamed whitely through the darkness as she got out of bed. "I'll be dressed in two minutes. I'm going along."

"No way."

She turned on a bed lamp. "If you're going to act like a herp, you can't stop me from acting like a reporter, can you?"

She was a lovely girl, Eastman thought, and she glowed with youth and fulfillment. She was in love with Converse—or whatever word they used for love these days. He felt the bite of regret and envy, and mourned for his own irrecoverable youth.

Converse, who was carrying his snake-catching stick, a pillowcase, and a large flashlight, looked at the waiting taxi in surprise. "How did you know I would come? After all, your boss gave me the boot this morning."

Eastman said gravely, "Well, I'm a pretty good judge of character, you know."

"I really behaved like a shit this morning," Converse said.

They got in the cab and Eastman said to Holly, "Where can we drop you?"

She shook her head. "I'm going with you."

Eastman started to protest. Converse said, "Save your breath, captain. I tried."

"She might get hurt."

"Don't worry, I'll see to it."

The driver was looking back at them through his protective glass. Eastman said, "Where do I tell him to go?"

"The Boys Gate, 100th Street and Central Park West," Converse said. The snake's territory was somewhat closer to the east side, but he was more familiar with the approach from the west. "Then into the park, and I'll tell him where to let us out."

"Police business," Eastman said. "Make time."

The driver's shoulders shook with laughter. Eastman thought, The Hawaiian shirt never fooled him, he had me made all the time. The taxi sped up Eighth Avenue, cheating on all the red lights. Converse and the girl were holding hands. Eastman tried to remember the last time he had held hands with a woman, including his wife.

The cab made good time until it reached 86th Street, and then it began to crawl and, finally, stop at the tail end of a long line of stalled traffic.

"What's this all about?" Eastman said to the driver. "Can you see anything?"

"Fya rengines," the driver said. "Fya rengines and cop cars."

Eastman rolled down his window and heard a clangorous, dissonant blend of emergency sounds: sirens, bells, wailers, hooters. A brightness caught at the tail of his eye. He pushed the door open and ducked his head out beneath the cab's roof.

"Christ Almighty," he said, "the whole goddamn park is on fire."

EIGHTEEN

OPERATION PILLAR OF Fire had begun at the first tick of midnight; thus, the night had technically become "tomorrow," and none would be able to accuse the Reverend Sanctus Milanese of having borne false witness.

Approximately sixty Puries took part in Operation Pillar of Fire. They were divided into eight squads of equal size and a larger ninth. The eight "diversionary" squads were designated by consecutive letters of the alphabet, A through H. The ninth went by the letter S for Serpent. There was at least one young woman in each of the eight squads A to H, but none in squad S. All, men and women alike, were dressed uniformly in black trousers or slacks, black polo shirts, and black socks and shoes. Squads A to H carried three five-gallon drums of gasoline. Squad S carried five drums, and was armed with shovels, axes, hoes, rakes, baseball bats, and roughly hewn forked sticks; many of the axes, shovels, hoes, and rakes were so recently purchased that they still bore the manufacturers' bright labels on their hafts.

Because they were aware of the police surveillance of the Tabernacle and the Reverend's mansion, the members of Operation Pillar of Fire assembled at widely dispersed points. They entered in cars (one each for squads A to H, two for squad S) through nine different gates, ranging the length and width of the park. Several of them passed patrolling police cars, but there were no incidents; they were indistinguishable from any other cars driving through the park. The squads were dropped off as near as possible to their assigned destinations, after which the cars drove away.

The "diversionary" sites were spread throughout the park, and away from the prime target area. The two southernmost locations were slightly to the west of the menagerie and along the Bridle Path near the Dalehead Arch. The northernmost sites were located in the Conservatory Garden to the east, near the Vanderbilt Gate, and on the Great Hill, almost directly across the width of the park to the west. One group penetrated to a wild area among the twining paths of the Ramble, another was on the opposite side of the Lake from the Ramble at Cherry Hill. A seventh group was at the King Jagiello monument a slight way from the 79th Street transverse, and an eighth in the center of the East Meadow.

Later, many people were to express astonishment that a plan of such detail and complexity could have been mounted in the four hours since the Reverend had returned from the East Side Hospital. But that was not at all the case. The operation, in a different form, had already been drilled meticulously for the

past three days. At its inception, without prior
knowledge of the actual hiding place of the black
mamba, Operation Pillar of Fire had been a scat-
tershot affair, in which more than twenty-five of the
most promising wild areas of the park were to be set
on fire, in the hope that the snake would be driven
from cover. It was to have involved almost two hundred Puries.

Although he had given his sanction to the plan,
and authorized intensive training of personnel, the
Reverend Milanese had been aware of its quixotic,
hit-and-miss nature, and might never have allowed it
to become operational. But when Graham Black had
pinpointed on a Parks Department map the precise
location of the snake, everything changed. Immediately, eight of the original squads were activated
as diversionary units, and a ninth formed around a
nucleus of Christ's Cohorts.

Operation Pillar of Fire was under the overall command of its architect and field general, Buckley
(Buck) Pell, a former Marine Corps sergeant and
veteran of the fighting in Southeast Asia. After his
expulsion from the Corps with a less-than-honorable
discharge for, in the words of his commanding officer, "undue savagery," Buck Pell had undergone a
sea change, repented of his massively godless past,
and joined the Church of the Purification. He
became one of the organizers and leaders of Christ's
Cohorts.

Buck Pell had trained his squads to concert pitch,
and their performance was exemplary. Each squad,
A to H, arrived at its target area no later than five
minutes past midnight. They proceeded without
delay to saturate the ground, the bushes, and the
lower branches of trees with gasoline. The leader of

the squad, meanwhile, had laid a trailer, a ten-foot length of fast-burning fuse leading outward from the target area. With the exception of the leader, the squad then withdrew approximately fifty feet from the critical area. At exactly 12:15, the leader—and each of the other leaders of squads A to H—lit the end of the trailer fuse.

Although there had been extensive safety drills, a few minor accidents occurred, mostly when squad members stumbled on rough ground or collided with each other in the darkness. There was one serious incident. It involved a Purie girl whose clothing, carelessly wetted by gasoline, had caught fire. Although the press was later to speak of her as becoming "a human torch," in the event she had been quickly rescued by her companions, who rolled her in a blanket and extinguished the flames. She suffered only minor burns.

After they piled out of the cab, the driver yelled, "Hey, who's gonna pay?" and Eastman knew that he was elected. Partially because he was an honest cop, but mostly because he was the only one left. Converse had taken off like a shot, with Holly right behind him.

He yelled after Converse, knowing that he wouldn't pay any heed, even supposing he could hear him over the racket of sirens and bells and hooters. He tossed some bills into the cabbie's lap and started running. But he knew he would never catch up.

Twenty years ago, maybe, but not now. Still, he ran, favoring his bad knee. The street intersections were a mess. There were cops and squad cars at every corner, frantically trying to shunt passenger cars off Central Park West and into the side streets. To Eastman's experienced eye, it looked hopeless. All over the park, orange flames were shooting up, enveloped in thick black smoke boiling upward to the soiled sky.

He tried to keep Converse's angular running figure in sight, but it was already becoming complicated. From nowhere, with their infallible talent for smelling out trouble, people were pouring onto the scene of the disaster, eternally hopeful of a cleansing tragedy that would reinforce their doting belief in the surpassing wickedness of their city.

The two cars holding the ten men comprising squad S pulled off the East Drive at the point where it intersected with the Police Department connecting road to the West Drive. The squad members piled out of the cars, and formed on Buck Pell. The cars drove off at once.

Buck Pell gave a hand signal, and began to run. The squad followed his long-legged stride on the double, awkward with their burden of gasoline drums, shovels, axes. Buck Pell led them quickly into brush, where they were hidden from the road. They stopped only once in response to a hand signal. Crouching low to the ground, Buck Pell shone a tiny flashlight on the map Graham Black had marked for the Reverend Milanese, studied it briefly and ran on again. He led the squad through heavy brush to the landmark rock that overlooked the hollow where Graham Black had been bitten. He pointed down into the hollow, and in a whisper warned his men to be on the alert, to move slowly, to check out exactly where their foot was going to land, to make sure they didn't spill any of the gasoline on their clothing.

He led the way into the hollow, carrying one of the gasoline drums himself.

As he ran, Converse began to attract followers, people who, seeing someone run, were sure he had inside information and would lead them to the scene of action. But they dropped off after a block or two, either because they lacked stamina, or were diverted by something else, or simply because he was taking too long to get someplace.

But Holly wasn't giving up. By now he recognized the sound of her footsteps, smooth and regular, and although she didn't seem able to catch up with him, she was holding her own. He felt a surge of possessive pride—beautiful girl, beguiling smiles, and a good runner, too! But he didn't slow up for her. He pounded on, awkward but tireless. He had always been able to run, from boyhood on, it was his one athletic skill. He was almost unaware of the clamor of police cars and fire engines roaring by, and of the flame and smoke that kept heaving upward all over the park.

When he turned his head for a glance at Holly, he was surprised to see Eastman behind her, head down, running doggedly. He felt sorry for Eastman, he was too old and heavy for the pace. But he couldn't wait for him. The Boys Gate was just a few hundred yards away now. When he looked behind him again, Eastman was still well back, but Holly was no longer in sight. He felt a pang of regret, followed at once by a sense of relief. He wouldn't have to worry about her now, he could concentrate a hundred percent on trying to catch the black mamba before it could be destroyed by a pack of maniacs.

• • •

After he had emptied his own gasoline drum, Buck
Pell surpervised the activities of the members of
squad S, keeping a sharp eye on their movements. A
few of his troops were gagging from the concentrated
stink of the gasoline in the still air, and he grinned.
So far as he was concerned, gasoline smelled
beautiful, and what it did was even better.

When he had first broached Operation Pillar of
Fire, a few people had protested that green vegetation wouldn't burn. It was a common fallacy, and
nobody knew it better than he did. Every time he had
torched a hootch in Nam, all the green stuff in the
neighborhood went up too, a nice little bonus of
defoliation. The reason was that gasoline made the
hottest of all fires, and the heat would almost immediately parch out the foliage around it, and the
green stuff wasn't green anymore and it would burn
like tinder. Look at the way the diversionary fires
were blazing all over the park—that was green stuff,
and it was burning real good.

When the gasoline drums had been emptied, Buck
Pell chased his squad all the way back to the big rock.
He would have liked to push them even further, he
had that much respect for the range of gasoline fire,
but then they wouldn't be able to see much. Once
they were on their way he laid his trailer fuse. It
would have been fun to use twisted toilet paper—he
had once set a whole village on fire with a toilet paper
trailer—but timing was important and toilet paper
wasn't all that dependable.

When he noticed that one or two of his men were a
little slow getting back to the rock, he sang out with
some of the old Marine Corps zip. Minus profanity,

of course, which he had given up when he joined the Church of the Purification.

"Move it, move it, you Puries there. Move it, you hear!" He watched the laggards light out for the rock on the double. "Okay, now. I'm gonna touch it off. And when the fuse burns down to the gasoline, she's gonna blow. If the snake is in there, it's gonna get burned up good, but we wanna know about it. I want every eye peeled on the fire. She's gonna burn real bright, so if the snake is in there, you'll see it. Make sure you check out the trees. Look sharp, you Puries, look sharp. And if you see it, I want you to sing out, and I want to *hear* you sing out. Any questions?"

They shook their heads, or said "No," and one or two of them, like old grunts, sang out a crisp "No questions, sir." Grinning, Buck Pell crouched over the fuse end and cupped his hand around his lighter.

Deep in its burrow, the snake felt the vibrations of footsteps. They moved around for a long time, very close to the burrow. The smell was heavy and rich and alien, and the snake was alarmed. It was the disturbing smell, after the footsteps had receded, that made the snake glide upward toward the second hole of the burrow and stick its head out.

It saw the shadowy figures standing on the rock. Another figure was running in the direction of the rock. Nearby, on the ground, a bright sputtering flame was approaching. The snake slid out of the burrow, and, for the moment, watching the brightness crawling toward it, did nothing.

As soon as the fuse was lit, Buck Pell turned and ran for the rock in long, rangy, ground-covering strides. Someone put a hand out and hauled him up. Seconds later, with a *pffft,* there was a blinding burst of flame.

"Look sharp, you Puries," Buck Pell shouted. "Peel them eyes."

The squad members were leaning forward, peering intently, shading their eyes with their fingers. Suddenly, one of them screamed, "There it goes."

Buck Pell caught a glimpse of the snake, behind the flames, and it was moving so fast that he knew it was not burned or injured.

"Okay," Buck Pell shouted, "let's go get him!"

He had to restrain some of his squad, who, in their eagerness, seemed intent on going straight forward into the burning hollow.

"No, goddamn," Buck Pell shouted, "around it, around it. Forgive me, Lord, for cussing. Let's go." He headed off in a wide arc to his left, his troops streaming after him. "Move it," he shouted over his shoulder, "get the lead out, you Puries!"

NINETEEN

ONCE, BEFORE HE pulled so far ahead that Eastman had trouble seeing him, Converse turned and looked back. He wants to make sure he's losing me, Eastman thought, the treacherous bastard, so he can play Good Samaritan to that stinking snake. He tried to turn on an extra burst of speed, but just then a squad car pulled up onto the curb and cut him off. Both doors fanned open and two cops came running toward him.

One of them yelled, "Freeze!" and put his hand on the butt of his revolver. "Freeze, you!"

For an instant, Eastman considered ramming into the cop and knocking him ass over teakettle. But the guy's partner was running up, and he already had his gun in his hand.

Panting, sucking air, Eastman yelled, "On the job," and started to reach for his I.D.

"Freeze," both cops yelled at once, and the second

cop crouched and brought his piece to bear, holding it in that terrific two-handed grip he had picked up from television. "Don't make a move!"

"Shit," Eastman said.

There were so many police vehicles on the scene that they were forced to compete with each other for access to the park. Once inside, they streamed onto the main auto routes and walkways, searching for suspects.

The Puries, squads A to H, had left the areas of their fires once they were certain they were burning satisfactorily, but they did not flee. They walked through the park in formation, singing hymns. They offered no uniform resistance to being gathered in by the police, although there were a few minor clashes. The net also swept up a few innocent muggers.

All of the detainees were piled into squad cars and then transferred to patrol wagons with a capacity of twenty persons. They were taken to the Central Park Precinct, where they were booked, charged, investigated, and fingerprinted. Because the Central Park Precinct had no lodging facilities, the suspects were dispersed for the rest of the night to the Two-oh, the Two-three, and the Two-four. The females were sent to Midtown North.

As he rounded into the park, Converse saw flames and black smoke boiling upward almost directly to the east, and he knew that the Puries had ignited the snake's territory. Bastards, they would roast it! But he ran on, though he was certain there was no way he could save the snake now. Even supposing it had not died in the flames, but had been driven out into the open, were the Puries going to stand by and allow him to bag it? Still, the snake might fool them. In Africa, during the seasonal burning of the dried grass, black mambas frequently survived by remaining in a burrow under a dead tree or a disused ant heap. Since it was natural to the species and would help explain how it had escaped detection for so long, it was reasonable to suppose that the snake in the park had found such a burrow.

A few hundred yards short of the snake's territory, Converse heard excited voices. He stopped. The voices came closer, and then they came into view, black-clad Puries running, waving their improvised weapons.

He watched as they streamed past him in a loose formation that he remembered vaguely from his ROTC days as an infantryman's extended order drill. From their purposiveness, it seemed certain that they had flushed the snake and were on its trail. From the way they were running they seemed to think the snake would move ahead in a straight line. But, of course, it would zigzag to take advantage of natural concealment, and it might even double back, although the flames would prevent it from returning to its territory. On the other hand, the Puries might actually be on its trail.

Converse hesitated, indecisive, then, on instinct, ran after the Puries.

One of the cops handed Eastman's I.D. back to him and said, "Sorry, captain, but you know how it is."

"No," Eastman said. "Tell me how it is. And put that gun away."

Both cops returned their revolvers to their holsters. The second cop said, "Well, we sure are sorry, captain."

"Tell me how it is," Eastman said to the first cop. His voice was shaking with anger. "Go ahead, tell me how it is."

"Well, we see this guy running—"

"Which guy running are you talking about?" Eastman said. "Me?"

"Yeah. You're running, going like hell, and I spot you, and I says to Joe, my partner—"

"There were fifty goddamn people running," Eastman said. "Why me?"

The cops looked at each other, and after a moment the first one said, "Well, sure there was all these other people running, but we spotted you and we said, we *both* said, Hey, that big guy, he looks big and tough, you know, well, you know, captain, what I mean, you should of seen what you looked like, what you look like. . . ."

"You dumb sonofabitch," Eastman said, "I know exactly what I look like. I look like a cop." He glared at the first cop. "Don't I?"

"Yeah, come to think of it. . . ."

"Don't I?" Eastman said to the second cop.

"You sure do, captain."

"Now that we got that straightened out," Eastman said, "I'm commandeering your car. Let's get moving."

"I don't know, captain," the first cop said, "we got our orders from the sergeant, we gotta—"

"Get in that car, you pair of shitheads," Eastman yelled, reaching under his shirt, "or I swear I'll shoot you both dead right in your fucking tracks."

• • •

Because the fires were dispersed over so wide an area, six fire companies were eventually brought into the park. By the time the firemen reached some of the fires the gasoline vapors had already burned off and the color of the flames had changed from black to a dirty brown.

The spread of the individual fires varied, depending on the contiguity of trees and bushes in the surrounding terrain, but none, fortunately, posed a threat to any of the park's structures. Since hydrants were unavailable in most of the affected areas (hydrants were emplaced only on the East and West Drives, in the transverses, and adjacent to buildings), the firemen were obliged to use pumpers for their source of water. In the case of the most difficult of the fires, the pumpers of two companies emptied booster tanks as well as their regular tanks, and were faced with the alternative of running a stretch to the nearest hydrant or using a hard-suction hose, a device which, dropped into a lake or pond, would suck up water rapidly and impel it at the nozzle with force. In the event, pumpers from other companies responded to the emergency with untapped tanks. Presently, the smoke from even the most stubborn of the fires changed from brown to white, and at this indication of abatement, the firemen breathed easier.

But even after the fires were well under control, it would be a long night for the firemen. In most of the areas where the fires were ignited, the vegetation had been compacted and dried for years, and would continue to smolder with the persistence of peat. For hours after the flames had died, the firemen would be overhauling the areas, raking and chopping until no spark remained.

* * *

"What do you think they put sirens in these things for?" Eastman yelled. "Turn it on. Turn it on."

But the wailing of the siren was just another instrument in the orchestra of official noises, and progress was slow. Eastman knew he could make better time running, but he needed the respite for the sake of his thumping heart and heaving chest. Both sides of Central Park West were jammed with spectators. Through a gap in the crowd Eastman caught a glimpse of Holly Markham. She was sitting on a bench, her head slumped toward her breast, her fists pressed hard into her diaphragm. Stitch in the side, Eastman guessed, and thought, If that splendid girl was my girl, I'm damned if I'd let any lousy snake keep me from giving her comfort.

The squad car found an opening and plowed ahead to the Boys Gate. Eastman directed the car to the West Drive, and then realized that he didn't know where to go. To the left, a group of Puries ran by, brandishing shovels and axes. A moment later he recognized Converse. Eastman screamed at the cop driving the squad car to stop, but the cop's reaction was slow. By the time he got out, the Puries and Converse were both out of sight. He took three deep breaths, slowly, and then ran after them.

The snake crawled into a thicket and rested, its eyes fixed on the bobbing lights that had been clinging to it in pursuit. Suddenly, a light shone directly into its eyes, and behind the light the snake could make out a shadowy figure.

Bill Hextall, at the extreme right flank of squad S, saw the snake when his flashlight beam reflected in its eyes. The snake, except for its head and neck, was hidden in brush. Hextall stared at the snake in fascination, then, as its head withdrew, let out a hoarse shout.

He saw the other members of the squad stop. He continued to shout until they started to run back toward him. He pointed toward the thicket where he had seen the snake, and half a dozen of them began to beat the area with their weapons. Then someone spotted it, gliding across an open area, speeding westward, where it disappeared into brush. Shouting, squad S took up the pursuit.

They picked up its trail again as it was crawling through the children's playground near the Boys Gate. It fled before them and ran through the opening into Central Park West.

Afterwards, in gloriously embroidered detail, a dozen or more citizens were to claim the honor of having been the first to see the snake slither out of the park and onto the pavement of Central Park West. Several others pinpointed the real discover as a well-dressed man wearing a pinstriped seersucker suit with shirt and tie, and a cocoa straw hat. This man, who shouted in a strangulated voice described predictably by those who heard it as sounding like "a man having his throat cut," saw the snake reverse itself and curve back toward the shelter of the park retaining wall.

The commingled voices of the crowd, including those who never actually saw the snake themselves, combined overtones of fear, horror, terror, revulsion, triumph, and pure excitement. The more prudent among them pushed backwards; others poised themselves in a balance that would allow them to retreat if the snake came toward them; still others pressed forward. From north and south along Central Park West, new crowds of people, hearing the screams and shouts and sensing a denouement, converged on the scene.

Given the stifling heat and the bodily reaction to the release of their emotions, it was little wonder that everyone in the crowd was pouring sweat. The mingled odor of burned foliage and petroleum was suffocating, and massive clouds of smoke were drifting murkily across the leaden sky.

Into this scene, a cop, who had been directing traffic at an intersection, arrived with drawn gun. He stood well back from the snake, which was crawling along the base of the retaining wall, aimed at its elevated head, and pulled the trigger. The shot struck the stone wall a full foot to the left of the snake, ricocheted, and tore a hole in the door of an unoccupied car parked at the curb.

The snake swerved outward from the wall, and, with the crowd retreating before it, crawled toward the curb and ran up into the open door of a taxi which had just pulled up, and which contained a man and two women in its back seat.

Squad S poured out of the park behind Buck Pell.

The snake panicked in the close confines of the taxi. It struck out at the flailing legs, bit once, twice, a third time, perhaps the same leg. Then it succeeded in turning around, and it dropped to the pavement, already squirming forward, its whiplike tail following. It ran toward the entrance to the park, but there were many figures blocking its path. It changed direction to its left and the figures moved with it; to the right, and the figures moved with it. It stopped, piled its length into a coil, lifted its head high, hissed dryly, opened its mouth wide, and swayed menacingly.

The sound of the crowd carried into the park, and
Eastman knew that the snake had been found. He
lowered his head and ran, making outrageous
demands on his heavy, out-of-shape body, grunting
and sobbing as he fought for breath.

And if I have a stinking heart attack, he thought,
there will be no inspector's funeral, just the ordinary
burial of a fat cop who died rather normally in line of
duty, and thank God for the pension, though it won't
be enough to see the boys through college and so
they'll drift into the NYPD, and start accumulating
pensions of their own, which, God willing, they'll
collect before they get so fat that they die in the simple act of running.

He heard the sound of a shot.

Converse had lagged behind the Puries, poking in
some underbrush, when he heard the shot from outside the park. He began to run. By the time he burst
out of the park, hurdling the stone wall, only dimly
aware that the plodding figure he had passed was
Eastman's, the snake was in the center of a ring of
black-clad Puries, which in its turn was surrounded
by a massed, concentric ring of onlookers.

Holding the Pilstrom tongs over his head, he
strained to break through the crowd to the inner ring.
Pushing, pleading, using his shoulders and elbows,
he tried to make a passage for himself. Once, when
he raised his head to take a deep breath, he caught a
glimpse of Holly, her face pale, her body cramped by
the press of other bodies.

"Close on in," Buck Pell shouted, "but slow,
careful."

With their weapons extended, the Puries shuffled forward, contracting their circle. The snake turned its head to follow their movements, hissing, its anterior rigid and swaying, mouth wide open. Suddenly, as the ring pressed in, it began to crawl forward. The crowd gasped and recoiled. A Purie leaped forward, and, half running to keep pace with the snake's movement, smashed the flat side of his shovel down on its curving posterior quarter.

"Death to the Devil," he screamed.

The snake rolled over completely, writhing, coiling over on itself. A ragged cry rose from the crowd, half horror, half exultation. Writhing, knotted, the snake moved forward again, its shattered rear dragging behind.

Buck Pell signaled, and the Puries of squad S closed in, flailing downward with their weapons. The snake's head rose, and it launched a strike at a Purie that fell short. A swinging blow from a rake knocked the snake flat. Its body squirming, knotting, it tried to right itself. The head came up, but a second blow struck it to the ground, bleeding. It flopped over on its back, and its light underside was turned up before it succeeded in righting itself. As it started to crawl forward, Buck Pell went to meet it, an ax raised high over his head. He braced himself, and brought the bright axhead down in a gleaming arc. Sparks flew from the pavement, and a chip, white at its edges, flew off into the crowd. The snake's head was severed just behind the neck. Near it, the long body, oozing blood, pulsed and shuddered and writhed.

Converse was still struggling against the density of the crowd when he saw the axhead flash upward and then down. He heard the thud and ring of the ax, and, from the crowd, a concerted gasp like a sudden gust of wind. At the same time, whether in awe or revulsion or both, the crowd eddied back, flowed around him, and he stood at the forefront. The black mamba's head and writhing body lay on the blood-smeared pavement, no more than six inches apart, but grotesquely out of line with each other.

The man who had wielded the ax, grinning triumphantly, bent over suddenly and reached downward.

Converse screamed, "No! Don't touch it! No!" But he was too late. The man had already picked up the severed head.

The snake's gaping mouth snapped shut over Buck Pell's hand; each of its fangs injected a minim of venom.

Buck Pell drew back his hand reflexively. The snake's recurved teeth held their grip. Buck Pell whipped his hand downward sharply, and the head fell free. It struck the pavement, bounced slightly with the force of its descent, and rolled a few inches before it subsided, mouth open, eyes staring.

A Purie stepped forward, lifted his leg, with the knee flexed, and brought his foot down squarely on the snake's head. The crowd screamed, surged forward, and, in a frenzy of competition, fought to reach the bloody pulp of the snake's head with their stamping feet. The Puries of squad S began to beat the snake's twisting body with their weapons.

TWENTY

EASTMAN WATCHED A squad of blue-helmeted TPU
cops form a wedge and start to bull their way through
the crowd. If they were going to try to collar the
Puries, they were in for serious trouble. Maybe the
crowd would allow them to take some names, but
that was the limit. Never mind that the Puries had
burned up Central Park—they had killed the killer,
hadn't they? They were the heroes of the hour,
weren't they? He shrugged. Maybe the cops would
have sense enough to act prudently.

The crowd murmured ominously and offered
resistance to the passage of the TPU wedge. Walk
away from it, Eastman told himself, you're just an
Emergency Service cop on special assignment whose
job is now finished, even if somebody else did it for
you. Fade out of the picture, you're too old to brawl
with an aroused citizenry.

He saw someone burst out of the crowd like a cork

popped from a bottle, elbows flailing, face dark and scowling. It was Converse, still carrying his snake-catching stick. For a moment they came face to face.

Eastman started to speak, but Converse muttered, "So long" and moved on.

Sore loser, Eastman thought. He listened to the voice of the crowd. It was swelling to a roar, peppered with obscenities. He saw fists being formed.

He sighed, and began to push his way through the crowd, toward the stalled TPU wedge. "Police. Make way. Police officer."

A hand reached out from somewhere and ripped his Hawaiian shirt down the front.

Marvin Thurman, a television reporter assigned to shooting "man in the street" reactions, spotted the Police Commissioner's limousine two blocks south of where the snake had been killed. The P.C. and the mayor were in the car, which was barely able to move because of the hordes of people who had poured out into the street.

Pushing his microphone through the window of the limousine, Thurman said, "Mr. Mayor, have you been informed that the snake has been killed?"

The mayor's pale, unshaven face lit up. "Wonderful. I didn't doubt for an instant that New York's finest would once again display their ability to cope with a difficult and unique problem." He turned to the P.C. "Congratuations, Commissioner, to the dedicated and tireless men of the NYPD."

Thurman, who was far too clever for his own good, refrained from telling the mayor who had killed the snake. Instead, he said, "What about the Puries? What will be done with them?"

"They will be prosecuted for arson, and all the

other crimes they have committed, to the fullest extent of the law.'' The mayor pounded on the side of the limousine for emphasis, and the commissioner, who was devoted to his car, winced. "There is no room for lawlessness and vigilantism in this great city, and it will be punished accordingly."

"I see," Thurman said. "Does that include the Puries who killed the snake?"

The falling open of the mayor's mouth was recorded for posterity in full color. So were the rapid changes his complexion underwent from ashen to bright pink to nearly black. But the epithet he flung at Thurman—"cocksucker"—went unrecorded because the Police Commissioner, with lightning-fast anticipation, had covered the microphone with his hand.

A police detachment, led by a Deputy Inspector, in deference to the subject's importance, arrived at Purity House, and was admitted without incident. The Reverend Sanctus Milanese, who was fully dressed and obviously expecting the visit, offered no objections to accompanying the police to headquarters. He was fully cooperative and jovial in manner.

As he was being helped into his red-lined cape he said smilingly to the Deputy Inspector, "I can come to no harm since I am under the divine protection of a holy trinity—God, my attorney . . ." He nodded to the distinguished white-haired man by his side. " . . . and the grateful people of New York who, when all others had failed, I delivered from the cruel and merciless limb of Satan."

But once outside the mansion, perhaps at the sight of the television cameras, the Reverend's demeanor changed. Spreading his cape, he dropped to his knees, made a steeple of his hands beneath his chin, and turned his face upward to the skies.

"Dear God," he said in a hushed tone, "I give Thee thanks. Again hast Thou prevailed over Evil, wielding, as the sword in Thy strong right arm, Thy faithful and humble followers, the members of the Church of the Purification. For Thy great trust, O Lord, we do bless Thee and rejoice. Amen."

It might have been high noon, Converse thought, as he walked aimlessly southward on Central Park West. At 2 o'clock in the morning, streets were alive with people, some streaming toward the center of the action, others returning from it, all of them feeling, perhaps justifiably, that they were actors with a role to play in the drama. He was astonished to see how many children were out, some as young as six or seven, apparently unattended by parents.

The streets were still clogged by official vehicular traffic. Police cars, fire engines, several ambulances. The fires in the park all seemed to be under control but smoke still climbed upward from a half-dozen different areas. The heat of the night seemed to have intensified, the humidity had thickened, and, where it reflected neon, the sky was the color of dirty blood.

"Hey, Mark, wait up."

Her voice reached him from the rear, and it sounded winded, so that he knew she must have been chasing him. She looked terribly pale, and he guessed that she had witnessed the slaughter of the black mamba.

She said, "I got a stitch in the side before, that's why I dropped out. First time that's ever happened to me."

"Yes, well. . . ." He really didn't feel like talking

to anybody, even Holly. "It's nothing to be ashamed of."

"For me it is. I ran the marathon in the park the last two years and both times I damn near finished. I got blisters."

They were walking slowly, ambling, and people were staring at the Pilstrom tongs. A kid, about two inches taller than a fire hydrant, tried to grab the tongs. Converse lifted it beyond his reach and scowled at him. The kid collapsed to the pavement in laughter.

Holly said, "I just don't want you to get the idea that it would have been any trouble keeping up with you."

"Yeah."

"What does yeah mean?"

He noticed that she was carrying a pad and a ballpoint pen. "You were in the right place for a scoop, right?"

"You're going to have to stop using that word. Anyway, there were more reporters there than civilians—the dailies, the wire services, the television, the radio, and a reporter and a photographer from my own paper." She put the pad and pen into her bag. "I just made a couple of notes. You know, the old fireplug reaction."

He looked straight ahead as they walked, but he was aware that her face was turned up to him, in some sort of silent pleading or, at least, serious questioning. From time to time her shoulder brushed against him. Then she reached for his hand. He withdrew it from her.

"Okay," she said. "You want me to go away?"

He shrugged.

"I guess I can take that any way I choose," she

said. "I choose to take it as meaning that you don't want me to go but are too tight-assed to say so. Well, all right, but I can be tight-assed, too, and if I don't get any response soon—"

He reached down and took her hand.

"Better," she said. "But talk to me. Or at least look at me."

He said, choking with anger, "I could have bagged it. There wasn't any need to kill it."

She shook her head. "There *was* a need. The situation cried out for an execution, for catharsis."

"They savaged it to bits." He swore under his breath. "Screw it. Screw everything. Things will be better in Australia."

"You're thinking of going to Australia?"

"What's wrong with Australia?"

"It's too far."

"By plane?" He glanced at her face. "Oh, you mean too far from *here?*"

"I mean too far from *me.* Didn't you, for Chrisesake, know that's what I meant?"

"I'll only be gone a couple of months. Wouldn't you wait that long?"

"I could try, but we're living in a very impatient century. Nobody ever waits for anybody anymore."

He said, "You're not being reasonable."

"Right. Not being reasonable—that's what it's all about, Buster."

She looked angry, and there were tears in her eyes. Goddammit, Converse thought, I can't make up my mind this fast. I need time—say until we reach the next streetlamp.

The flames had swept over the burrow and scorched the earth black. They had set the fallen tree afire, and seared the two entrances, but they had not reached inside, and if the snake had remained in the burrow she might have survived unharmed.

She had mated in the spring at the breeding grounds near Elisabethville, and laid her eggs in the burrow three days ago. If they survived hunting animals and the winter cold, they would hatch out in the spring. Each egg that came to term would produce a twelve-inch-long black mamba, resembling the full-grown snake in every particular except color. Each would be light green on top, and pure white on the underside. Each would be highly aggressive, in the way of young snakes, and its venom, from the very instant of birth, would kill a large rat.

The snakes would grow very rapidly toward their mature size of ten or eleven feet. But, long before then, their venom would be potent enough to kill a man or a horse.

The eggs were approximately the size of a hen's eggs, oval in shape, and white in color. There were thirteen of them.